M

LEABHARLANN CHONTAE
LIATROMA
LEITRIM COUNTY LIBRARY

The Wrong Miss Richmond

WITHDRAWN

By the same author

Rakehell's Widow
Hide and Seek
The Makeshift Marriage
A Change of Fortune

The Wrong Miss Richmond

Sandra Wilson

LEABHARLANN CHONTAE
LIATROMA
LEITRIM COUNTY LIBRARY

ROBERT HALE · LONDON

© Sandra Wilson 1989
First published in Great Britain 2010

ISBN 978-0-7090-9000-7

Robert Hale Limited
Clerkenwell House
Clerkenwell Green
London EC1R 0HT

www.halebooks.com

The right of Sandra Wilson to be identified as
author of this work has been asserted by her
in accordance with the Copyright, Designs and
Patents Act 1988

2 4 6 8 10 9 7 5 3 1

Typeset in 10.5/14pt Classical Garamond
Printed in the UK by the MPG Books Group

1

Curzon Street; September 10, 1803

M Y DEAR SIR,
     I am in receipt of your letter offering to release me from the projected match with your daughter, Jane, and hasten to reassure you that such a course could not be further from my mind. My recent fortunate inheritances may have advanced my circumstances beyond anything to which I had hitherto hoped to aspire, but my regard for Miss Richmond has not altered at all. I may not have yet made her acquaintance, but I know in my heart that she is the bride for me.

In your letter you mention going to Bath next month to take the cure, and that you will be taking Sir Archibald Fitton's house in Johnstone Street. It is now my intention to visit Bath at the same time, staying at my aunt's residence in Royal Crescent, which is at present not in use. Perhaps the autumn ball at the Upper Assembly Rooms would provide an ideal opportunity for me to make Miss Richmond's acquaintance? If you are in agreement, I trust you will let me know.

I will close now, but please believe me when I say that I look forward with all my heart to meeting the lady who will one day soon be Lady St Clement.

I am, my dear sir,
Ever sincerely and faithfully,
Robert Temple
Lord St Clement

The candlelight swayed over the dark drawing room as Robert sanded the letter, folded and sealed it, and then wrote the name and address: Mr Henry Richmond, Richmond House, Stroud, Gloucestershire. Then he put the quill down and rose from the chair.

He was tall, with broad shoulders and slender hips, and everything about him was unmistakably patrician. His face was fine-boned and very handsome, and his thick dark hair was worn long enough to brush his high collar at the back. He had arresting eyes, gray and long-lashed, and there was a sensitivity about his mouth that told of a readiness to smile. He looked very sophisticated and stylish in formal evening clothes, a black velvet coat and cream silk breeches, because he hadn't long returned from dining at Carlton House with his longtime friend the Prince of Wales. At twenty-nine he was in his prime, and such was his charm and ready wit that he was regarded throughout society as one of its most attractive scions.

Until recently his only fault had been a distinct lack of funds, a state of affairs brought about by his late father's profligacy at the gaming tables of St James's. The green baize had been responsible for the frittering away of the Temple family fortune, almost to the point of sacrificing Bellstones, the Somerset country seat that had been in the family since the time of Queen Elizabeth. Bellstones had been spared at the eleventh hour because Robert's widowed father had met with a fatal riding accident while following the Exmoor staghounds, and Robert had inherited the financial shambles he'd left behind.

But now money was no object at all for the new Lord St Clement, who'd unexpectedly come into two vast inheritances because of the sudden deaths of two distant cousins. From the very edge of penury he'd been raised to the heights of great wealth, and there wasn't an estate in the realm that he could not have afforded to purchase; but Bellstones was his pride and joy, and, modest as it was by some standards, he was content to retain it as his country seat.

It was the significant change in his financial circumstances that had brought into doubt the future of his forthcoming betrothal to Miss Jane Richmond, a young lady whose respectable fortune had originally made her an entirely suitable proposition for an impoverished lord. In society's opinion, and in the honorable opinion of Miss Richmond's father, it was one thing for a lord to embark upon a match because he required a wealthy wife, and because the lady's father had long cherished an ambition for his daughter to marry into the aristocracy; it was quite another for one of England's richest lords to continue with such a modest arranged match when his new situation could bring him a titled bride from the highest families in the land. If Robert and Jane had formed a deep attachment, then it might have been understood, but they hadn't even met, and society, as well as Mr Richmond, was going to be astounded to discover that the match was still very much on.

The candle on the escritoire was the only light in the sumptuous white-and-gold drawing room, and its flame still swayed slightly as Robert went to pour himself a glass of cognac from the decanter on the marble console table by the window. There wasn't a sound in the house, for it was late now and the servants had retired. Folding back the shutter, he looked out at wet, deserted Curzon Street. It was a dismal September night, the rain lashing visibly in the pools of light beneath the streetlamps. Such weather paid no compliments, even to the elegance of Mayfair.

Swirling the cognac, he stared at the rain. He was tired of London, tired of the endless round of parties, balls, assemblies, and dinners, and above all tired of the scandal-mongering and whispering that were part and parcel of the *beau monde's* existence. Indeed, sometimes he thought gossip was the *raison d'être* of the grand circles in which he moved. Gossip and Robert Temple had always gone hand in hand, for he seemed to attract it, especially where his private life was concerned. His looks had long made him the darling of the opposite sex; indeed there was a certain salacious list in circulation that placed his name at the very top when it came to prowess between the sheets. London had recently been much entertained by a shocking incident on the steps of fashionable St George's, Hanover Square, when two bold and famous actresses, Mrs Pickering of the Italian Opera House and Miss Jennings of Astley's Royal Amphitheater, had both arrived in their carriages, intent upon waylaying him as he left after a friend's wedding. Neither lady had met him before, but both intended to add him to her list of conquests and, coming face-to-face, they'd swiftly begun to argue, the disagreement culminating in a fearsome exchange of blows that had brought the street to a standstill.

London had curled up with mirth about it, but Robert hadn't been at all amused, for he'd found the whole thing extremely embarrassing. He wasn't a monk, far from it, but he disliked having his name connected with ladies he knew nothing about. His amorous activities had occasionally merited a little whispering, but nothing on the scale that surrounded him now, and he was heartily tired of it. With each passing day the thought of returning to Bellstones and Exmoor's wild freedom became more inviting, as did the prospect of marrying Miss Jane Richmond. He smiled at his reflection in the window, raising his glass. 'Our health and happiness, sweet Jane,' he murmured.

On that same wet, windswept September night, a single light glimmered in Richmond House, a fine old mansion overlooking the town of Stroud, right on the edge of the Cotswold Hills. Stroud was built upon wool, for thereabouts the streams ran fast and clear, ideal for the many mills producing the fine woolen cloth for which Gloucestershire had been famous since the Middle Ages. Richmond House was constructed of Cotswold stone, with lichen on its many-gabled roof, and ancient ivy climbing its walls. In daylight it was a landmark visible from all around, but on such a night as this it vanished in the gloom, detectable only by the lamp burning in the bedroom of Christina, elder of Mr Henry Richmond's two daughters, and half-sister to Jane.

Christina was twenty-five years old, and considered quite pretty, with large lilac eyes and a cloud of long dark-brown hair, but she was unmarried, and likely to remain so. Two important factors conspired to keep her a spinster: she was too bookish by far, and she wasn't an heiress like Jane, whose fortune had been inherited from her mother, the second Mrs Richmond. To Christina, the pages of a book were much more important than the dubious delights of socializing, and she made no effort at all to rectify this undoubted fault in her character. She was content with things the way they were, for she'd yet to meet a man who'd even remotely aroused her heart. As far as she was concerned, there were far too many perils in arranged matches, from the unhappy thought of a lack of respect between both concerned, to the awful prospect of falling in love with a husband who took his many pleasures elsewhere. Nothing less than a love match would do for her, which would have been all very well had she conducted her life in such a way as to meet prospective suitors, but since she steadfastly resisted all occasions that might have led to such introductions, a love match seemed very unlikely indeed.

Jane Richmond, on the other hand, was possessed of a very outgoing character, and at just eighteen was eagerly anticipating every ball, assembly, and other social gathering she could possibly attend. The sisters couldn't have been less alike, but in spite of this they were very close indeed, and it had been Christina who'd at last prevailed upon their father to break with convention and allow an impatient Jane to embark upon the Marriage Mart. In Mr Richmond's opinion, things should have been done in the correct order, with Christina finding a husband, and then Jane, but since he was at last persuaded that his elder daughter was likely to remain unmarried, he'd agreed to attend to his younger daughter's future first. A chance encounter with Robert Temple at an Oxford University reunion had led to the projected betrothal, a betrothal which now seemed very much in doubt.

There was a fire in the bedroom hearth, for the September nights had been unseasonably cool, and the glowing logs cast a warm light over the sisters as they sat on the floor toasting bread on long copper forks. The difference between them had seldom been more apparent, for Christina was neat and precise in a mauve sprigged-muslin wrap, her dark hair tied back with a ribbon, but Jane was bright in buttercup yellow, her russet curls tumbling in profusion about her shoulders. Taller than Christina, and willowy rather than rounded, she had the sort of melting brown eyes that played havoc with the male heart. She was effervescent, impulsive, headstrong, and full of life, but her mood at present was a little depressed, for she could only fear that the exciting match with Robert Temple was about to crumble away to nothing.

Her brown eyes were luminous in the firelight as she stared at the toast on the end of her fork. 'He's bound to want to be rid of me now, for I'm hardly the sort of catch such a man could want, am I? He could have a duke's daughter if he wanted, or a widowed countess, someone of breeding and wealth.'

'We don't know that,' replied Christina gently.

Jane glanced wryly at her. 'No, but we can have a pretty good idea.'

'He was very eager for the match in the first place; indeed, I always felt there was more to it than just an arranged contract that happened to suit both parties.'

'You've said that before, but I can't think it's true. I simply seemed a good proposition because although I don't have aristocratic blood, I bring a handsome inheritance. Why else would a lord take a modest landowner's daughter as his bride? If it was a love match, I wouldn't be worrying like this, but I've never met him. I know from the miniature he sent that he's very handsome, and I know that he can write a charming letter. I also know that certain scandals have attached to his name of late....'

'Perhaps completely unjustly.'

'So much smoke without fire?'

'You can hardly expect him to have led a cloistered life.'

'No, and anyway, it doesn't really matter, because all I'm saying is that I don't *know* him. I've no idea at all what he's thinking right now.'

'Then let's look at it from a different angle. What does *he* know about *you*? You've seen his miniature, but equally he's seen yours, so he knows that you're very beautiful indeed. He's also read your very pretty letters.'

'*Your* very pretty letters,' reminded Jane sheepishly.

Christina blushed a little. 'He doesn't know that.'

'No, I suppose not.' Jane glanced at her. 'If the letters you wrote for me proved anything, it was that you're wasting yourself by being so determined to molder away.'

'I'm not moldering away, I'm quite happy like this.'

'Yes, but ...'

'You know what happened earlier this year, when I was unwise enough to accept Aunt Brooke's invitation to stay with her in London. The visit was a disaster from beginning to end, and I loathed everything about London. I just had to cut my stay short and come back here – I couldn't stand it a moment longer. I doubt if Aunt Brooke will ever forgive me.'

Jane nodded. 'The communication she fired at poor Father was enough to blister the vellum.'

'I told him *you* should have been the one to accept the invitation. It would have been a simple matter to plead illness on my part and dispatch you instead, but he would insist upon things being done correctly.'

'I must admit that if I *had* gone, I'd have made the most of it.'

'Yes, there's no doubt about it. You've always longed for London. We're chalk and cheese, aren't we?' Christina smiled.

'But we blend very well.'

'Exceeding well. Mind that toast! It's going to burn!'

Jane gasped, snatching the fork back from the fire and inspecting the singed offering on the end. 'Oh, no, it's done to a cinder!'

'Never mind, I think we've made more than enough,' said Christina, looking at the little silver toast rack keeping their midnight feast warm by the hearth.

The room was quiet for a while, the silence broken by the scraping of the knife upon the toast. Jane watched her elder sister, taking fresh note of her flawless complexion, glossy dark hair, and lovely lilac eyes. There was no doubt about it, Christina Richmond was her own worst enemy, for she had looks enough to attract the right sort of husband, even if her lack of fortune would deny her the Lord St Clements of the world.

Christina perceived the long look, and correctly interpreted its meaning. 'Don't say it, Jane, for you know what my attitude is.'

'I sometimes think you're psychic,' grumbled Jane, accepting a slice of buttered toast.

'I'm nothing of the sort, I've just been your sister long enough to read you like one of my books.'

'I wish *I* could read *you* as well,' declared Jane with feeling, 'but sometimes I just don't understand you at all. It's beyond me how anyone could prefer a book to a ball.'

Christina smiled. 'Eat your toast.'

Jane poked her tongue out, but applied herself to the delicious hot toast.

For a while they ate in companionable silence, listening to the rain on the window outside, but then Jane sighed, her thoughts returning to Robert Temple. 'Oh, Christina, I *do* so want to be Lady St Clement, I want it more than anything else in the world. When I think of the moment I saw his portrait for the first time ...' Her voice trailed away as she remembered.

Christina remembered too, for she'd been with her in the library. Their father had told them Robert was said to be one of London's most handsome gentlemen, and that the ladies apparently found him irresistible, but nothing had prepared them for the arresting male beauty of the painted face in the little golden frame. The striking gray eyes had seemed alive, and the lips curved in a way that suggested an imminent smile; Christina had been transfixed, but Jane's breath had caught on a joyful gasp and she'd snatched up the miniature, dancing ecstatically around the room.

Jane gave another sigh, licking her fingers and gathering her skirts to get up from the floor. 'Much as I'd like some more toast, I suppose I'd better go to my room. Father and I are setting off early for Cheltenham.'

'I wish you well.'

'Are you *sure* you won't change your mind and come with us?'

'To watch Father take the waters for three days, and you cavorting on every available dance floor? No, thank you very much.'

'It would be much more agreeable if you were there.'

'I don't think you'll have time to notice my absence. You have invitations for every afternoon and evening, which means you'll be in bed every morning until nearly noon. The fact that I'm not there is hardly going to make any difference, is it?'

'No, I suppose not.' Jane shook out her yellow skirts, and then smiled down at her. 'Very well, I'll let you off this time, but next time we go anywhere, I shall insist.'

'For a younger sister, you're an incorrigible bully, Jane Richmond.'

'But I'm absolutely adorable as well,' said Jane, bending to kiss her on the top of the head. 'Good night, Christina.'

'Good night.'

Christina remained by the fire after the door had closed. The flames reflected in her eyes and glinted on her hair as she gazed into the glowing heart of the flames. What did the future hold? Was Jane still going to be Lady St Clement? Only time would tell.

2

THREE WEEKS LATER, early on a crisp October morning, a smart green traveling carriage set out from Richmond House *en route* for Bath, some thirty miles away to the south. The team came swiftly up to a spanking pace, scattering the fallen autumn leaves, and the coachman's whip cracked once as he urged the horses along the Bath road. Late in the afternoon, after a midday halt for luncheon at the Petty France Inn, the carriage would reach number 14A Johnstone Street, the house rented from Sir Archibald Fitton, an old friend of Mr Richmond's from Oxford University days.

The three passengers, Mr Henry Richmond and his two daughters, were in excellent spirits because they now knew beyond a doubt that the match with Robert Temple was still on. The letter from Curzon Street had arrived on the day Jane and her father returned from Cheltenham, and its cheering contents had done more to alleviate Mr Richmond's gout than the spa waters.

Jane had been in the seventh heaven ever since, bubbling with excitement and happiness. She was eagerly anticipating her first meeting with her future husband at the autumn ball in the Bath Assembly Rooms, and she'd quite worn poor Christina out by constantly rehearsing every possible conversational opening gambit. She'd dressed with great care for this important journey, choosing a three-quarter-length golden velvet pelisse and trained white muslin gown. A plumed golden velvet hat rested on her red hair, and she fidgeted impatiently with the strings of her reticule, sitting right on the edge of the seat opposite her father and sister.

Mr Richmond glanced fondly at her, confident that such a delightful creature could only enchant the eminent husband arranged for her. Mr Richmond was a tall kindly man with warm brown eyes, and in his youth had been considered very good-looking. A black tricorn hat rested on his gray-wigged head, and he wore a fur-trimmed Stroud-wool cloak. His hands were thrust deep into a warm muff, and his gouty foot rested gingerly on a little stool. He was a Tory of the old order, an ardent admirer of the retired prime minister, Mr Pitt, and a seasoned detractor of the perfidious Bonaparte. He mistrusted France, and said so, often, but at present his contented thoughts were on Jane and her dazzling future.

He knew no such contentment where his elder daughter was concerned. Christina was seated beside him now, her nose deep in a large volume of *The Adventures of Gil Blas*. He despaired of her, for she was quite determined to defy any attempt to find her a husband, and she had no intention at all of looking for one herself. Looking at her now, her dark hair falling in three heavy ringlets from beneath her dove gray velvet bonnet, her daintily feminine figure sweet in a matching dove-gray spencer and gray-and-white-striped silk gown, he couldn't credit that she was so stubbornly and unreasonably set upon remaining single. He'd tried everything, from gentle persuasion to browbeating, but she'd remained adamant on the matter, and now he was resigned to her decision. He wanted his daughters to be happy as he'd been, for he'd loved both his wives, and had been loved by them, but only Jane seemed about to follow in his footsteps.

He leaned his head back, thinking of his marriages. Christina's mother, Joan Stapleton, had been the daughter of a Gloucestershire clergyman, and she'd died in child-bed. After a subsequent, bitterly painful love affair, he hadn't wanted to marry again, but then Georgiana Vesey had come along. She'd been a lady of very good family, and her romantic elopement with a widower of modest means hadn't pleased her relatives at all. She'd been disinherited during her lifetime, but after her death from a sudden fever, just after Jane was born, the Veseys had relented, and the considerable inheritance that should have been Georgiana's had come to her daughter instead.

Mr Richmond sighed quietly, reflecting on his youth. He'd been devastated by the loss of his first wife at Christina's birth, but after a few years had been persuaded by his friends to reenter the social scene, taking himself to London for a while and leaving his daughter in the country. He'd discovered that he had wit and charm enough to survive very nicely in the capital, and he'd fallen in love again. Oh, how he'd fallen in love! But who could not have tumbled head over heels for a creature as enchanting as Alicia Partington? She'd been so adorable, with laughing green eyes and a mane of golden hair, and she'd shown herself to be flatteringly interested in the young Gloucestershire widower. But although she'd been bewitching, she'd also proved to be faithless, as he'd discovered in Chelsea on a memorable September afternoon in 1784. His eyes clouded as he recalled the pain of that day. He'd quit the capital almost immediately, and within two months had met and married Georgiana Vesey. Ah, sweet Georgiana, she'd brought him such brief happiness, leaving him a widower for the second time only ten months after their marriage; and leaving him, too, with a second daughter, Jane. He hadn't left Gloucestershire again, nor had he met anyone he'd wished to make his third wife, but in spite of Alicia's sins, she still crossed his mind from time to time. If only she'd been faithful, how different might things have been? Clearing his throat a little noisily, he dismissed Alicia from his thoughts, and looked out of the carriage window as the autumn countryside swept by.

Luncheon at the Petty France Inn was a crowded, rather disagreeable affair, for the establishment was the first stage out of Bath, and the last stage in, which meant there were many other travelers availing themselves of its table. There was no pleasure to be had in lingering over the excellent beefsteak pie, not when one's neighbors' elbows were digging into one all the time, and the moment the horses were ready, the journey to Johnstone Street was continued.

It was four in the afternoon when the carriage at last breasted notorious Swainswick Hill, and Bath could be seen spreading up the slopes of the valley below. The elegant terraces, crescents, circuses, and squares were white in the October sunshine, and the Gothic splendor of the abbey church rose majestically above the surrounding rooftops, close to the shining curve of the Avon.

Descending the steep hill, the carriage joined the main London highway, driving southwest into the heart of the spa. The city was a little past its real heyday, when Beau Nash had reigned supreme, but it was still a very fashionable resort. Many fine carriages thronged the streets, and there were stylish ladies and gentlemen strolling on the raised pavements, pausing to look at the windows of the shops.

The carriage drove down Walcot Street toward Pulteney Bridge, for Johnstone Street lay across the river in the fairly new development built on the former Bathwick estate. Jane's excitement could barely be suppressed now that they were actually in Bath, but Christina hardly glanced up from the absorbing pages of *Gil Blas*.

Pulteney Bridge spanned the Avon next to a weir that was swollen by the autumn rain. It was a splendid bridge of superb classical lines, built over with charming shops, so that from the pavement it was impossible to tell it was a bridge. Since it was the only way of crossing the Avon into the other part of Bath, it was also a dreadful bottleneck, and for some reason today seemed to be particularly bad, with traffic reduced to a crawl because of the crush.

It was Jane who first perceived that the cause of the jam was something taking place in Sydney Gardens, the famous Vauxhall or pleasure gardens, that lay about a half-mile ahead, on the edge of the town. A great diversion was in progress, for the whole of Bath seemed to have turned out.

As the weary coachman inched the carriage forward, Jane got up to lower the window glass to see what was happening. After a moment she gave an excited gasp. 'Look! Oh, do look! It's a balloon!'

Mr Richmond sat forward sharply. 'One of those infernal aerostations?' he growled disapprovingly.

'Yes. Oh, *please* look!' Jane was entranced, gazing over the rooftops in the direction of Sydney Gardens.

Christina was roused from the book at last, closing it carefully and setting it on the seat beside her before getting up to squeeze next to her excited sister.

A large crimson-and-blue globe floated serenely in the sky, about three hundred feet up in the air. It was a very novel sight, and Jane stared breathlessly at it, her imagination completely captured. A long rope appeared to be anchoring the balloon to the ground, descending from the golden car slung beneath the globe, and vanishing among the trees of the pleasure gardens. There was a single figure in the car, a daring young pilot who was brandishing a Union Jack to and fro, much to the delight of the crowds.

Still very disapproving, Mr Richmond reluctantly got to his feet, lowering the other glass to peer out.

Jane continued to gaze at the balloon. 'Oh, it's the most wonderful thing I've ever seen,' she breathed. 'Isn't he a hero of the air? I wish I was up there with him.'

Christina heard their father's angry reaction to this last remark, and nudged her sister warningly, but it was to no avail, for Jane's attention was fixed intently on the balloon. 'What must it be like to fly like a bird?' she mused wistfully. 'How magical it must be to float up there, gazing down upon everything.'

Mr Richmond drew irritatedly back inside. 'Close the window at once, ladies,' he commanded, sitting down and replacing his swollen foot carefully on the stool.

Jane didn't hear. Christina nudged her again, sharply this time, and with sudden realization she pulled quickly inside, pouting with disappointment. 'May we not watch it, Father?'

'No, missy, you may not,' he snapped.

'But ...'

'Such engines are vulgar and disreputable, and if I perceive you – either of you – marveling at it again, I shall be obliged to reprimand you most severely.'

Christina knew when it was wise to submit, and she lowered her eyes meekly, resuming her seat, but Jane didn't always know when to stop. 'I don't think it's so very reprehensible just to *look*,' she declared, still pouting.

Mr Richmond's eyes darkened. 'That's quite enough, young lady, you aren't Lady St Clement yet. Aerostations are an abomination, and it isn't without reason that those who ascend in them are called balloonatics. The subject is now closed, is that quite clear?'

They stared at him, astonished by his vehemence.

'Is that quite clear?' he repeated.

'Yes, Father,' they replied.

'And if that thrice-cursed fellow is making ascents from Sydney Gardens, you are both forbidden to go anywhere near. Is that clear as well?'

'Yes, Father.'

'Good.'

For once it was too much, even for Christina. 'Father, is something wrong?' she ventured hesitantly, for she'd never seen him so fierce before, except, perhaps, when he spoke of Bonaparte.

'No. Should there be?' he replied testily.

'No, it's just ...'

'Yes?'

'Well, you *are* being rather, er, forceful.'

'I have my reasons, oh, yes, I have my reasons,' he answered with great feeling; then he looked away, signifying that the conversation was most definitely at an end.

The sisters looked askance at each other, still very puzzled. Why did he loathe balloons and balloonists so much?

No further mention was made of the offending object in the sky, and several minutes later it descended out of sight into the Sydney Gardens Vauxhall. The traffic began to move again, and the carriage crossed the bridge, entering the short length of Argyle Street. A hundred yards or so later they were negotiating Laura Place, the elegant circus off which Johnstone Street led.

Johnstone Street was a short cul-de-sac of fine three-story town houses, and number 14A, the property of Sir Archibald Fitton, was almost on the corner of Laura Place. The house next door, number 15, was right on the corner, and a small crowd was gathered on the pavement outside, gazing not in the direction of the pleasure gardens, but up at a pedimented second-floor window, as if waiting for something.

The coachman edged the team past the crowd, and drew up by the graceful wrought-iron railings of number 14A. Mr Richmond alighted first, lowering himself gingerly to the pavement and taking care not to jar his sore foot. As he assisted his daughters down, a stir passed through the crowd, and someone called out, 'Mr Pitt! Mr Pitt!'

Mr Richmond turned as quickly as his foot would permit, looking up at the pedimented window as everyone began to cheer.

Someone had drawn the net curtains aside, and a man had appeared. He was tall and very slender, his face puffy and unwell, and his powdered auburn hair was tied back with a black ribbon. His clothes were formal, making him seem even more frail, and he was immediately recognizable as *the* Mr Pitt, for his questing nose had appeared in countless political cartoons. He was still only forty-three, but ill health had aged him, and perhaps long public service had as well, for he'd become prime minister at the incredible age of only twenty-four, and had held the office for eighteen years before resigning.

Mr Richmond stared openmouthed. 'Upon my soul, I do believe I've taken the house next door to Pitt himself!'

Christina smiled. 'I knew he was supposed to be coming here for the cure, it was in *The Times* a week or so ago.'

'By Gad, how splendid,' breathed her father. 'Maybe I'll manage to get an introduction, and then I'll persuade him to get back to the helm, where he belongs. We need him to stand up to the French!'

Christina glanced at the unfortunate Mr Pitt, who didn't look in any condition to be at the helm, or to take on the French.

Jane drew her aside as Mr Richmond continued to stare up at his hero. 'Trust you to have read *The Times*, Christina Richmond.'

'It happens to be very informative.'

'And excruciatingly dull. Oh, do stop looking at that window, I want to talk about the balloon!'

'Sh, or Father will hear,' Christina warned anxiously. 'You'd be wise to forget all about balloons, Jane.'

'Father is being very unreasonable.'

'Maybe, but he's still our father, and what he says is law.'

Jane sighed crossly, turning to look toward Sydney Gardens. 'I *would* like to see it, and I'd *adore* to fly in it.'

'Put any such notion from your head, Jane. You're here to meet Robert Temple, and you'd be exceeding foolish to do anything that might even remotely jeopardize the betrothal. Ladies don't make ascents in balloons, certainly not unmarried ladies about to make grand matches!'

Jane's eyes flashed, and suddenly she was very much the spirited redhead. 'I sometimes think you haven't got an adventurous bone in your body, Christina.'

'There's a difference between being adventurous and being head-strong, which latter trait you appear to have perfected over the years!'

Jane scowled, at her, and then gathered her skirts to sweep into the house.

Christina sighed, for although she loved her sister dearly, there were times when she could cheerfully have strangled her. The balloon wasn't important, but Robert Temple was. She glanced toward Sydney Gardens, strongly suspecting that Jane wouldn't forget about the balloon; indeed, if there was a chance of sneaking off to see it at close quarters, the future Lady St Clement was quite foolishly capable of doing just that.

3

S IR ARCHIBALD FITTON was a gentleman of taste, as the interior of
his residence bore elegant witness. Furnished in the French style,
it was a gracious dwelling that both Christina and Jane found very
much to their liking, although their father cast dark glances at all
things French, except, perhaps, champagne and cognac.

Christina's bedroom was at the rear of the house on the first floor,
looking over a walled garden and two hundred yards of open land
sweeping down to the Avon, not far from Pulteney Bridge. Bath rose
from the far bank, presided over by the tower of the fifteenth-century
abbey church.

The room was blue and white, with striped cotton on the walls
above low white paneling, and ruched white silk at the two tall shuttered windows. The Aubusson carpet was beautifully patterned in the
same colors, and so was the tapestry-upholstered armchair before the
fire, but refreshing contrast was provided by the lemon silk hangings
of the bed. A dressing table covered with frilled white muslin stood
against the wall between the windows, and there was an inlaid table
beside the bed. In the corner to one side of the carved marble fireplace there was a washstand, and in the other corner there was an
immense wardrobe with mirrors on the doors. Paintings and more
mirrors adorned the walls, a domed clock and some silver-gilt candle-
sticks stood on the mantelpiece, and an open potpourri jar had been
placed on the hearth, filling the warm air with the scent of roses.

The short October evening was drawing to a close, and because
the windows faced almost due west, the sunset shone brilliantly in on
Christina as she sat reading in the armchair by the fire, waiting to go
down to an early dinner.

She wore a satin gown the same lilac as her eyes. It had a golden belt with a clasp fixing the high waistline immediately beneath her breasts, and long tiffany gauze sleeves gathered at her wrists. The fashionable train spilled over the carpet, and the low scooped neckline was graced by the only item of jewelry she'd chosen to wear tonight, a dainty pearl choker necklace bequeathed to her by her mother. A fringed white shawl rested lightly around her shoulders, and her dark hair was twisted up into a loose knot, leaving a froth of little curls to frame her face.

The pages of *Gil Blas* turned slowly as she whiled away the minutes before dinner. Her father intended to follow the Bath regimen to the letter, which meant very early mornings indeed, hence the disagreeable hour set for dinner. As always, *Gil Blas* absorbed her, so much so that she gave a start when the clock began to chime half-past six. She closed the book, smiling a little as she wondered if the stay in Bath would lead to her father's realizing his great ambition, meeting Mr Pitt.

The door burst open suddenly, and Jane came in in a flurry of rose-pink organdy muslin. A diamond-studded comb flashed in her carefully pinned hair, and a knotted pink-and-white shawl trailed along the floor behind her. She was holding a letter that had just been delivered, and her eyes were bright with excitement and pleasure. 'Oh, Christina, he's written to me again! It's a perfect letter, simply perfect!'

'What else could such a paragon write?' murmured Christina, setting *Gil Blas* aside. 'Am I going to be permitted to read it, or is it too passionate for my delicate sensibilities?'

Jane gave her a pert look. 'I've a mind to keep it from you now.'

'But you won't, because you wish to flaunt it,' observed Christina accurately.

'Certainly I do, wouldn't you?'

'Probably.' Christina held out her hand for the letter, which was written on the same fine vellum as all the others.

Curzon Street
October 3, 1803

My dear Miss Richmond,
The singular joy I feel because you are to be my wife is such that I am compelled to write to you again. The moment of our first

meeting will be precious indeed, and you may believe sincerity dictates my pen when I assure you that time will pass on leaden feet until the evening of the autumn ball.

I am, yours very simply,
Robert Temple

Jane watched breathlessly. 'Isn't it perfect? Isn't it the most perfect letter ever written?'

'Well, I don't know that I'd go quite *that* far ...' began Christina teasingly.

'Don't be infuriating, just admit that he's quite wonderful and that I'm the most fortunate creature on earth!'

'Very well, I admit it on both counts,' replied Christina, returning the letter.

Jane held it against her heart, twirling joyfully so that the perfume from the potpourri jar moved richly around the room. 'I'm so happy I think I might burst!'

'Oh, please don't do that, not in my bedroom, anyway.'

Jane ignored her. 'I'm going to be the envy of the world at the ball, and I'm going to exult in every second of it!' she cried, laughing.

Such happiness was infectious, and Christina found herself laughing as well, but then Jane suddenly stopped twirling, a lightning change of mood making her serious. 'What if I bore him?'

Christina stared at her. 'Bore him? *You*? Hardly.'

'No, I mean it, Christina. You know what we've heard about him, about the many ladies he's, well, he's known ...'

'So?'

'So I'm a green country girl, I've never been to London, and I don't know anything about high society. Why, *you* know more about it than I do!'

'Gentlemen like to play the field, Jane, but they don't want their wives to have done the same.' Christina got up, taking her sister's hand. 'Don't you think it would be strange if such a gentleman *hadn't* associated with the opposite sex?'

Jane lowered her eyes. 'I know, but I can't help feeling dull. How can I possibly be as interesting as an actress? I haven't had any experience at all.'

'I should hope not. Listen to me, Jane Richmond. Husbands should be experienced, for then they can know how to please – no, to pleasure – their wives.'

'Christina!' Jane was shocked at such a worldly observation.

'Well, it's true. A wife should be innocent, and she should be taught everything by a loving, knowledgeable husband. At least, that's what *I* would wish.'

'Is that the sort of thing you read in your books?'

Christina grinned. 'It's the sort of thing I read *between the lines* in my books.'

'Perhaps I should take up reading.'

'Why bother when you'll soon have a real flesh-and-blood husband to occupy your time.'

Jane was still staring at her. 'How can you look so demure and yet say such outrageous things?'

'Being demure doesn't preclude me from thinking.'

'Evidently.' Jane's gaze became quizzical. 'Which must lead me to again ask the obvious.'

'Why don't I put myself out to find a husband?'

'Yes.'

'For the same old answer, because I wouldn't settle for anything less than a love match. Oh, please don't take offense, for I don't in any way wish to denigrate your match with Robert Temple, but you have to admit you seem to have been fortunate.'

'You might be as well.'

Christina shook her head. 'I'd rather remain as I am.'

'But ...'

'Please, Jane, just leave it alone.'

'Oh, very well. For the time being.'

Christina sighed. This conversation had taken place in so many different ways over the last few years that she really didn't think there could be any more variations on the same theme.

Jane went to one of the windows, staring out at the silhouette of Bath Abbey against the blood-red sunset. Thoughts of the balloon returned. 'Christina, I do think Father's being grossly unfair about the balloon. It's quite ridiculous for us to be forbidden even to go to Sydney, Gardens.'

'I agree, but Father quite obviously has his reasons.'

'Which are to be kept a mystery.'

'That's his privilege.'

Jane glanced at her over her shoulder. 'I still think balloons are wonderful,' she said slowly.

For once, Christina didn't detect anything untoward in her sister's manner. 'I've found out a little about this particular one,' she said.

'You have? How?'

'Jenny told me.' Jenny was Christina's maid, who, together with Jane's maid, Ellen, and their father's man Edward, had traveled to Johnstone Street several days ahead of the family.

Jane left the window. 'What did she tell you?'

'Well, the aeronaut is a certain Mr William Grenfell, a dashing young gentleman who has recently been making ascents over London.'

'A gentleman?'

'Most definitely, and good-looking as well, from all accounts.'

Jane's eyes sparkled. 'Oh, how romantic. A handsome young gentleman pilot, soaring in the sky over London and Bath.'

'He makes only captive ascents, and started here only yesterday, which accounts for all the furor when we arrived. It's still very much a nine-day wonder.'

'Captive ascents? What does that mean?'

'The balloon is held to the ground by a long rope.'

Jane drew a sighing breath, her eyes still shining. 'Oh, I *do* so want to see it all properly.'

Christina was alerted at last. 'No,' she said firmly.

'Oh, but—'

'No! We've been forbidden, Jane, and that's the end of it.'

'We could just stroll along Great Pulteney Street one day soon—'

'No,' repeated Christina wearily. 'I'm not going to disobey Father, Jane, and under the present circumstances, *you* shouldn't even be thinking about it.'

'Because of Robert Temple?'

'Is there any need to ask? Of *course* because of Robert Temple. I know you only too well, Jane Richmond. You wouldn't be content with a mere stroll, you'd have to go into Sydney Gardens, and then you'd have to walk right up to the balloon. I wouldn't put it past you to then step into the balloon's car and instruct Mr Grenfell to take you up!'

'I wouldn't!'

'No? Forgive me if I view that assurance with a rather jaundiced eye. I'm Christina, remember? I've been with you all your life, and I *know* the sort of scrape you're capable of getting into. It isn't so very long since I caught you riding bareback in the lower meadow, and walking with that shepherd to look for lambs. Then you waded in the stream up to your knees, chased that peddler with a stick, argued with Squire James outside the church—'

'He was being positively beastly about the Reverend Hunter's sermon!' protested Jane indignantly.

'You still shouldn't have called him a boneheaded old clodhopper.'

Jane grinned. 'But that's exactly what he is.'

'Maybe, but *ladies* don't say such things,' answered Christina, struggling not to grin as well. 'Jane, your impetuosity has caused a great deal of trouble over the years, and you simply can't take a chance now. You're going to be Lady St Clement, so please, *please* behave like it.'

'I am behaving like it. I'm a reformed character, truly I am.'

'I wonder how many incorrigible miscreants have appeared before judges and said the selfsame thing?' mused Christina with some feeling.

Jane was offended. 'I'm hardly an incorrigible miscreant.'

'No? What else would you call someone who's constantly in hot water of one sort or another, albeit without Father ever knowing?'

'I've already said that I'm a reformed character. I don't intend to misbehave at all, Christina, I promise.'

'I sincerely hope so, otherwise I don't give this match with Robert Temple much of a chance. You really must curb your hotheadedness, Jane.'

Jane sighed. 'I know, and I will. I want this marriage, Christina – in fact I think I'm in love with Robert already.'

Christina smiled. 'Just you keep reminding yourself of the fact, and then behave accordingly.'

The dinner gong echoed dully through the house, and Christina adjusted her shawl. 'I'm hoping against hope that we're going to be spared roast beef and Yorkshire pudding just this once.'

'I hate to disillusion you, but when I crossed the landing just now, the aroma was suspiciously familiar.'

'Oh, I do wish Father would choose something else for a change. I swear I'll wake up one morning and find my head has turned into a Yorkshire pudding.'

Jane laughed, linking her arm. 'If you found yourself a husband, Christina Richmond, you'd be in charge of the menu and need never have roast beef ever again.'

'With my luck, I'd choose a husband who shared Father's culinary fixation,' replied Christina dryly.

They proceeded from the room and down the staircase, but at the bottom Christina felt obliged to issue another warning. 'For goodness' sake, steer clear of all mention of balloons. A safer topic of conversation would be the blessed Mr Pitt.'

'Safer, but as dull as dull can be.'

'Grin and bear it, sister mine,' replied Christina, pushing open the dining-room door.

They entered to see the immense joint of roast beef ready and waiting on the table.

4

THE STRICT REGIMEN of the Bath cure commenced before dawn for Mr Richmond, who rose before either of his daughters was awake. He was conveyed to the Cross Bath in a sedan chair, along with many fellow sufferers, immersed for an hour in the hot waters, and then wrapped in blankets from head to toe to be returned to Johnstone Street in the same sedan chair. He immediately adjourned to his bed to cool down, after which he'd take breakfast and then sally forth again, this time to the Pump Room to drink the water. It was his return from the Cross Bath that at last aroused his daughters from their slumber.

Christina awoke, stretching luxuriously in the lemon-silk-hung bed. She felt refreshed after such a long sleep, and didn't lie there for long. Flinging back the bedclothes, she slipped from the warm bed and put on her apricot wool wrap. Pausing only to drag a brush through her tangled hair, she left the room to go to sit with Jane for their customary early-morning dish of tea.

Her sister's room was at the front of the house, overlooking the corner of Laura Place. It was a gold-and-cream room, bright with early-morning sun because the windows faced the east. Jane's maid, Ellen, had already brought the tray of tea and attended to the fire, so the room was not only bright and inviting, it was comfortably warm as well.

Jane was sitting up sleepily in her immense four-poster bed, her red hair tumbling over the shoulders of her white satinet nightgown. She smiled as Christina entered. 'Good morning, I trust you slept as well as I did.'

'I think I must have done,' replied Christina, hurrying to kiss her cheek before going to the tray of tea next to the velvet fireside chair.

Jane watched her pour the tea. 'You're always disgustingly eager for your first cup of the day.'

'I *love* my morning tea,' admitted Christina, taking one of the dainty floral porcelain cups to her, and then returning to sit in the chair, stretching out her bare toes toward the fire.

They sipped the tea in companionable silence for a while, and then Christina noticed Robert Temple's miniature on the mantelpiece, the painted face caught in a shaft of sunlight. The eloquent gray eyes seemed to be gazing at her, and by a trick of the light the lips appeared to move. She lowered her cup.

Jane observed her. 'I'm of a mind to be piqued, for you appear to find my intended completely absorbing.'

'Well, he *is* rather striking, you have to admit.'

'I think he's beautiful,' sighed Jane.

'*Beautiful*? What sort of word is that to apply to a gentleman?' Christina smiled at her.

'A silly word,' admitted Jane, 'but it does seem appropriate. Oh, I can't wait for the night of the ball.' She sat up then. 'That reminds me, when Ellen came in a little while ago I instructed her to go to Madame Gilbert, the couturière in Milsom Street. I've been in such a tizzy about everything recently that I've lost weight, and when I tried on my new plowman's gauze evening gown last night, it positively hung. It has to be taken in before the ball, and last time we stayed here, Madame Gilbert was so very efficient with that badly torn pelisse.'

'She was indeed.' Christina smiled then. 'No doubt you'll soon be eating like the proverbial horse again, and the poor woman will have to let it all out again.'

Jane laughed. 'Probably. Actually, I've taken it upon myself to mention your gown in the message to Madame Gilbert as well. I hope you don't mind.'

'My gown? Why?'

'Well, when you tried it on before we left home, I admit I thought it the prettiest thing, and more bluebell than our woods in May, but on reflection I think the silk needs just a little adornment.'

Christina thought for a moment. 'You're probably right – you usually are where such things are concerned.'

'Only because I make the effort,' observed Jane slyly.

Christina gave her an arch look. 'You aren't going to start all that at *this* unearthly hour, are you?'

'Well, in the absence of any other diversion ...'

'There'll be diversion enough in a moment, for I believe I hear Father stirring from his bed. He'll be expecting his breakfast in a moment, and then the chair will be here to bear him away for his obligatory three glasses of the water.' Christina finished her cup of tea and got up. 'Shall we inspect the house after he's gone? I mean *really* inspect it, every nook and cranny from attic to cellar?'

'Oh, yes, like we did in Queen Square the last time we were here.'

'It's settled?'

'It's settled.'

Mr Richmond did indeed call for his breakfast shortly afterward, and his daughters were astonished at the veritable mountain of bacon, kidneys, scrambled eggs, and sausages he devoured; evidently immersion in Bath's hot waters gave one a more-than-just-hearty appetite!

He departed for the Pump Room at nine o'clock precisely, and was most pleased to find himself following the great Mr Pitt's chair through the town. He gave little thought as to how his daughters were going to amuse themselves on their first morning; he was too intent upon how he was going to achieve an introduction to England's great leader.

The moment he'd departed, Christina and Jane commenced their promised inspection of the house, beginning with the attic. There wasn't a corner of roof space they didn't pry into; they were even impudent enough to go through the contents of a large sea chest, and all was well until an enormous spider ran over Jane's hand. Spiders were the one thing she couldn't bear at any price, and with it shuddering squeal she gathered her orange muslin skirts to flee to the safety of the floor below. Spiders weren't Christina's favorite creatures either, and in a moment she was following her sister, the hem of her dark-blue dimity gown covered with dust and the ribbons on her day cap fluttering around her head. On reaching the landing below, she suddenly realized how very funny they must both look, and she began to laugh. For a moment Jane wasn't amused, but then she had to smile as well, and after that they elected not to poke around where they had no business to be.

They continued with their inspection, but decorously this time, refraining from opening cupboards and drawers which were none of their concern. They'd completed the bedroom floor and were on their way down to the ground floor, when something made Christina glance back at Jane's room. The door was open, affording a clear view through the windows at the front of the house: there, floating serenely just above the rooftops of the houses opposite, was the balloon.

Christina's steps faltered, and her breath caught on an amazed gasp, for there was nothing captive about this flight; the balloon was as free as a bird. 'Look! Oh, look, Jane!' she cried, turning to hurry back up the stairs.

Jane saw the balloon as well, and with an excited squeak she followed. They ran to the bedroom window, raising the sash and leaning out to stare at the incredible sight hovering in the air across the street. They weren't alone in watching, for a great crowd filled the pavements and thoroughfares, and the traffic was in a terrible jam as vehicles attempted to turn and follow the great spectacle in the sky.

Mr William Grenfell's crimson-and-blue balloon was wondrous to behold, and more splendidly accoutered today than it had been before. The gilded car, seemingly empty, was swathed with golden satin, and there were immense oars and wings, made of white silk stretched over wooden frames, protruding from the sides. These oars and wings were evidently intended to row the balloon backward and forward, or up and down, but there wasn't anyone in evidence to employ them. Union Jacks, still rolled around their poles, rested against the inside of the car, and the ropes of the huge net enclosing the balloon itself were fluttering with red pennants. There were Latin mottoes painted on the globe, and Christina could make them out quite clearly. *Negata tentat iter via*, and *Spernit et humum fugiente penna*, she read, calling upon her school lessons to translate them as 'He dares journey by forbidden ways' and 'Even the earth he spurns on flying wing.'

As Jane stared at the balloon, Christina had a wry thought. 'I wonder what Father would say?' she murmured. 'We're actually being wicked enough to gaze upon an aerostation.'

'Without a balloonatic in sight,' observed Jane in puzzlement. 'Look, the anchor rope seems to have broken! Yes, that's what happened, it was making a captive ascent and the rope broke! But where's the pilot? Oh, you don't think he's fallen out, do you?'

Christina looked at the golden car again, detecting a slight shuddering that told of occupancy after all. 'No, I think he's still in the car,' she said reassuringly. 'He's doing something right inside, where we can't see. Yes, there he is!'

The pilot appeared suddenly, leaning over the edge to thrust something out that plummeted to the street below, scattering the crowd. With a dull thud, the object, a sandbag, struck the pavement, burst open, and showered sand in all directions. A second sandbag followed, and the pilot watched anxiously to see if the balloon rose to a safer level above the rooftops, for at the moment it was in imminent danger of striking the line of chimneys. There was a great cheer from the ground as the balloon obliged, floating up just sufficiently to spare both the car and the chimneys from disaster. Hearing the cheers, the pilot was showman enough to wave cheerfully down at the onlookers, although he must have been very apprehensive indeed about what was to happen to him.

Mr William Grenfell was a flamboyant young gentleman, with blond hair and a good-looking, sunburnt face. He wore a full-sleeved white shirt, unbuttoned at the throat, and his gray silk neckcloth hung loose. His waistcoat was made of fine electric-blue armazine, and his trousers were striped in gray and white. It was this latter item of apparel that caught Jane's astonished attention. 'Why, he's wearing trousers! I thought only sailors wore such things.'

'Trousers are set to be the new fashion for all gentlemen,' replied Christina.

'They are? How do you know that?' demanded Jane, tearing her attention from the balloon and its pilot to look at her sister.

'I read it in a journal,' replied Christina, grinning. 'Reading is very informative, you know. You should try it.'

'I shall ignore your sarcasm,' responded her sister, leaning out of the window again. 'I don't believe it about trousers, anyway, they're *not* going to become universally fashionable. Nothing will ever take the place of breeches, you mark my words.'

THE WRONG MISS RICHMOND

'You're probably right. I think he looks a little foppish, don't you?'

'Maybe a little, but he's very dashing, isn't he?' Jane gazed admiringly at the young pilot, who had by now perceived them leaning from the window.

The removal of the more immediate danger had evidently bolstered his spirits, for a broad grin spread across his face and he waved boldly at them.

Christina refrained from responding, knowing it would hardly be the thing, but Jane forgot herself completely, leaning forward even more and waving back with complete abandon.

Appalled, Christina pulled her back inside. 'You mustn't, Jane!'

'Why not? I'm only waving.'

'You're not, you're positively jumping up and down with enthusiasm!'

'But it's so exciting,' protested Jane, wrenching her arm free and leaning out again.

A breath of wind had lifted the balloon, and Mr Grenfell had put the two ladies from his mind. His back was toward them now, and he was tugging upon a rope that hung down from inside the neck of the balloon. He kept tugging, then glancing up at the billowing orb above, as the breeze wafted him away over the rooftops in the direction of Argyle Street and Pulteney Bridge.

Jane craned her neck to watch, only drawing back inside when the balloon had drifted completely out of sight, pursued by the great gaggle of people and vehicles on the ground. She glanced hopefully at Christina. 'I don't suppose we could...?'

'No, we could not.'

'But Father only said we weren't to go to Sydney Gardens.'

'He said we weren't to have anything to do with the balloon, and he meant precisely that,' replied Christina firmly.

Jane sighed a little petulantly. 'Father's being very tiresome.'

'A trait you've more than inherited.'

Jane smiled ruefully. 'What an acid tongue you have, to be sure.'

'Come on, I've a mind to sit out in the garden.'

'Oh, all right.' Jane glanced wistfully out of the window again. 'I still think the balloon is the most exciting thing I've ever seen, and I'd love more than anything to actually make an ascent.'

'Do that and you'd have to marry Mr Grenfell, for to be sure, you'd have compromised yourself out of any hope of becoming Lady St Clement,' replied Christina, taking her arm and steering her from the room.

5

THE GARDEN AT the rear of the house was, in its way, as stylish and superior as the residence itself, for Sir Archibald was very horticulturally inclined, and expected flowers to bloom throughout the year, even though he was seldom there to see. He employed two full-time gardeners to attend to matters, and their endeavors did him proud, for although it was October, the flowerbeds were very colorful indeed.

There were asters and dahlias, Michaelmas daisies and goldenrod, and a rose arbor that was still adorned with sweet-scented pink blooms. Ivy grew over the perimeter wall, pansies, geraniums, and nasturtiums edged the stone-flagged paths, and lily pads floated on the raised pond. The fruit trees were heavy with apples and pears, and two maids were engaged in picking walnuts from a gnarled tree growing against the wall. The gardeners were busy, one preparing potted fuchsias to overwinter in the greenhouse, the other taking cuttings from a laurel bush by the path leading to the coach house at the bottom of the garden.

After strolling all over the garden, Christina and Jane at last sat down on a wrought-iron bench that was sheltered by the wall. A sumac tree grew next to it, its foliage just on the point of turning into the fiery autumn glory that made it such a popular addition to any garden.

Christina surveyed the garden with immense approval. 'I admire Sir Archibald's taste, for this is indeed a splendid October garden.'

'As colorful as the ball will be.'

Christina had to smile. 'Are we back to the ball again? I swear you talked of nothing else every inch we walked along those paths.'

Jane gave her a sly look. 'Well, we could always talk about the balloon....'

'No, thank you very much.'

'Then I shall talk about the ball. You do think Madame Gilbert will be able to prepare our gowns in time, don't you?'

'I'm sure she will. She's already sent word that she'll see us today, and I'm quite certain she'll be only too glad to do any necessary work, if only so that she can crow to the world that she's saved the day for the future Lady St Clement.'

'I hope you're right.'

'Stop worrying, Jane, everything's going to be all right.'

'I can't help worrying. I want to look absolutely perfect that night.'

'And so you will. That plowman's gauze is exquisite, and suits you more than anything else I've ever seen you in. Robert is going to be charmed when he sees you.'

Jane flushed a little with pleasure. 'Do you really think so?'

'Stop fishing for compliments,' replied Christina, smiling.

'Beast.'

Across the Avon the bells of the abbey began to ring out, a joyous sound that echoed all around so loudly that at first they didn't clearly hear the shout of warning.

'Watch out below!'

Christina gave a start, glancing around. 'What was that?'

'Mm?'

Something, Christina didn't know what, made her glance up into the sky suddenly, and her heart almost stopped with shock, for there, floating barely thirty feet overhead, was Mr Grenfell's balloon. It was descending toward them, its shadow suddenly blotting out the sun.

The pilot's face peered anxiously down from the car. 'Watch out below!' he shouted again, holding another sandbag aloft ready to toss down in an effort to lighten the balloon.

Jane glanced up with a shocked gasp, then gathered her skirts and fled toward the house. For a moment Christina was too startled to move, but then she collected her wits, dashing from the seat just as the sandbag hurtled earthward, thudding in a bombburst of sand on the path behind her.

The two maids picking walnuts ran shrieking into the house, and the gardeners left their tasks with some alacrity, making for the relative shelter of the coach house.

Jane had halted by the French window into the dining room, and she caught Christina's arm, staring up with a mixture of alarm and fascination at the balloon as it billowed above the garden. The ejection of the sandbag had been to no avail, for the car was only just above the fruit trees now, and Mr Grenfell could be seen frantically tugging at the rope that vanished into the neck of the balloon.

Christina pressed her hands to her mouth as the car swung slowly from side to side, snapping the topmost twigs of the pear tree. Still more height was lost, and with a dreadful splintering sound the car crashed further into the tree. Pears tumbled to the ground, rolling in all directions, and leaves fluttered after them. Mr Grenfell gripped one of the ropes supporting the car, which was tilting alarmingly to one side as the balloon continued to descend, and Christina could see now that the globe was deflating, its surface rippling in the breeze.

At last the car became wedged between the branches, remaining at a precarious angle. The pilot held on for dear life as the balloon settled over the trees, the orb shrinking all the time so that in a few minutes it would look like a huge crimson-and-blue sheet draped there to dry in the sun.

Christina took a hesitant step toward the tree. 'Are ... are you all right?' she called, her voice almost lost in the continuing pealing of the bells.

More pears fell to the ground as Mr Grenfell struggled to ease himself from the car on to the relative safety of a branch. Torn leaves and broken twigs followed the pears as he lowered his legs before dropping down on to the grass. His full-sleeved shirt was torn and spoiled, and his gray silk neckcloth had disappeared altogether. Pausing only to straighten his waistcoat, he came toward Christina, who'd been joined by Jane now.

Smiling more than a little ruefully, he sketched an elegant bow. 'A thousand apologies, ladies. I trust my sudden arrival hasn't frightened you too much,' he said, raising his voice above the abbey bells. He was well-spoken, and close to, was decidedly good-looking, with roguish green eyes. He ran his hand through his disheveled blond hair, his glance lingering admiringly on Jane for a moment. 'I'm mortified to have come such a humiliating cropper. Indeed, Icarus and I would appear to have rather too much in common for comfort at this very moment. That was my first free flight, and was definitely unplanned; first the anchor rope broke, and then the flap valve jammed open.'

Jane had been staring at him, but now looked toward the balloon. 'The ... the flap valve?'

'Yes. It's used to release hydrogen and thus lower the balloon. On this occasion it chose to remain open, releasing hydrogen all the time.'

Jane was none the wiser. 'Forgive me, but I don't know what hydrogen is either.'

'Perhaps you know it as inflammable air,' he replied, the admiration still plain in his green eyes as he looked at her. When she was being prettily puzzled, Jane was quite devastatingly appealing to the opposite sex, and Mr Grenfell was no exception to the rule. He gazed at her, suddenly tongue-tied.

Christina felt uncomfortable, and not only because he was obviously captivated by her sister; their father might return at any moment, and the Lord alone knew what his reaction would be to finding the loathed aerostation actually ensconced over the pear tree.

Even as the dread thought crossed her mind, there was an angry roar from the French window behind them, clearly audible above the bells. 'I say, sir! You, sir! What's the meaning of this outrage?' Mr Richmond stood there, his gouty foot held up carefully from the ground as he leaned on his stick. He was glowering at the unfortunate pilot.

Mr Grenfell tore his gaze away from Jane, looking in some surprise at the quivering, furious figure behind them. He sketched another bow. 'Mr William Grenfell. Your servant, sir.'

'How *dare* you violate this garden, sirrah! How *dare* you place your infernal contraption on these premises! I won't have it, d'you hear? I won't have it!'

'I ... I apologize most profusely, sir ...' began the aeronaut, a little taken aback by the other's strong tone.

'That's not good enough, sirrah! Tampering with the laws of

nature brings retribution, as this debacle has more than proved. Leave this property at once, sir.'

'But, sir, my balloon....'

'Can remain where it is for the moment. It's *you* I wish to see removed from this garden. Out, sir, this very minute, or I'll have the authorities upon you for trespass!'

Seeing there was no reasoning with him, Mr Grenfell turned apologetically to Christina and Jane. 'My apologies are sincerely meant, ladies, and I trust that you at least forgive my intrusion.'

Jane smiled at him, her brown eyes large and lustrous. 'Of course we do, Mr Grenfell.'

He took her hand, raising it to his lips. 'May I know your name?' he inquired.

'Miss Jane Richmond, and this is my elder sister, Christina.'

He gazed into her eyes, not even glancing at Christina. 'I'm honored to make your acquaintance,' he murmured.

Mr Richmond was almost beside himself with rage. 'I ordered you off this property, sir, and yet I perceive you to be still very much in evidence! I intend to have you ejected!' Turning, he stomped painfully back into the house, shouting for the butler to go for a constable.

Christina quickly put a warning hand on the pilot's arm. 'I think you'd better leave, Mr Grenfell.'

He nodded reluctantly. 'Is he always like this?' he asked with some feeling.

'Only where balloons are concerned, I'm afraid,' she replied. 'Come this way, I'll show you out through the coach house. Jane, you go and calm Father down, otherwise he really will bring the constables.'

'All right.' Jane gathered her skirts and hurried into the house.

Mr Grenfell stared wistfully after her, but allowed Christina to draw him away along the path.

The green traveling carriage loomed in the shadows of the coach house, and a cat slipped away like a wraith into a corner, disturbed in its hunting. There was a strange murmuring sound from beyond the outer door, a sound that became suddenly clear as Christina opened the door to allow the pilot to escape. A fairly large crowd had congregated on the open land sweeping down to the river, having evidently followed the balloon's disastrous progress. The only reason the murmuring hadn't been heard earlier was that the abbey bells were still pealing out gladly.

The aeronaut turned apologetically to her again. 'I really am sorry about all this, Miss Richmond.'

'You hardly did it on purpose, Mr Grenfell.'

'May I inquire when I will be permitted to retrieve my balloon?'

'How long will it take you?'

'With my men, about an hour, I should think.'

'My father is due to call on Mr Tyson, the master of ceremonies, at two o'clock, so if you come then ...'

'Thank heaven for Bath ritual,' he said, smiling. 'Will you and Miss Jane be at home then?'

'Yes, sir, but I think it a little remiss of you to ask,' she replied coolly, knowing that the question was solely owing to his ill-concealed interest in Jane.

He had the grace to smile ruefully. 'I don't mean to be obvious, Miss Richmond.'

'Nevertheless that is what you are being, sir. Perhaps I should inform you that my sister is soon to be betrothed, and that therefore any hopes you may be entertaining of furthering her acquaintance should be well and truly quashed.'

Disappointment entered his green eyes. 'Then quashed they will have to be,' he murmured, taking her hand and kissing it. 'À bientôt, Miss Richmond.'

'Mr Grenfell.' Uncomfortably aware of the curious stares of the onlookers, she drew gladly back into the coach house, closing the door.

As she hurried through the garden to the house, Jane came out to meet her. 'It's all right, Christina, I've persuaded Father that there's no need to send for anyone.'

'Thank goodness.'

Jane glanced back toward the coach house. 'I take it he's made good his escape?'

'Yes, but he's returning later to collect his balloon. I've told him to come when Father goes to the master of ceremonies at two.'

'Oh, good.'

'We're not going to have anything more to do with him, Jane,' warned Christina.

'Oh, but—'

'Nothing whatsoever,' repeated Christina firmly.

Jane sighed, gazing at the balloon, which had now collapsed sadly all over the tree, hanging so limply it was hard to believe it had ever been inflated to float above the rooftops.

Christina looked crossly at her. 'Just remember why you're here in Bath, Jane Richmond.'

'I won't forget.'

'Mr William Grenfell would like nothing better than for you to forget,' replied Christina. 'I thought he would melt away when he gazed into your eyes.'

'Oh?'

'Don't use that airy tone with me, I know you too well. You enjoyed exerting your charm over him like that.'

'And if I did?'

'It was misplaced, Jane. Now, then, I'm going to try to wheedle Father into allowing the balloon to be taken away this afternoon when he's out.' Christina walked on into the house.

6

M R RICHMOND WASN'T at all pleased with his elder daughter, whom he saw fit to blame on several counts. As the elder sister, she should have ushered Jane into the house the moment the balloon appeared, instead of remaining outside to watch the entire disgraceful episode, and she certainly shouldn't have encouraged a conversation with the pilot, escorted him from the premises in full view of a staring crowd, or gone so far as to tell him when it would be convenient for him to retrieve his balloon!

As he at last grudgingly consented to allow Mr Grenfell to collect his property from the pear tree, Christina was left wondering greatly what lay behind the vitriolic dislike. Balloons weren't exactly a common occurrence – indeed they were very few and far between – and yet he'd somehow formed what appeared to be a completely unreasonable antagonism toward them. It was very intriguing, so much so that she was on the point of asking him outright what it was all about, when Madame Gilbert, the couturière, arrived, preventing the question.

The dressmaker knew all about the balloon's undignified descent into the garden, for the news had traveled the length and breadth of Bath, and it was to learn all about the incident that the talkative Frenchwoman had hastened so promptly to Johnstone Street. She was very adept indeed when it came to subtly extracting every morsel of information, especially from someone as basically unwary as Jane, and by the time she left with the two ball gowns, she knew exactly how much the future Lady St Clement admired balloons and balloon-ists. It wouldn't be long before Bath society heard all about it, for Miss Jane Richmond was a very interesting person – how could she not be, when she was set to marry one of England's most eligible gentlemen?

During the couturière's visit there had been little Christina could do to stop Jane's indiscreet revelations, but the moment the Frenchwoman had departed, Jane was left in no doubt at all what her elder sister thought of her lack of wisdom; she was also warned that Mr Grenfell's return that afternoon was an occasion that would now require the utmost prudence. Jane, belatedly chastened, promised faithfully to be very good, but it was a promise that was thrown to the four winds when she was again faced with the temptation of learning more about the mysteries of ballooning.

At a quarter to two precisely, Mr Richmond embarked in a sedan chair to be conveyed across Bath to the residence of the master of ceremonies, a gentleman of the utmost importance. It was unthinkable that any new arrival in Bath should fail to pay such a call, for Mr Tyson wielded absolute power over every social function of consequence, and could bar any individual, even the father of the future Lady St Clement.

The anxious Mr Grenfell had evidently been waiting secretly nearby with his small band of assistants from Sydney Gardens, for the moment the sedan chair disappeared along Argyle Street in the direction of Pulteney Bridge, the pilot hastened to the door, after first instructing his assistants to go around to the rear of the house with the wagon they'd brought for the balloon.

Mr Richmond had left strict orders that his daughters were to remain in the house while the 'accursed aerostation' was collected, and Christina stood at her bedroom window, watching everything from a discreet and safe distance, and thinking that Jane was in *her* bedroom, writing an overdue letter to Aunt Brooke; but Jane wasn't in her room, she'd slipped downstairs to the dining room in order to watch the rescue exercise more closely.

Christina found it all interesting as well, watching as Mr Grenfell instructed his men, several of whom had climbed the pear tree in order to tease the collapsed orb of rubberized taffeta, for that was what she'd discovered the balloon was made of, away from the sharp twigs and branches. Two more men were engaged in unfastening the ropes holding the golden car, which was lowered with great difficulty to the grass. The oars and wings were treated with great care, for they were very fragile and had miraculously survived the crash intact.

At last the balloon itself was recovered, and after a brief inspection for any tears in the taffeta, it was carefully folded into a manageable bundle and carried out through the coach house to the waiting wagon. Then the car was carried out as well, laden with the ropes, flags, oars, wings, and other equipment, and Mr Grenfell prepared to call briefly at the back door to inform the waiting butler that all had been completed.

It was then that Christina realized to her horror that Jane had been by the French window in the dining room, for her sister's dainty redheaded figure suddenly emerged into view in the garden, hurrying across the grass to speak to the pilot. Christina watched in the utmost dismay as a brief exchange took place, then Mr Grenfell smiled and nodded, kissing Jane's hand before walking away after his assistants. Jane paused for a moment, then gathered her skirts to hasten into the house again.

Christina didn't delay, but almost ran from her room and down the stairs, determined to find out what was going on. She was just in time to hear her sister instructing the butler to serve a tray of tea in the drawing room.

'Jane? What are you doing?' she demanded with grave misgivings.

Jane's brown eyes met hers very briefly. 'I thought it only polite to take a dish of tea with Mr Grenfell,' she replied a little airily, for it was plain she knew she'd again allowed her impetuosity to get the better of her common sense.

Christina stared at her in disbelief. 'You ... you thought *what?*'

Jane bit her lip. 'Well, it's only good manners,' she replied, realizing there was little point in attempting to justify her *faux pas*.

'Oh, Jane!'

'I couldn't help it, Christina. I was watching everything from the dining room, and there are so many things I want to ask about the balloon that I simply *couldn't* allow him to leave without speaking properly to him.'

'And what if Father should return?'

'He won't. Not yet, anyway.'

'And when he does, he'll hear all about it. Jane, haven't you got any sense? You've already allowed your tongue to wag unwisely to Madame Gilbert, who'll have set the tale in motion around Bath that Robert Temple's prospective bride is disgracefully eager to know all about Mr Grenfell's balloon, and now you compound the sin by actually inviting Mr Grenfell himself to take tea in this house! What if Robert should hear?'

Jane lowered her eyes guiltily. 'I just didn't think.'

'Now, where have I heard *that* before?' responded Christina acidly, 'Oh, Jane, after all your promises, all your protests that you're a reformed character, you have to go and do this! It's really too bad of you. It's also too bad of Mr Grenfell, who should have done the gentlemanly thing and politely declined.'

'It's hardly his fault,' objected Jane immediately.

'Oh, yes, it is. He made his admiration only too plain this morning, so much so that I felt obliged to inform him that you are about to become betrothed; he really shouldn't have accepted your invitation.' Christina sighed crossly, for she was displeased with them both, but Jane had presented her with a *fait accompli*.

The drawing room was at the front of the house, its fine windows gazing out over the street. It was a handsome room with silver-blue damask on the walls, and chairs and sofa upholstered in royal-blue velvet. The white-shuttered windows boasted tasseled, ruched curtains that were raised and lowered by means of silver ropes, and on the floor there was a superb French carpet patterned in blue, cream, and gray. Above the marble fireplace there was a portrait of Sir Archibald Fitton, and on the wall between the windows there was a gilded cartel clock made by Sam Jones of Bath. The foremost item in the room, however, was a very fine forte-piano by Rolfe of Cheapside, which occupied a prime position in front of the windows. Jane was a very talented musician, and had declared the instrument to be very fine indeed when she'd played it after dinner the evening before.

The sisters sat on the sofa, waiting in silence for the butler to announce Mr Grenfell. A maid brought the tray of tea, setting it carefully on the table and withdrawing with her eyes downcast in a way that told Christina there was a great deal of speculation going on in the kitchens.

45

At last there were steps in the hall, the door opened, and the butler announced the pilot. 'Mr William Grenfell.'

In the few minutes since he had accepted Jane's foolish invitation, William Grenfell had taken care to make himself as presentable as possible. His coat had been tidied of every speck of fluff, his blond hair had been combed, and his trousers were immaculate. He smiled warmly at Jane, and then bowed over Christina's hand. 'I'm honored to be asked to join you like this, Miss Richmond.'

'Please sit down, sir,' she replied, indicating a chair that was closer to her than to Jane, but to her further annoyance, he affected not to notice, choosing one that placed him near Jane, who smiled at him.

'I trust your balloon hasn't come to too much grief, Mr Grenfell,' she said, as Christina poured the tea.

'There's only a little damage, Miss Jane, and I expect to be airborne again tomorrow,' he replied, avoiding Christian's eyes as he took a cup.

'With better luck than today, I hope.' Jane smiled again.

'With a serviceable flap valve, that's for sure,' he replied, smiling.

Jane was anxious to commence her cross-examination. 'Mr Grenfell, this morning you spoke of inflammable air. I believe you called it hydrogen?'

'Yes, Miss Jane.'

'I'm afraid I'm extremely ignorant, and I don't know anything about it. What exactly is hydrogen?'

He smiled again, unable to help gazing into her eyes. 'It has another name as well, phlogiston, but hydrogen is the name given to it by the Frenchman Lavoisier. It's what causes the balloon to rise.'

She was fascinated, and fascinating. 'Really? Where do you get it from?'

'We, er, we manufacture it from iron filings, acid of concentrated vitriol, and water,' he murmured, bewitched by her loveliness.

'How very scientific. I confess I'm all admiration. What first interested you in balloons, Mr Grenfell?'

'As a boy I saw a print of Lunardi's balloon when it was on display in the Pantheon in London. Lunardi was, as you probably know, the first man to ascend in a balloon in England, and when I read an account of his voyage, and subsequently the voyages of others, I was inspired to attempt to follow in their illustrious footsteps.' His glance slid a little guiltily toward Christina, who was eyeing him in silent wrath.

Jane's enthusiasm was intense, and her brown eyes shone as she sat forward. 'What is it like to fly, Mr Grenfell?' she asked breathlessly. 'Is it really as wonderful as I think?'

'Miss Jane, nothing can compare with the sensation of floating away from the earth. It's more than a wondrous experience, it's an introduction to perfect bliss. There is silence, remoteness, and serenity, and one flies with the spirits of Phaethon, Daedalus, and Icarus.'

He was very eloquent, and Jane was entranced. 'Oh, just imagine,' she breathed longingly.

Christina sipped her tea. 'Phaethon, Daedalus, and Icarus?' she murmured thoughtfully. 'Mr Grenfell, of those three, only Daedalus survived intact.'

He couldn't fail to be aware of her disapproval. 'Er, yes, and it is upon him that I presume to model myself.'

'Indeed? I thought the other two must be your heroes, for to be sure, you emulated them rather well when you descended on to our pear tree this morning.'

Jane shot a dark look at her. 'Christina!'

Unperturbed, for he deserved to be prodded, Christina continued to sip her tea.

Jane turned to him again. 'I don't care what my sister says, Mr Grenfell, for I think it's all absolutely marvelous. Tell me, have ladies ever ascended?'

'Why, yes. Mrs Sage made a captive ascent with Lunardi, but the first lady to make a free flight was young Madame Thible, who in 1784 made a flight lasting forty-five minutes, reaching a height of eight thousand feet. It's said that she sang like a nightingale all the time, charming the King of Sweden, who was watching.'

Jane was rapt. 'Oh, I'd sing like a nightingale too!'

He gazed at her. 'Would ... would you like to make an ascent, Miss Jane?' he ventured slowly, studiously ignoring Christina.

Jane's breath caught. 'Oh, yes.'

'It would please me immeasurably to grant you your wish. Would you, and Miss Richmond, of course, honor me by being the first ladies to ascend with me?'

Jane was completely overwhelmed. '*Could* we? Oh, *could* we?'

'I'd be delighted, Miss Jane,' he murmured.

Christina put down her cup, unable to believe her fluff-headed sister was actually going this far. There was no excuse, no excuse at all. Crossly she rose to her feet. 'Mr Grenfell, I fear we cannot possibly take you up on your offer, for our father wouldn't approve at all.'

Jane's face fell. 'Oh, Christina!'

'Don't you "Oh, Christina" me. You promised you'd conduct yourself decorously, and you haven't even attempted to.'

Jane flushed at that, lowering her eyes quickly to her cup.

William cleared his throat uncomfortably, knowing that Christina's anger was justified. 'Er, forgive me, Miss Richmond, for I spoke out of turn.'

'Yes, sir, you did,' she replied crushingly. 'I told you earlier today that my sister is about to be betrothed, and so it ill becomes you to behave as you are, just as it ill becomes her to encourage you.'

Jane was thoroughly mortified, hanging her head to hide her blushes.

William was acutely embarrassed now. 'Perhaps I should leave....'

'Yes, sir, perhaps you should,' responded Christina, allowing him no quarter.

He put his cup down. 'May I inquire whom Miss Jane is to marry?' he asked.

'Lord St Clement.'

He stared at her. 'She's *that* Miss Richmond?'

'How many Miss Richmonds abound in Bath, Mr Grenfell?'

'Forgive me, I just hadn't put two and two together.' He drew a long breath. 'He's a formidable rival for any man,' he murmured with some feeling.

Something in his manner told Christina that he and Robert Temple were acquainted. 'You know Lord St Clement, Mr Grenfell?' she asked, praying he didn't.

'Good Lord, yes, we go back a long way. Our families are neighbors in Somerset, and I went to Oxford with him.'

Her heart sank, for now there was little chance of Robert Temple *not* hearing about this dreadful tea party.

William looked at her. 'I confess I had no idea Robert was in Bath.'

'He isn't as yet – he's coming here by the end of the week to attend the autumn ball. He and my sister are to be introduced then.'

'I see. Well, I can tell you that you won't be disappointed in him; and I can be equally certain that he won't be disappointed in Miss Jane, for she is in truth the most delightful, enchanting—'

'*Mr* Grenfell!' Christina was fast losing what little patience she had left.

He quickly and politely took his leave, resisting the temptation to linger over Jane's dainty hand.

Silence reigned in the drawing room as he left the house, and it continued to reign very heavily for a minute or two until Jane gave a stifled sob and fled to her bedroom.

Christina gave vent to her anger. Standing up, she seized a cushion and hurled it across the room. She could cheerfully have choked her sister *and* the overbold William Grenfell; and she was displeased with herself, for she should have forbidden the pilot to enter the house. Now she'd have to face their father, who'd be furious that his orders had been so willfully disobeyed. She, Christina, would bear the brunt of his wrath, for she was the older daughter and therefore held to be responsible. And in this she *was* responsible; why on *earth* had she permitted the invitation to stand?

With a sigh she sat down on the sofa again, leaning her head back to stare at the chandelier shimmering from the ceiling. How she wished she was back at Richmond House, where there were no difficulties. By being indiscreet with Madame Gilbert, Jane had already seen to it that Bath society would be whispering about Robert Temple's future wife's considerable interest in the balloon, and if William Grenfell's visit to the house had been witnessed, as it undoubtedly had, then the whispering would increase. The whispers were bound to reach Robert's ears, if not from the gossipmongers, then from William himself, who was such an old friend.

It had to be faced that this day's utter foolishness could have placed the St Clement match in jeopardy.

7

WHETHER ROBERT TEMPLE would hear the story or not remained to be seen, but fate was at least kind enough to keep it from Mr Richmond.

He returned from the master of ceremonies by a rather round-about route, having been instructed by that erudite gentleman to take out certain subscriptions for the duration of the stay in Bath. He called first at the Assembly Rooms at the top of the town, then at a circulating library in Milsom Street, and at the Theater Royal in Orchard Street. Last, and very reluctantly, he took himself to the Sydney Gardens Vauxhall, it having been pointed out to him that to be absent from certain forthcoming diversions would be socially disadvantageous. Keeping up appearances was all-important, especially when one's daughter was about to be betrothed to one of England's most desirable gentlemen, and so Mr Richmond had felt he had no option but to take out a subscription to the pleasure gardens; but he remained determined that neither of his daughters would have anything to do with William Grenfell or the balloon that was at the center of so much vulgar interest.

Arriving back at the house in Johnstone Street, Mr Richmond found everything calm and apparently normal. The butler took his hat and gloves, and said nothing at all about William Grenfell's brief presence in the drawing room. Christina had by now inveigled Jane from her room, and the sisters had patched up their differences. Seated demurely in the drawing room, they were both engaged upon their embroidery as their father entered. Detecting nothing amiss, he informed them all about his visit to the master of ceremonies, and the various subscriptions, making certain that they were both still well aware of his feelings regarding the balloon. Jane looked her father directly in his eyes and murmured her compliance; Christina felt so wretchedly guilty that she avoided his gaze, confining herself to a dutiful nod. She glanced accusingly at Jane, warning her with a fierce look that any more nonsense like today's would almost certainly lead to utter disaster. Indeed, today might yet lead to disaster, for William might see fit to inform Robert all about it; but for the moment, at least, they'd escaped.

In the week before Robert's arrival and the ball, Mr Richmond and his daughters led a very full social life. Bath was a very regulated place, with clearly defined activities that were expected of its visitors. While Mr Richmond took the cure, his daughters sallied forth to the circulating library, went shopping, walked on Beechen Cliff, the wooded hill overlooking the spa from the south, visited a number of exhibitions, and took tea in the Assembly Rooms. In the evening they attended the theater with their father, or responded to the various invitations that continually arrived through the door. Miss Jane Richmond was a person of note, and everyone was anxious to make her acquaintance, although it had to be said that Madame Gilbert's tittle-tattle had raised a mixed reaction. For every person who thought Jane's interest in the balloon was an indication of her admirable spirit, there were two who thought it revealed her foolishness and unsuitability for the grand marriage she'd been fortunate enough to secure.

The balloon continued to make its captive ascents from the pleasure gardens, and the crowds continued to flock to watch, but as the days passed, it became less of an attraction. As the days passed, too, Jane was very mindful to conduct herself with perfect decorum. She didn't put a foot wrong, and was everything the prospective Lady St Clement should be, much to her proud father's delight.

Christina found the week very trying indeed, for a dizzy social life was the last thing she found enjoyable. She longed for it all to be over, so that she could return to the peace and quiet of Stroud. She was glad enough to withdraw into the background, leaving her sister to revel in being the center of attention, but all the time she was conscious of the dread possibility that William Grenfell might acquaint Robert with the facts concerning the invitation to tea. Such information about his prospective bride might lead Robert to think Jane entirely unsuitable.

It was a dread that lingered for Christina until almost the end of the week, when a chance encounter with William in the Orange Grove gave her the opportunity to broach the subject. She was alone at the time, Jane having accepted an invitation to drive with Lady Joan Newton to see an exhibition of porcelain at Shockerwick House on the London road. As tactfully and delicately as she could, Christina brought the conversation around to what had happened at their last meeting. William hastened to reassure her that not a word would pass his lips, and she was much relieved; she was less than pleased when he continued by saying that he looked forward to their next meeting, which would be at the autumn ball, a function he had every intention of attending.

She sighed to herself as she walked back to Johnstone Street. Jane was a trial that ought not to be inflicted on anyone, least of all a long-suffering half-sister who wanted nothing more than a quiet life! William was far too attracted to his friend's future wife, and that future wife was too impulsive to keep a firm hold on common sense; they'd both require close watching at the ball.

There was one moment during that week when Christina, not Jane, emerged as the center of attention. It happened outside the Pump Room, when she was seated on a bench reading *Gil Blas* while waiting for her father, who'd taken an unconscionable length of time. Mr Pitt emerged, attended by his usual gaggle of followers. He was looking a little better than he had done at the beginning of the week, although still far from healthy. Something about Christina's neat figure on the bench attracted his attention. Ignoring everyone else, he approached her, apologized for his boldness, and inquired if the volume she was reading was indeed *The Adventures of Gil Blas*. Startled, she stammered that it was, and he remarked that he'd guessed it to be so because the volume was bound in precisely the same way as his own copy. He told her that the book was his favorite reading, giving him endless pleasure, and he hoped that it was proving as rewarding to her. Almost overcome, and more than a little aware of the envious stares of the onlookers, she replied that she was enjoying the book very much indeed. He gave her a warm smile that transformed him, then took his leave, proceeding to his waiting sedan chair and according her another smile before being conveyed away.

Mr Richmond had emerged to hear of the incident with mixed feelings. He was delighted that at least one of his family had spoken to the great man, but he was pinched to the quick that after all his efforts, he hadn't been the one.

On the day of the ball, Robert Temple's elegant dark-blue traveling carriage bowled into Bath along the London road, its team of high-stepping grays drawing much attention because their manes and tails had been left unfashionably long and unplaited. It was an eye-catching drag, driven with masterly ease by a coachman in scarlet livery, and there wasn't a head that didn't turn in admiration as it drove along the Paragon, making for Bath's most exclusive address, the Royal Crescent.

Robert hardly glanced out at the streets; he was too deep in thought about how things would go at the ball that night. He wore a gray great-coat with a black astrakhan collar, over a charcoal coat and cream breeches, and his long legs were stretched out on the seat opposite, his Hessian boots polished so much that they gleamed. His top hat was tilted back on his dark hair, and the diamond pin in his neckcloth glittered in the sunlight shining in through the carriage window.

The moment was almost upon him when he'd meet his Miss Richmond. Had he made the right decision where she was concerned? Was it really wise, in his changed circumstances, to take a rather insignificant landowner's daughter as his bride? He knew that the *beau monde* of London didn't think it was wise, they'd made their opinion very clear indeed, and he could only suppose that Bath society would feel the same way. When he'd been impoverished, the marriage had been regarded as one of convenience and necessity; now it was regarded as a misalliance. The Richmonds simply weren't good enough for a man of Lord St Clement's present exalted standing, and society wanted him to drop them in favor of an aristo-cratic connection that was considered more in keeping with his new circumstances.

He drew a long breath, glancing out at last as the carriage entered the curving magnificence of Royal Crescent. Let society think as it chose, he intended to make Jane Richmond his bride.

The carriage pulled up at the curb by his aunt's residence, and he alighted, pausing for a moment to gaze around at the superb elegance of the crescent, and the matchless view over Bath in the valley below.

Turning, he looked across the road and down over the grassy slope toward the heart of Bath. Something caught his eye, a crimson-and-blue globe suspended in the air above Sydney Gardens. A faint smile touched his lips, for he recognized the balloon. So, his old friend William was in Bath, was he? It would be good to see him again.

Pulling his hat forward a little, Robert turned on his heel to enter the house, pausing only to acknowledge the brief greeting of his next-door neighbor, a very crusty military gentleman, Major General Sir Harold Penn-Blagington.

As darkness fell, Christina and Jane prepared for the ball. Christina sat at her dressing table while her maid, Jenny, put the final touches to her hair. Jenny was the daughter of one of Mr Richmond's game-keepers and intensely loyal to the family. She was a fair-haired country girl, with a rather buxom figure and china-blue eyes, and her starched cream cotton dress crackled as she moved. She was clever with her mistress's shining dark hair, combing it expertly up into a knot at the back of her head, and teasing many thin ringlets into a tumble to the nape of her neck. The knot was then adorned with little mother-of-pearl flowers which went well with the necklace Christina's mother had left her, and which she wore tonight.

Madame Gilbert had done well with the bluebell silk gown, adorning its bodice, puffed sleeves, and trained hem with countless tiny pearl beads that again echoed the necklace. A white shawl rested over Christina's arms, and she wore long white gloves. A fan and reticule lay waiting on the dressing table before her.

The door opened behind her, and Jane came in in the pink plowman's gauze that had needed taking in. Madame Gilbert had excelled, for it was impossible to tell that the dress had been altered at all. The delicate gauze, adorned with silver satin spots, shimmered and glittered at the slightest movement, and the scoop neckline was daringly low, but stylishly so. Turbans were all the rage, and Jane's red hair was almost concealed beneath one made of silver satin, from which sprang several tall ostrich plumes. A feather boa dragged on the floor behind her, her eyes were bright, and her cheeks flushed. She looked anxiously at her sister.

'How do I look?'

'Exquisite.'

'Do you really think so? I wondered if I should wear the lime silk tunic dress after all ...'

'No,' said Christina quickly, 'you look quite perfect as you are.'

'I want to look my very best, and somehow I don't feel I do.'

'But you *do* look your best,' reassured Christina, getting up and going to her, but as she did so, the clasp on her necklace gave way and it fell to the floor. 'Oh, no!' she cried, bending to retrieve it.

Jenny hurried over to her. 'I think there's something wrong with the fastening, Miss Christina. I had quite a job doing it up.'

Christina inspected the necklace. 'I can't see anything wrong.'

'Maybe you should wear the diamond pendant, Miss Christina,' Jenny suggested.

'No, it wouldn't look quite right with all the pearls on my gown.'

'But you may lose the necklace at the ball,' observed Jenny sensibly.

Christina examined the clasp again. There really didn't seem to be anything wrong with it, and she could only conclude that Jenny hadn't fastened it properly. 'I'll wear it,' she declared then, giving it to the maid to put on for her.

Reluctantly Jenny did as she was told, testing the clasp several times when the necklace was in place, and then asking Jane to look at it as well. Jane obliged, and had to concede that it all seemed very safe and firm.

Christina smiled. 'Are you both quite sure?'

'Yes, Miss Christina.'

'Yes, we are,' concurred Jane.

'And does the rest of me look well enough for the great occasion?'

Jane surveyed her from head to toe. 'You'll do.'

'Thank you.'

'Maybe Mr Pitt will be there to single you out.'

'I hardly think he'll attend a ball.'

'Maybe he's smitten with you. After all, you have *Gil Blas* in common.'

'I rather think our virgin minister is too set in his ways to pursue anyone.'

Jane was a little shocked. 'You really shouldn't call him that. If Father heard you ...'

'But Father didn't hear me,' replied Christina wickedly.

There was a tap at the door, and the butler announced that the chairs were at the door and it was time to leave.

Jane caught Christina's arm nervously. 'Oh, I feel quite sick!'

'Take a deep breath.'

'That *never* works!'

'Then we'll have to leave without you,' replied Christina airily.

'Don't be beastly.' Jane laughed ruefully then. 'I wish I was as cool, calm, and collected as you.'

'Then you'd be as dull as me as well. Come on.' Christina took her hand, leading her toward the door.

They descended to the entrance hall, where their father was waiting, resplendent in formal black. The frills of his white shirt had been starched and ironed so that they protruded at right angles from his chest, and his white satin waistcoat was modishly quilted. His white silk breeches sported fine gold buckles, and his stockinged calves were very well made indeed, so much so as to be the envy of many a footman reduced to wearing calf pads. As he turned to greet his daughters, Christina was struck that in his youth he must have been a very personable young man, for he was still good-looking.

He took their hands. 'My dears, you both look charming.' His glance then rested on Jane alone. 'I'm sure young Temple will be bowled over, absolutely bowled over.'

'I hope you're right, Father,' she replied in a voice shaking with nerves.

He patted her hand reassuringly, then looked at Christina. 'How you can look so very lovely and yet be determined to become an old maid is quite beyond me. You're truly the most exasperating creature in the world. Have I ever told you that?'

'Yes, Father, frequently.'

'But to no avail, it seems,' he observed dryly. 'Now, then, shall we go?'

He offered them both an arm, and they emerged from the bright warmth of the house into the dark chill of the October night.

8

LINKBOYS WITH SMOKING torches preceded the chairs all the way to the Assembly Rooms. It seemed that all of Somerset was attending the ball, for a throng of chairs and carriages was converging on the same destination. Guests from out of town arrived in carriages, but those who resided in Bath used the much more convenient and maneuverable chairs.

The Assembly Rooms, designed in the middle of the previous century by John Wood the Younger, were very austere indeed from the outside, the plain elevations giving no hint of the splendors to be found within.

From the vestibule, with its fine chandelier, everyone proceeded through to the octagon room, which was situated in the heart of the building, and from where access could be had into the three principal reception chambers – the tea room to the right, the card room directly ahead, and the splendid one-hundred-foot-long green-and-gold ballroom to the left. The octagon room was always a terrible crush on occasions like this, and its four perfectly placed fireplaces were completely hidden by the press of guests. The seats by these fireplaces were the special preserve of elderly spinsters and chaperones, who jealously guarded their places against all corners. The room was already uncomfortably hot, even though it was cold outside.

The ball had been in progress for nearly an hour, but by no means all the guests had arrived, for it was at present quite a fashion in some circles to attend several card parties before going to the main function of the evening. In the ballroom the master of ceremonies was in complete command, supervising the dancing and seeing that

THE WRONG MISS RICHMOND

all went as smoothly and agreeably as possible. Mr Tyson was elderly now, but ruled with a rod of iron, and wasn't above pointing a disapproving cane at anyone observed committing even a tiny offense, such as innocently taking up a position other than the one indicated at the commencement of a contredanse. The orchestra was situated in a semicircular apse high in the green-and-gold wall halfway down the great room, and as it began to play, a sea of people began to move in unison beneath the line of exquisite chandeliers suspended from the hipped roof. In the day the light was provided by the windows set high in the wall between Corinthian columns, but at night, when the chandeliers were lit, everything was illuminated by a warm glow. Those guests who weren't dancing occupied tiers of scarlet stuff sofas against the walls, surveying the floor with a very critical eye, for half the pleasure of a ball was the opportunity to find fault with one's peers.

There was quite a queue of new arrivals waiting for their names to be announced, and as she waited with her father and sister, Christina glanced carefully around, wondering if Robert Temple had arrived yet. She scanned the scene, knowing she'd recognize him immediately from his portrait, but there didn't seem to be any sign of him.

They reached the front of the queue and the steward rapped the floor with his cane. 'Mr Henry Richmond, Miss Richmond, and Miss Jane Richmond,' he announced.

There was an immediate stir, for it was no secret that Jane's first meeting with Robert was to take place at the ball. Quizzing glasses were raised and fans put to whispering lips as everyone studied the turnout of Bath's most-talked-of young woman. Jane's cheeks flushed prettily, and she kept her lovely eyes downcast as she and Christina proceeded into the ballroom on their proud father's arm. Even those who hadn't seen her before could tell which of the Miss Richmonds was the prospective Lady St Clement, for there was a glow about Jane that was quite unmistakable; she'd never looked more lovely, and guests who'd come with a sour attitude toward the match had to concede that whatever faults she had, a lack of beauty certainly wasn't one of them.

Mr Tyson hastened toward them immediately, for it was one of his duties to choose partners for the more important guests' first dance.

He'd already made his selections, and for Jane he produced a young clergyman of somewhat dull and horsey appearance but excellent family. Christina was presented to a stout viscount in clothes so unbecomingly tight they seemed to have been poured over him, but although he looked clumsy, he proved to be a dainty dancer, leading her through a very commendable Làndler. Mr Richmond had no intention of antagonizing his gout, which had been relatively docile for the past few days, and so he politely declined the master of ceremonies' offer to secure him a lady partner, choosing instead to occupy one of the sofas at the edge of the floor.

Over the next hour there was still no sign of Robert. Jane succeeded admirably in hiding her great nervousness, dancing every dance and leaving Christina to dutifully sit with their father. Christina danced only the first dance, not because she wasn't asked, but because she wished to sit with her father. It wasn't an onerous duty, for he was hardly dull company, and anyway, it gave her a legitimate excuse to withdraw a little from the social hurly-burly she disliked so much.

Just as a polonaise ended, and Jane's latest partner, a young guards officer, returned her to her family, William Grenfell approached the sofa. The pilot wasn't in the pitch of high fashion tonight; indeed, he was as discreetly and correctly turned out as all the other gentlemen. His black coat was tight-fitting, having to be left unbuttoned to show off his white satin waistcoat, frilled shirt, and crisply starched neckcloth. His white silk breeches were of excellent cut, his patent-leather pumps exceedingly shiny, and there was no sign now of the rather outrageous aeronaut whose balloon had come to grief on the pear tree. His blond hair was carefully combed, and his manner was very conventional and proper as he bowed.

'Good evening, Mr Richmond. Miss Richmond. Miss Jane.'

Christina inclined her head, but her father glowered. William appeared to bring out the very worst in him, for he didn't even accord the pilot a nodding acknowledgment.

Jane smiled. 'Why, Mr Grenfell, what a pleasure it is to see you again.'

William glanced a little uncomfortably at Mr Richmond, then smiled at Jane. 'The pleasure is entirely mine, Miss Jane.'

'You're too kind, sir,' she murmured in reply, wafting her fan to and fro in a way that a dismayed Christina judged to border on the coquettish.

'Jane ...' she began in an urgent undertone.

Jane ignored her. 'Tell me, Mr Grenfell, how is your balloon?'

'Grounded again, I fear. The flap valve is being very obstinate.'

'Oh, dear. Then we must trust that you solve the problem as quickly as possible, must we not?' Jane smiled one of her most enchanting smiles, and Christina couldn't help see the effect it had upon William, who reddened, and swallowed.

Mr Richmond was still delivering the pilot a very lengthy snub, gazing squarely past him. Christina had never known her father to behave like this before; it was very embarrassing indeed, but even though William was obviously embarrassed as well, he nevertheless held his ground, encouraged to do so because Jane showed herself prepared to be engaged in conversation. Christina didn't know what to say or do in such circumstances, and she was cross with all three of them.

William then proceeded to make things more difficult than ever by asking Jane to dance with him. 'Miss Jane, would you do me the inestimable honor of dancing with me?'

Christina looked at Jane with quick warning, but it was already too late, for the invitation had been promptly accepted. 'I'd be delighted to dance with you, Mr Grenfell,' Jane said, smiling as she placed her hand in his, rising quickly from the sofa before either Christina or her father could say anything.

Mr Richmond was dumbfounded, staring after his younger daughter as she swept on to the floor with the loathed pilot. For a moment it seemed he was about to call her back, but Christina hastily put a restraining hand on his arm. 'It's too late, Father. If you say anything now, you'll only draw very unwelcome attention.'

He saw the wisdom of this, and so remained angrily silent, but his expression was very dark indeed.

On the floor, Jane knew full well she should have declined the invitation. Her father had made his feelings about William Grenfell only too plain, but as the handsome pilot smiled into her eyes, and told her she was divinely beautiful, she sighed and smiled in return. 'I'm very flattered, sir.'

'It isn't flattery, for you outshine every other woman here,' he said, being bold enough to draw her hand to his lips.

'You shouldn't pay me such compliments, Mr Grenfell,' she reproved, blushing still more as she quickly pulled her hand away.

'I know I shouldn't, and if it offends you ...'

'I'm not offended, sir,' she replied, her lovely eyes meeting his, 'but you still shouldn't do it.'

'I envy Robert Temple with all my heart,' he said softly.

The orchestra began to play a minuet.

Christina and Mr Richmond watched from the sofa. Mr Richmond was still angry, and Christina felt obliged to warn him again that he might yet attract undue interest. 'Father, it is a ball,' she said tactfully, 'and Mr Grenfell is hardly an undesirable element.'

'That, my dear, is a matter of opinion.'

'So it seems, but you shouldn't scowl at them like that, for it will be remarked, which is the last thing we want tonight. Remonstrate with Jane afterward by all means, but all she's actually done is dance with a gentleman of whom you disapprove, which disapproval isn't known to everyone else here present.'

'I take your point,' he replied, looking away from the floor. 'That pernicious Icarus is an insolent young pup, and *she*, indiscreet minx, isn't doing all she might to discourage him. Remonstrate with her later? I'll make her foolish ears ring!' His glance swung back to the pair on the floor. 'Look at her! See how she smiles at him!'

Christina followed his gaze and said nothing, for Jane was making it quite plain that she found William Grenfell's company very pleasing, and under the circumstances it was very unwise indeed. Robert Temple might arrive at any moment, and it wouldn't do for him to see his future wife smiling so frequently into the admiring eyes of his old friend.

Even as this dire possibility crossed her mind, the steward's staff rapped again, and a buzz went around the ballroom as Robert Temple's name was announced at last, but on the floor, Jane and William continued dancing unawares.

Christina looked at the man her sister was to marry. He was the image of his portrait, and in the flesh even more breathtakingly handsome than she'd expected. He was tall, his dark hair was a little disheveled, and she felt she could see how gray his eyes were, even across the room. There was something about him that would have set him apart in any company, an unruffled poise that told of the exalted circles in which he was accustomed to move. He wore a dark-purple velvet coat and white silk breeches, and a jeweled pin glittered in the rich folds of his lace-edged neckcloth. She gazed at him as he paused by the doorway, toying with a spill of lace at his cuff. There was something utterly compelling about him, something that had her complete attention. Suddenly the noise of the ballroom seemed to fade all around her. The orchestra was still playing, people were still dancing and talking, but she couldn't hear anything except the quickening of her own heartbeats.

The master of ceremonies had hurried over to him now, and was leading him around the floor toward the sofa. He smiled at whatever the bustling Mr Tyson was saying, and acknowledged a number of greetings from friends and acquaintances, but his gray eyes were suddenly on Christina. A spell was winding seductively around her, a forbidden spell that was so subtle she could do nothing to resist. His lips softened into a lazy smile that was directed solely at her. Her heart was beating wildly now, and still the ballroom was muffled and remote. She was hardly aware of the master of ceremonies as he introduced him to her father, but every sense was suddenly alive as at last he was being presented to her.

Her hand trembled as she extended it.

His white-gloved fingers were warm. 'I'm so glad to make your acquaintance, Miss Richmond,' he murmured, raising her hand to his lips.

His voice was low and quite softly spoken, and his eyes held her captive. She somehow managed to reply. 'And I yours, my lord.'

He smiled again, and a shiver of wanton pleasure passed through her. Emotions she'd never experienced before coursed wildly along her veins. She was shaken and confused. Whatever she'd expected on first meeting Robert Temple, it hadn't been this. Not this.

9

HIS DUTY HAVING been discharged, the master of ceremonies returned to his other tasks.

Robert looked at Mr Richmond. 'Forgive me for arriving late, sir, my only excuse is that my aunt's cook fell suddenly ill and I waited until the doctor had examined her.'

Mr Richmond, who thought highly of his own cook at Richmond House, was concerned. 'I trust it isn't serious.'

'A surfeit of her own rich cuisine would appear to be at the back of it, sir,' replied Robert, smiling again, 'but since she is much treasured by my aunt, who in turn is much treasured by me, I felt it only right that I should wait to hear the diagnosis. My aunt is a formidable lady, and it wouldn't do to offend her.'

'I don't believe I know your aunt,' said Mr Richmond, doing his best not to glance toward Jane, who was still dancing unawares with William.

'Lady Chevenley. She departed from Bath last month to stay at my country seat, Bellstones, and I sincerely hope that you will meet her when you are my guests there.'

'Your guests?' replied Mr Richmond.

'Yes. It would seem appropriate and more than desirable for you to stay at Bellstones once we have agreed all the tiresome details of the betrothal.' Robert smiled at Christina again.

Mr Richmond saw the invitation as absolute proof of Robert's commitment to the match, and he beamed.

The dance was ending at last, and Jane was sinking into a graceful curtsy, still ignorant of her future husband's arrival. William seemed unaware as well, for they lingered on the floor as the other dancers dispersed.

Mr Tyson announced the next dance, a cotillion, and for a terrible moment Christina was afraid that Jane and the pilot would take their places in one of the sets, but they began to leave the floor at last, still smiling and talking together.

Robert suddenly looked at Christina. 'Miss Richmond, I trust you will not think me forward if I ask you to honor me with this next dance?'

She was taken completely aback, for it was hardly proper for him to dance with her before he'd been introduced to Jane.

She might not have known what to reply, but her father, who wished to speak sternly alone to Jane if at all possible, seized his opportunity. 'Of course she'll dance with you, my lord, she'd be delighted.'

Robert held his hand out to her, and hesitantly she accepted, only too aware of his touch. As they stepped on to the floor, she was aware, too, of the curious glances they were receiving, for a great many people thought it odd that Lord St Clement should be leading the elder Miss Richmond out instead of the Miss Richmond he was supposed to be marrying.

Christina was sensitive to everything about him, as if a current was passing between them. She saw the way his dark hair curled at the nape of his neck, how soft his lips were when he was about to smile, how graceful he was as he moved; she drank in every detail, unable to help herself, and she was totally bewildered by the force of feeling that had suddenly been aroused in her. She danced in a dream, still hearing hardly anything but the beating of her heart.

At the sofa, Mr Richmond was confronting Jane and William, his gaze fixed upon his daughter in particular. 'Well, missy? What have you to say for yourself?'

She was immediately defensive. 'Father, I merely accepted Mr Grenfell's invitation to dance. Is that so heinous a crime?'

'Yes, missy, it is. You're very well aware of my feelings where this latter-day Helios is concerned, and not only did you choose to defy me, you also allowed him to ogle you in a most obvious way!'

Jane drew back, both mortified and indignant. 'Father, how *could* you say such a thing!'

William was torn between guilt and a similar indignation. 'I say, sir, that's a little strong....'

'No, sirrah, it isn't strong enough! You've made your interest in my daughter disgracefully clear. You're most definitely surplus to requirement, sir, and I'd be obliged if you'd spare us your presence,' replied Mr Richmond coolly.

Jane was utterly shocked. 'Why are you being so horrid, Father? I really haven't behaved all *that* badly.'

'Oh, yes, you have, missy. As to why I'm being so horrid, as you're pleased to term it, well, what else do you expect when you cavort so intimately with this blackguard and don't even notice the arrival of the man you're expecting to marry!'

She stared at him. 'He's here?' she said at last, glancing quickly around.

'He most certainly is, and he is at present dancing with your sister.'

William cleared his throat awkwardly then. 'I, er, I think I should perhaps take my leave of you, Miss Jane.'

'And not before time,' agreed Mr Richmond cuttingly.

William took Jane's hand. 'Thank you for honoring me with a dance, Miss Jane,' he said softly.

'It ... it was a pleasure, Mr Grenfell,' she answered, suddenly conscious of the glances of many of the guests. Spots of color marked her cheeks, and she snapped open her fan, moving it to and fro before her hot face.

As William withdrew, Mr Richmond eyed her again. 'I think you may count yourself lucky that Temple doesn't appear to have noticed your conduct.'

'Are ... are you sure?' she asked hopefully, looking toward the floor and picking out Christina and Robert as they danced.

'Fairly certain. I tell you this, missy, you'd better be a model of excellence from now on. Mr William Grenfell is to be a thing of the past, is that clear?'

'Yes, Father.'

'It had better be, or you'll be returning to Stroud without a match!'

She bit her lip, lowering her eyes.

On the floor, Christina was still moving in something of a daze. The cotillion progressed, step by step, turn by turn, and in her confusion she forgot that it ended with a forfeit, a kiss on the cheek from her partner.

Robert smiled, stepping close. His arm was briefly around her waist, and his lips brushed warmly against her cheek. She felt weak and not in control, sensations alien to one usually disciplined and calm. Oh, this was so very wrong. She shouldn't feel like this about him, she *mustn't* feel like this about him ...

As the floor cleared and a country dance was announced, he drew her to one side of the ballroom, not the side where Jane and Mr Richmond waited by the sofa. Still holding her hand, he looked into her eyes. 'Maybe I'm again being a little premature, Miss Richmond, but I feel we will do well together. I consider myself very fortunate indeed to have secured you as my bride.'

Stunned, she stared at him. He thought *she* was Jane?

Her reaction puzzled him. 'Miss Richmond?'

'I ... I think you've made a mistake, my lord,' she said at last, a flood of hot color staining her cheeks.

'Mistake? In what way?'

'I'm not the one you are to marry, my lord.'

Now he stared. 'I don't understand. You *are* Miss Richmond, aren't you?'

'Yes, but I'm Miss Christina Richmond. It's my sister, Jane, who is to be betrothed to you.'

'Miss *Christina* Richmond?' Obviously taken quite by surprise, he ran his fingers through his hair, giving a rather embarrassed laugh. 'Deuce take it, I had no idea ... Forgive me.'

'There is nothing to forgive, sir, for you've evidently been misled in some way.' She was too flustered to meet his eyes.

He drew her hand through his arm then, ushering her to a quieter corner and turning her to face him again. 'As you will by now have gathered, Miss Richmond, I had no idea that your father had two daughters.'

She was puzzled. 'But how could you possibly mistake me for Jane? You were sent her miniature, and I'm not even remotely like her to look at.'

'I received the miniature, it's true, but it was in what the Irish call "smithereens", broken beyond all repair. It didn't occur to me that there might be sisters, because I was informed that Miss Jane Richmond was the *only* daughter of Mr Henry Richmond and his wife, Georgiana Vesey.'

'Which is quite true, for Georgiana was my father's second wife. Jane and I are half-sisters.' She gave a self-conscious smile. 'Jane has inherited a fortune from her mother's family, which is why the younger Miss Richmond is the one you hope to marry, my lord.'

His gray eyes moved over her face. 'Fortunes aren't everything, Miss Richmond, and although it may be presumptuous of me to say so, you are more than lovely enough to have found a husband before now. May I ask why you are still single?'

The question took her a little aback. 'I … I'm quite happy to remain as I am, my lord, and I'm quite content for my sister to marry before me.'

His gaze seemed almost intense. 'Which can only mean that you haven't given anyone your heart.'

She had to look quickly away. Until tonight that had been true, but it wasn't anymore.

Her silence was misinterpreted. 'Now I have indeed offended you. Forgive me.'

'You haven't offended me,' she replied, taking a long breath and making herself look at him again. 'We … we're beginning to cause comment, my lord, and as I see my sister is with my father now, perhaps it would be best if we…?'

'Yes, of course. But, Miss Richmond…?'

'Yes?'

'I trust this unfortunate misunderstanding will not blight our future friendship?'

'Of course not, it's forgotten already.'

'Would that I could forget as promptly,' he replied, smiling at her. 'If your sister is only half as lovely and charming as you, I shall count myself exceeding fortunate.' He offered her his arm.

Their progress around the crowded floor was punctuated by many pauses to speak briefly to his numerous friends and acquaintances, most of whom were openly curious about Christina's presence at his side, instead of Jane. He passed it off by replying that in his opinion it was a wise bridegroom who first made allies of his prospective in-laws, an explanation that was accepted with much amusement. Christina was careful to conduct herself as properly as possible, for she was aware that the Richmond family was on trial tonight, and that Jane's conduct with William Grenfell hadn't gone unnoticed. By the time she and Robert were at last approaching the sofa, and Jane, Christina was satisfied that the damage had been repaired; she was far less satisfied with what had happened to her own small world, which was suddenly in complete disarray.

As Mr Richmond hastened to at last effect the long-awaited intro-duction between prospective bride and groom, and Jane raised her magnificent eyes to meet Robert's, Christina discreetly drew aside, in need of a moment or two to compose herself for the remainder of the ball.

She felt utterly wretched, and strove to hide the fact behind a smile. There was a pain deep inside, and it was a pain she knew she had no right to feel. Love at first sight was a phenomenon she'd hith-erto believed existed only in books and poems, but now she knew it did indeed happen, for it had happened to her tonight. From the moment he'd entered the ballroom, she'd been utterly lost. She was the victim of unkind fate, falling head over heels in love with the one man she could never have, for he was to marry her sister.

10

IT WAS JUST before dawn when the three sedan chairs returned to Johnstone Street.

Christina retreated thankfully to the privacy of her bedroom, where she lay wide-awake, watching the dawn lighten the sky outside. She'd often wondered what it would be like to fall in love, but she'd never dreamed it would feel like this, so desolate and full of hurt. How she'd endured the rest of the ball, she really didn't know, for every minute had been an ordeal. Robert and Jane had made such a delightful couple that they'd soon captivated the entire gathering, except, perhaps, for the unfortunate William Grenfell.

Jane's rather too enthusiastic enjoyment of the young pilot's company before Robert's arrival, and then Robert's unexpected invitation to his bride's sister to dance with him first, had soon been forgotten by everyone, and by the end of the ball it was generally agreed that Lord St Clement and Miss Jane Richmond were ideally suited. Of course there were still those who murmured that Miss Richmond was too lowly for the match, but even they were forced to concede that with looks, vivacity, and charm such as hers, it wouldn't be long before the famous marriage of convenience became a love match of the highest order.

There had been a moment, while Robert was observed deep in conversation with his old friend William Grenfell, when Christina had feared the young pilot's own feelings for Jane might persuade him to forget his promise, but it seemed that he'd resisted the temptation to tell tales about Jane's indiscretions, for Robert's manner didn't change at all, and it was clear he hadn't been told anything even remotely untoward about his lovely prospective bride's previous conduct.

At the end of the ball, Mr Richmond had invited Robert to dine with them the following evening, and Jane had lingered a moment with him before hurrying after her father and sister to the waiting chairs. Christina hadn't been able to bring herself to look at Robert as he'd waved farewell; she'd been close to tears throughout the evening, and was striving to contain them until she was alone. Now she was alone, but the tears hadn't come. She stared at the cracks of morning light piercing the shutters, listening to the first street calls as the early traders went about their business. Birds were in full morning song in the garden, and across the river the abbey bells began to peal. It was set to be another glorious autumn day, and somehow she was going to have to cope with what had happened; she couldn't confide in anyone, it was something that was going to have to remain secret.

Mr Richmond was in such ebullient spirits after the success of the ball that sleep eluded him as well, for he rose only a short while after retiring, calling to the butler to have a chair wait at the door to take him for his daily immersion at the Cross Bath. Jane, exhausted by the excitement, slept on and on, not even stirring when her father returned to take to his bed for the necessary cooling off. Breakfast came and went, Mr Richmond went to the Pump Room and returned, and still Jane slumbered on, but Christina was up and about, busying herself with various tasks in order to take her mind off her unhappiness. Letters were written, instructions were issued to the cook, and an hour was spent on her embroidery before she felt she simply had to escape from the house for a while to be completely on her own. She was presented with an excellent excuse when her father grumbled that the circulating library in Milsom Street had failed to send someone with his London newspapers, a service for which he'd paid handsomely and which he therefore expected to be prompt and faultless. Christina immediately volunteered to go for them herself, and at just gone noon, accompanied by Jenny, she set off gladly from the house in the October sunshine.

She wore her dove-gray velvet spencer and gray-and-white-striped silk gown, with ringlets tumbling from beneath her bonnet, and to all intents and purposes she appeared lighthearted and carefree.

The short extent of Argyle Street was very busy, with the noise of constant traffic echoing between the elegant houses. There were curricles and cabriolets drawn by high-stepping blood horses, gleaming town carriages with liveried coachmen, gentlemen mounted on superb thoroughbreds, delivery wagons of every color and description, chattering pedestrians, and, of course, the ubiquitous sedan chairs. Not all the pedestrians were walking toward the center of the town, for quite a number were obviously making for Sydney Gardens, in the hope that William Grenfell's balloon would make another of its celebrated ascents.

Christina reached Pulteney Bridge, where the narrower confines exaggerated the noise. An ox wagon had somehow become stuck in a rut, causing even more congestion. Men were shouting, the oxen were giving voice of their own, and a dog was barking. Christina and Jenny hurried along the pavement, anxious to escape from the furor, but as they reached the far side of the bridge, instead of walking up into the town, Christina turned to the left, where a paved terrace edged by a wrought-iron railing overlooked the river.

The noise of the traffic jam was overwhelmed by the roar of the weir. Downstream some men were fishing, and a sailing barge was moored at a tree. There were a lot of trees, their leaves either on the point of turning to autumn colors or already in their full glory of scarlet, russet, and gold. Looking across the river, past the gardens of Argyle Street, Christina could see the rear of Johnstone Street, and her own bedroom window, where a maid was polishing the glass.

Jenny drew discreetly to one side as her mistress looked down at the water as it spilled over the weir. Christina sighed. How she wished last night had all been a dream, and suddenly she'd wake up to discover nothing had happened at all, that Robert Temple hadn't affected her, and that she, Christina Richmond, was her old unruffled self.

'Miss Richmond?'

With a gasp she turned, for it was Robert.

He was crossing the terrace toward her, looking very Bond Street in a pale-green coat with brass buttons, a dark-green brocade waistcoat, and tightly fitted cream cord breeches. A discreet gold pin was on the knot of his unstarched neckcloth, and the golden tassels on his highly polished Hessian boots swung to and fro as he walked. A pearl-handled cane was in his gloved hand, and he removed his top hat as he bowed on reaching her. 'Good morning, Miss Richmond, or is it good afternoon?' He smiled.

Flustered, she did her best to appear natural. 'I believe it's good afternoon, my lord.'

'Have I discovered you on your way into town, or on your way home?'

'I'm going to the circulating library in Milsom Street. They've been remiss enough to forget my father's London papers.' She marveled that somehow she was contriving to sound quite normal, for in truth she was all at sixes and sevens again. He had such an effect on her that she was sure he must be able to read her like one of her books. She was trembling inside because she was face-to-face with him again.

He didn't seem to be aware of anything as he leaned on the iron railing, his top hat and cane swinging together as he looked at the view. 'Bath is very lovely, is it not?'

'Yes.'

He glanced at her. 'I'm glad to have encountered you like this, for last night's gross error on my part has been preying on my mind.'

'There's no need, truly.'

'But there is, Miss Richmond, for I could tell by your subsequent manner that I'd upset you more than you'd admitted.'

Her subsequent manner? He'd obviously noticed how she'd withdrawn into the background as much as possible. She colored a little. 'You're mistaken, my lord, for I certainly didn't take offense, nor was I unduly upset. If you noticed any, er, reserve, it was simply that I wished to leave the evening entirely to you and Jane. It would hardly have done for the elder Miss Richmond to look as if she wished to be at the center of things as well, would it?' She smiled.

He studied her. 'I *did* notice your reserve, and if it was simply as you say, then I can understand and appreciate your reasons, but I can't help feeling ...'

'Yes?'

'That there is something else concerning you. Is it perhaps that you have doubts about the betrothal? Maybe your sister isn't entirely happy about something?'

'Oh, *please* don't think that,' she said quickly. 'No woman on earth could be happier than Jane, believe me, and I don't have any doubts about the match, for I'm sure you and she were made for each other.'

He smiled. 'I'm relieved to hear you say so, Miss Richmond.' He looked at the river again. 'Did you know that you and I almost met earlier this year?'

She was startled. 'Did we? But how could that possibly be? I hardly ever leave Richmond House.'

'You ventured to London, did you not?'

'Yes.'

'We happened to attend the theater on the same evening. You were in Mrs Brooke's box. I understand she's your aunt.'

'Yes, although I fancy she now wishes me in perdition for the disaster I made of my stay.'

'Disaster?'

'I'm afraid I didn't much care for London life.'

'Is that why you cut short your visit?'

She stared at him. 'How did you know that?'

He smiled. 'You were pointed out to me at the theater as Miss Richmond of Richmond House in Gloucestershire, and as negotiations had begun between your father and myself, I was naturally greatly interested to meet you.' He gave a short, rather rueful laugh. 'At least, perhaps I should explain again that I was anxious to meet the young lady I believed to be Miss *Jane* Richmond. I attempted to introduce myself during the intermission, but your box was an intolerable crush and I couldn't get even close to you. So I decided to call upon you the following morning, but when I did, I was informed that you'd taken yourself back to Gloucestershire.'

She looked away. That night at the theater had been the last straw. She'd hated every minute of it, loathed her aunt's vapid friends and their endless empty chatter, and been appalled at the prospect of nearly three more weeks of such socializing. It had been too much, and she'd greatly affronted her aunt by announcing that she was returning to Stroud immediately.

He watched her. 'Perhaps you now understand why I was firmly under the impression that *you* were my prospective bride. You'd been pointed out to me as *the* Miss Richmond, and I subsequently didn't even have the miniature to correct the error, for as I explained last night, it was broken beyond all redemption when it arrived.'

'Well, I'm sure you were more than delighted when you met Jane,' she replied.

He didn't answer, for at that moment something in the sky caught his attention. 'It seems the inestimable William has taken to the air again,' he murmured.

Shading her eyes against the sun, she looked toward Sydney Gardens. Sure enough, the crimson-and-blue balloon was floating serenely in the sky, firmly anchored by its rope. 'He must have repaired the flap valve,' she observed without thinking.

'Flap valve? I had no idea you were well-versed in such technical matters, Miss Richmond.'

She colored again. 'I'm not, it's just that Mr Grenfell told us last night that he was grounded again because of the valve.'

'Ah, yes, I understand you and he are acquainted because he made a somewhat humiliating descent on to your apple tree.'

'It was a pear tree, actually.'

He grinned. 'I suppose he should be thankful it wasn't a thorn tree! But even thorns wouldn't have taught him a lesson, he'd still be intent upon attempting his first nighttime voyage.'

Her eyes widened. 'But isn't that exceedingly hazardous?'

'William revels in the hazardous, and has occasionally paid the price for his, er, valor, as your pear tree knows only too well. I understand your father wasn't very amused.'

'Father loathes balloons and balloonists – he calls them balloonatics.'

'Very appropriate. Tell me, why does Mr Richmond abhor such things so much? I, er, heard a little from William last night.'

'I really have no idea. I can only think that something must have happened in the past.'

He smiled, his hat and cane still swinging idly to and fro. 'If I'm perfectly honest, I noticed your sister last night before I approached you and your father.'

Her heart sank. 'You did?'

'Yes. I saw William, and naturally glanced at his partner. I thought him a fortunate fellow to be dancing with such a beautiful creature.'

She didn't know what to say, for if he'd noticed Jane dancing with his friend, he must also have noticed how openly pleased she'd been to be in that friend's company. But there was no way of telling now what he thought; his eyes gave no hint. Feeling uncomfortable suddenly, she turned to look at a clock on the wall above a nearby shop. 'I … I think I should get on with my errand, my lord, otherwise my father will never have his London papers.'

'Allow me to accompany you,' he said immediately, straightening.

'Oh, please, there's no need, for I have my maid.'

'But I'd *like* to walk with you, Miss Richmond,' he Insisted.

She smiled self-consciously. 'Then, of course …'

He offered her his arm, and they proceeded from the terrace, followed by Jenny.

Milsom Street was broad and gracious, with Palladian facades and elegant bow windows, and it climbed the lower incline of the same hill that was crowned by the Royal Crescent, the Circus, and the Assembly Rooms. It was a splendid street, boasting a variety of shops, from haberdashers, milliners, and dressmakers, to tailors, confectioners, and high-class grocers. There were repositories of art and music, superior lodging houses, and, of course, circulating libraries, and the one to which Mr Richmond subscribed was at number 43, on the east side of the street. It was much frequented by the better levels of society, and there were several fine carriages drawn up at the curb as Robert opened the door, ushering Christina and Jenny inside.

Bookshelves lined the walls from floor to ceiling, and there were ladders to reach those near the top. Tables laden with journals and various newspapers stood around, and there were several ornate writing desks where letters could be penned, paper, ink, and quills being provided for a small fee.

A smart young man in a brown coat and spotted silk neckcloth was serving behind a counter in the center of the floor. He was new to Christina, who instinctively disliked his manner. Two ladies were taking out subscriptions, entering their names in the ledger he placed before them. He informed them that a subscription of half a guinea would give them access to all the latest novels, magazines, reviews, and so on for a whole year, whereas three shillings would do the same for only three months. The ladies decided upon the latter, as Mr Richmond had done nearly a week before.

While Robert waited by one of the writing desks with Jenny, Christina approached the counter. The young man attended to her complaint, explaining in a rather superior way that the boy they usually employed to deliver for them had been taken ill that morning. Placing the newspapers for number 14A Johnstone Street on the counter, he was about to move on to the next customer, a clergyman, when Christina realized that *The Times* was missing.

'Sir,' she said quickly, 'I'm afraid this order isn't correct.'

The young man paused, raising an eyebrow and pursing his lips. 'Not correct?'

'There isn't a copy of *The Times*.'

'Ah, yes, well, I'm afraid we only have one copy left, and that is reserved for Count Bleiburg, who has intimated that he may possibly require it.'

More than a little incensed, she stood her ground. 'Sir, this Count Bleiburg may indeed *possibly* require it, but my father *definitely does* require it, and since a subscription has been taken out, and the necessary extra payments made, I rather think—'

'The count subscribes as well, madam,' replied the young man superciliously, looking down his nose at her in that arrogant way some assistants had when they gave themselves the airs and graces of the less-likable customers they were there to serve.

'Nevertheless—' she began again.

'I'm sorry, madam,' he declared, intending to close the conversation forthwith.

She felt Robert move to her side. 'Miss Richmond, is there any way I can be of assistance?' he murmured.

'It appears I cannot take the last copy of *The Times*, even though we've ordered it.'

'Why not?'

'Because a certain Count Bleiburg might require it.'

'*Might* require it?' Robert's eyes moved to the man behind the counter. 'Is this true?'

'Er, yes, sir ...'

' "Yes, my lord," ' Robert said, correcting him coolly.

'M-my lord?' stammered the young man, feeling very uncomfortable before Robert's steady gaze.

'Lord St Clement.'

The young man's eyes widened. Lord St Clement and Miss Richmond? *The* Lord St Clement and Miss Richmond? His face paled as he thought he'd clashed with two of the most-talked-of persons in Bath. 'I, er, I may have been mistaken about the newspaper, my lord,' he said quickly, reaching for another ledger.

'Oh, I'm quite sure you're mistaken,' murmured Robert.

With a shaking finger the flustered assistant went down a list of names, then closed the ledger with a snap, smiling a little too brightly. 'Yes, indeed, I was entirely in the wrong, Count Bleiburg wishes to have a newspaper tomorrow, not today.' Hastily reaching under the counter, he produced the contested copy of *The Times*, placing it neatly with the rest of Christina's order. 'I do apologize,' he said, looking so uncomfortable that Christina would have felt sorry for him, had she not remembered how very unpleasant he'd been before Robert's intervention.

As she took the newspapers, the young man spoke again. 'May ... may I take this opportunity to wish you both well for the future?'

Color rushed into her cheeks. 'Oh, I ...' she began.

But Robert smiled coolly at the assistant. 'Yes, sir, you may.'

As they emerged into the daylight again, followed obediently by Jenny, Christina looked accusingly at Robert. 'My lord, that wasn't well done.'

'No? Didn't you want the newspaper?' he inquired lightly, grinning.

'That wasn't what I meant. That man thinks you and I are ...'

'Maybe he does, but in actual fact he merely wished us well for the future, and what harm is there in that?'

'But I'm the wrong Miss Richmond.'

He turned to face her. 'Well, I'm the right Lord St Clement, so he wasn't entirely incorrect, was he?' He looked at her in amusement. 'Would you like to go back in and explain his mistake?'

The thought of confronting the odious young man again was too much. 'No, thank you very much,' she replied.

He offered her his arm, and they continued down Milsom Street in the direction of Pulteney Bridge.

William Grenfell's balloon had vanished as they walked along Argyle Street, but the crush of traffic was as great as ever. There were so many pedestrians that Christina might never have noticed Jane hurrying from the direction of Great Pulteney Street toward the house – at least, she *thought* it was Jane, for the woman was the same height and build, had red hair, and was wearing a matching yellow pelisse and gown just like Jane's; but as Christina and Robert reached the pavement outside number 14A, the shutters at Jane's window were still closed, which could only mean that the lazybones occupant had yet to awaken.

Robert prepared to take his leave. 'Until tonight, then, Miss Richmond.'

Still puzzled about thinking she'd seen her sister, Christina looked blankly at him. 'Tonight?'

'I've been invited to dine with you.'

'Oh, yes, of course. Forgive me, I was thinking about something else. I was about to ask you to take a dish of tea with us, but I'm rather afraid my sister is still asleep.' She glanced again at the shuttered window.

'What a lie-a-bed she is, to be sure,' he replied, smiling. 'Until tonight, Miss Richmond.' Taking her hand, he raised it to his lips.

A shiver of pleasure ran secretly through her. 'Thank you for escorting me, my lord.'

'I enjoyed your company, Miss Richmond.'

'And I enjoyed yours, my lord.' Oh, *how* I enjoyed yours.

'*Au revoir.*' Bowing, he strolled off along the crowded pavement, and was soon lost from view.

Followed by Jenny, she went into the house, pausing in surprise as she saw Jane descending the staircase wearing the yellow muslin gown, having evidently divested herself of the matching pelisse.

Jane smiled. 'Don't look so startled, Christina, you *did* expect me to get up sometime today, didn't you?'

'Have you just been out?' asked Christina, as Jenny hurried up the stairs to await her.

'Out? Good heavens, no, I've only just roused myself from my bed. Why do you ask?'

'It's just that I thought ... Oh, it doesn't matter. Is Father in the drawing room?'

'No, he's gone out. A message was delivered from a Mr Middlemiss. Apparently they were at Oxford together, and Mr Middlemiss invited Father to lunch with him at the White Hart.' Christina put the newspapers down on a console table. 'I've just had the honor of Robert Temple's company.'

'Should I be jealous?'

'Hardly.'

'How did you meet him?'

'Oh, we just bumped into each other. He escorted me to the circulating library, routed a disagreeable young man behind the counter, and walked me back here again.'

'Why didn't you invite him in?'

'I was going to, but I thought you were still in bed. Your shutters are closed.'

'Are they?'

Christina looked at her a little incredulously. 'Surely you noticed! After all, they *are* inclined to darken rooms somewhat.'

Jane smiled ruefully. 'To be perfectly honest, I didn't have a clue what time it was when I woke up. I didn't give it a second thought. I was still half-asleep when I had the tea Ellen brought me, and I practically dozed off when she was combing my hair. I was just going to sit in the garden for some fresh air, to liven myself up a little. Will you join me? I do so want to talk about the ball.'

'Of course. I'll just go up and take off my bonnet and spencer.'

Gathering her skirts, Christina hurried up the stairs. She was just about to go into her own room when a movement in Jane's caught her eyes. The shutters were still closed, but Ellen could be seen by the open wardrobe. She was just putting away the yellow pelisse.

11

IT WAS DARK outside, and in her candlelit room Christina was dressed for the small dinner party she had no wish to attend. She'd considered pleading a headache in order to avoid seeing Robert and Jane together, but knew such a course was pointless. She was going to see them together a great deal from now on, and the sooner she became used to it, the better. But it wasn't going to be easy.

She sat by, the fire, the volume of *Gil Blas* open on her lap, but she gazed at the page without attempting to read. The firelight flickered over her, flashing deep purple through the amethysts at her ears and throat. She wore a cream velvet gown, trained, with a low square neckline and long tight sleeves, and there were more amethysts on the golden buckle of the belt immediately beneath her breasts. Her dark hair was pinned into a loose knot at the back of her head, falling in a single heavy tress past the nape of her neck, and there was a hint of rouge on her cheeks and lips. Her lilac eyes were luminous in the soft light as she closed the book and leaned her head back against the chair. In the space of a single day her life had been inexorably changed, and nothing would ever be the same again; and all because she'd looked into Robert Temple's gray eyes and lost her heart.

The minutes seemed to be ticking away so very slowly that she felt as if she'd been ready for hours. Glancing at the clock on the mantelpiece, she saw that it was a quarter to eight; Robert was expected at any time now.

Suddenly she heard Jane's excited gasp, and the rustle of her apple-green taffeta gown as she hurried into the room. 'Christina! He's here!'

'Are you sure?'

'Quite sure.' Jane looked exquisite, her red hair in a Grecian knot and a froth of curls around her face. Her apple-green gown shimmered in the candlelight, the glass beads on the dainty petal sleeves flashing like diamonds. There were diamonds in her necklace and on the tall golden comb in her hair, and she carried a delicate white shawl, its ends knotted so that they swung when she moved.

There was a knock at the front door of the house, and the sound carried up the stairs. Jane's breath caught nervously. 'Oh, I feel quite sick with nerves again.'

'There's no need,' said Christina, discarding the book and getting up. 'Just think what it was like when you were with him last night at the ball. He had eyes only for you, and tonight will be the same.'

'You *are* sure he didn't think anything untoward when he saw me dancing with William, I mean Mr Grenfell, aren't you?'

'Quite sure.'

Jane swallowed, pressing her palms against her skirts to steady herself. 'Shall we go down, then?'

'If you're ready.'

'I'm ready.' Jane smiled ruefully. 'What would I do without you, Christina? You're always here to comfort me, and I'm ashamed of how often I rely on you.'

Christina smiled. 'What else is a big sister for?'

On impulse Jane hugged her tightly, then turned to go down.

As Christina followed, she glanced along the landing at Jane's room, remembering how she'd seen Ellen putting the yellow pelisse away. 'Jane...?'

'Yes?' Jane paused on the stairs, looking quizzically at her.

Christina drew back from the question, for now wasn't the time. 'It doesn't matter.'

'What is it?'

'It really doesn't matter. Come on, or the gentlemen will wonder what's become of us.'

They proceeded down the stairs to the drawing room, where Robert had been shown into Mr Richmond's presence. Mr Richmond was in fine fettle because of the excellent way things were going where the betrothal was concerned. He wore a new burgundy coat and black silk breeches, and looked particularly well.

Robert wore an indigo velvet coat, and white silk breeches, and there was a sapphire pin on the knot of his white silk cravat.

The two men stood before the fireplace, and Mr Richmond was selecting a new clay pipe from the jar on the mantelpiece. They turned as the sisters entered.

Mr Richmond smiled, coming toward them. 'There you are, my dears. How very lovely you both look. I am indeed a fortunate man to have two such beautiful daughters.' He kissed them both fondly on the cheek, then turned to escort them to Robert, who took Jane's hand and drew it warmly to his lips.

'I believe I must have been born under a lucky star to have gained the hand of someone as lovely as you,' he murmured, looking into her soft brown eyes.

She blushed, lowering her glance demurely. 'I was the one to have been born under the lucky star, my lord, for in you I'm sure I will have the most perfect of husbands.'

'We meet again, Miss Richmond.' Robert turned to Christina.

She made herself look at him and smile. 'We do indeed, my lord.'

He took her hand then, drawing it to his lips as he had Jane's, and she steeled herself for the moment his kiss brushed her bare skin.

Mr Richmond filled his clay pipe with tobacco from his favorite jar, lit it with a spill held to the fire, and then drew a long satisfied puff. As a curl of the sweet smoke rose into the air, he went toward a small table on which stood several decanters and a number of glasses. 'An *apéritif* before we dine?' he inquired, picking up the decanter of pale sherry.

Dinner itself was every bit the ordeal Christina had known it would be, for not only did she have to watch Robert and Jane together, she also had to participate in a conversation that turned greatly upon Bellstones, Robert's Tudor mansion at the foot of Exmoor in Somerset. He quite evidently adored the house, and frequently referred to how much he thought Jane would come to love it as well.

Jane seemed prepared to love it no matter what, and she asked a great many questions, so that before long they knew the house had twenty-eight rooms, a baronial hall, suites once occupied by Queen Elizabeth and King Charles II, a series of particularly beautiful terraced gardens, matchless views of the high moors, a park where Queen Elizabeth herself had once ridden to the local staghounds, and a beautiful river that had its source in a lake on the moor.

Conversation also turned upon London, which Jane openly longed to visit. Robert had a wealth of anecdotes about the capital and its high society, and he was an amusing raconteur, keeping them greatly entertained. Christina observed him, thinking again how devastatingly attractive he was. It was small wonder that such a man had a reputation with the ladies, for there could hardly be a woman alive who didn't respond in some measure to him. One thing was certain: Miss Christina Richmond was responding, in spite of her deep desire to do the opposite.

Sir Archibald Fitton's cook had excelled herself for this important occasion, Mr Richmond having been firmly overruled by his daughters on the matter of roast beef, which dish they were determined would not grace tonight's table. Instead there was an exquisite puree of artichokes, magnificently garnished cutlets à la provençale, and deliciously light meringues à la crème, but tempting as the meal was, Christina ate very little.

She tried to be all she should be, for no one must even begin to guess the truth, and she discovered that she was a more-than-adequate actress, for they were all convinced she was as delighted as they with the way things were turning out.

The meal ended at last, and Christina and Jane adjourned to the drawing room, leaving the gentlemen to discuss the *minutiae* of the marriage contract over their port. Christina didn't go directly into the drawing room, but hastened first to the kitchens to congratulate the pleased cook upon the excellence of the meal.

Going to join her sister in the drawing room, Christina entered to see her standing at one of the windows. Jane had opened a shutter and was looking out at the cold starry sky. There was something a little odd about her, and Christina paused in the doorway. 'Is something wrong?'

Jane whirled guiltily about. 'No. Of course not,' she said quickly, closing the shutter.

'For someone who says there's nothing wrong, you look exceeding guilty.'

'Don't be silly.' Jane laughed lightly, going to sit on the sofa. The butler had put a silver tray on the table before it, with a coffeepot, some golden porcelain cups and saucers, a decanter of sweet apricot liqueur, and four little glasses.

Christina sat on a chair opposite, eyeing her. 'What is it, Jane?' she pressed.

Jane looked away. 'If I seem guilty it's because I happened to be thinking about Mr Grenfell.'

'I see.'

'No, you don't. It was only an innocent thought, about what Robert told you earlier today. I think it's far too dangerous to make an ascent in the dark, and I wish such a plan would be set completely aside.'

'I agree with you, but I also think that *you* should set *Mr Grenfell* completely aside,' warned Christina uneasily. 'He's nothing to you, Jane, beyond the fact that he's made his admiration disgracefully plain. You've somehow managed to get away with your questionable conduct so far, but no one can expect such luck to last forever, and if you do anything else, I doubt very much whether you'll emerge unscathed. You do want Robert, don't you?'

'Of course I do.'

'Then don't speak of Mr Grenfell, don't think about him, don't even remember his wretched name.' Christina leaned forward to pour two cups of the black unsweetened coffee.

'You don't have to lecture me,' complained Jane.

'Don't I?'

Jane fell silent, accepting her cup. After a moment she looked curiously at Christina. 'I think perhaps it's my turn to ask if something's wrong.'

'What do you mean?' Christina met her eyes.

'Well, since last night you've been a little ... Oh, it doesn't matter.' She laughed then. 'Actually, this sounds a little familiar, for I seem to recall you were about to ask me something just as we came down, and you also said it didn't matter.'

'So I did.'

'What was it?'

Christina paused, and then put down her cup. 'I was going to ask you again if you'd been out just before I returned from the circulating library.'

Jane stared at her. 'But I've already said—'

'I know, but when I went upstairs I saw Ellen putting your yellow pelisse away. When I thought I saw you returning to the house, I thought you were wearing the pelisse and gown, and when you actually came down the stairs, you *were* wearing the gown.'

Jane continued to stare at her for a moment, and then laughed. 'And because of that you think I've been up to something? No doubt you suspect me of creeping off to Sydney Gardens to see my other admirer.'

'Have you?' Christina held her eyes.

'No, I haven't. Of course Ellen was putting the pelisse away, she'd brought it out because she thought I intended to go out a little later. That's really all there was to it.'

Christina was forced to smile a little sheepishly. 'I must ask you to forgive me, but I really did think ...'

'Robert means too much to me, Christina.'

'I'm glad, for you obviously mean as much to him.'

'Are you really happy for us?'

'Of course I am.'

'And you *do* like Robert?'

'Very much. Why do you ask?'

'I don't know. You seem ... Perhaps it's me, I'm in such a state all the time, I sometimes don't know if I'm coming or going.' Jane laughed.

Christina laughed as well, but knew privately that in spite of her efforts, Jane had detected the change in her. From now on she, Christina, would have to try even harder to hide the truth about her feelings for Robert.

They'd commenced their second cup of coffee, and were discussing a forthcoming play at the Theater Royal, when the gentlemen joined them at last, and by Mr Richmond's beaming smile, they knew that everything had been satisfactorily agreed.

He rang for the butler, and instructed him to bring the large bottle of champagne that had been sitting in ice for several hours now, in anticipation of this auspicious moment, and when they all had a frothing glass, he smiled at Jane.

'It's all arranged, my dear, we've leaving for Bellstones at the end of next week, and you and Robert will be formally betrothed there on his birthday, the twentieth of this month.' He raised his glass. 'I wish you both every happiness, and trust that you will be as happy in your marriage as I was in both of mine.'

As they all raised their glasses, Jane's eyes sparkled like the champagne. Her cheeks were flushed with happiness, and she looked so radiant she was almost ethereal. Robert put down his own glass, relieved her of hers, and then pulled her close to kiss her on the cheek.

It was the perfect gesture, and Mr Richmond was suddenly so moved that tears sprang to her eyes. All along he'd prayed that the match would be a happy one, and now there seemed no doubt that it would be. Turning away to hide his emotion, he sought in his pocket for a handkerchief.

Jane and Robert were talking about the future, and Christina seized the moment to go to her father. 'You're not supposed to be wiping your eyes at a time like this,' she said gently, taking his arm.

He patted her hand fondly. 'I know, my dear, I know, but one day I'm sure I'll be wiping similar tears at the announcement of your betrothal.'

Seeing that Jane and Robert were still preoccupied, Christina smiled again at her father. 'I don't want to be betrothed, for I'm quite happy to remain with you.'

'You have so much to give, my dear, and you should have a husband to share it with.'

But I can never have the husband I want. The thought passed unbidden through her head, as she knew it often would from now on. She glanced briefly at Robert, and then back at her father, who was gazing wistfully into the fire. 'What are you thinking about?' she asked.

'Oh, the past.'

'Your marriages?'

'Not exactly.' He paused. 'About the one marriage that eluded me.'

She looked curiously at him, having long suspected that neither of his wives, although much loved, had been the great passion of his life. 'Who was she, Father?' she asked quietly.

He lowered his glance. 'Her name was Alicia Partington, and I knew her after your mother, and before Jane's.'

'Do you want to tell me about her?'

'No. She's very definitely a thing of the past, and will always remain so.' He drew a quick breath, smiling at her. 'Oh, the heart is a dreadful organ, my dear, it can raise you to the heights of joy or plunge you into the depths of misery. Sometimes I think your philosophy may be the wisest one after all, for at least you'll be spared unhappiness.'

Christina knew only too well the irony of this.

Jane remembered her father then, hurrying to him. 'Oh, I'm so very happy,' she said, hugging him tightly.

Christina knew it was time for her to give Robert her best wishes. 'I'm so very pleased for you both,' she said, forcing her voice to sound as warmly natural as it should be at such a time.

'Thank you.' He smiled.

'In my sister you have one of the sweetest, most adorable creatures in all England, my lord.'

He smiled again, catching her unawares by bending forward to kiss her on the cheek. 'I know that she is everything you say, Christina, but I also know that the same description more than applies to you,' he murmured softly.

The warmth of his lips made her feel weak, and he was so close that it would have been easy to slip her arms around him. Oh, to be able to hold him, to be able to taste his lips, to feel his heart beating close to hers. She had to hold her breath for a moment, to quell the torrent of forbidden emotion that welled up inside her, and it wasn't until she was in command again that she realized he'd addressed her by her first name.

12

AFTER SUCH A memorable evening, the next day could have been something of an anticlimax, but that was the last thing it was destined to be.

Mr Richmond was still mindful of keeping the dreaded gout at bay, and rose promptly at his usual hour to go to the Cross Bath. Then, after a very agreeable breakfast with his daughters, he removed himself from the house again, this time to go to the Pump Room for his daily glasses of the water.

As his sedan chair vanished around the corner into Argyle Street, Jane rose from the breakfast table and looked longingly out at the warm October sunshine. 'Shall we go for a walk, Christina?' she asked, the ribbons on her pink day cap fluttering as she turned to look at her sister.

Christina smiled, folding her napkin. 'Where shall we go? Beechen Cliff?'

'I rather thought it would be agreeable to stroll along the towpath of the canal.'

Christina gave her a suspicious glance, getting up from her chair and fluffing out her cherry muslin skirts. 'I'm sure Beechen Cliff would be much more sensible,' she said, knowing full well that the Kennet & Avon canal passed through Sydney Gardens.

'I know what you're thinking, but you're wrong,' said Jane a little haughtily. 'I'm a little tired of the wonderful view from Beechen Cliff, and just happen to think it would be pleasant to walk by water on a day like this. If you don't trust me to conduct myself correctly, we can walk *around* Sydney Gardens and join the canal on the far side. Would that do?'

Christina studied her for a long moment, and then decided that the discussion they'd had the evening before had probably had the desired effect where Mr William Grenfell and his balloon were concerned. 'All right, the towpath it is, but *beyond* Sydney Gardens. You may have made up your mind about things, but I suspect Mr Grenfell of very different notions.'

'William is a gentleman.'

'William?' Christina raised a very disapproving eyebrow.

'I mean, Mr Grenfell.' Jane looked out of the window again. 'The weather looks really warm. Do you think my pink velvet spencer will be sufficient?'

'Ample.'

'Good, because I do so like wearing it with this lawn dress.'

Half an hour later they emerged into the sunshine, setting off along Great Pulteney Street toward Sydney Gardens. Jane looked very pretty in her pink velvet and lawn, her straw gypsy hat tied on with an enormous pink satin ribbon. Christina wore her cherry muslin dress with its matching full-length frilled pelisse, and on her head there was a gray silk jockey hat with a long tiffany gauze scarf falling almost to her hem at the back.

The vista of Great Pulteney Street was closed by the porticoed facade of the Sydney Hotel, behind which rose the trees of the Vauxhall. It was through the hotel that access into the gardens was gained, and as a consequence there was a great deal of to-ing and fro-ing through the doors beneath the fine portico, but Jane didn't even glance toward the entrance as the sisters walked by, following the pavement of Sydney Place as it curved up the undulating hill on which the hexagonal gardens had been laid out. Very little of the gardens could be seen from outside, for they were surrounded by a high wall, but the trees were very fine in their autumn foliage, and the classical roof of a little mock-temple appeared toward the top of the hill.

Although the gardens were set on a rising slope, the canal passed at an angle through them, cut along a convenient dip in the contours. As Christina and Jane walked on, leaving the gardens behind, the land began to fall away again, revealing the canal as it led away to the east across open countryside. Some steps led down to the towpath, and soon the sisters were strolling beside the glittering water toward the nearby village of Bathampton.

The canal was always busy carrying barges to and from London, but there were a number of pleasure craft as well, for it was quite the thing to hire a small boat in Sydney Gardens to row out into the countryside. Ladies lounged on cushions, drawing their fingers idly through the water as several moorhens bobbed like corks on the wash of their boat. It was a lovely day, the autumn trees reflected in the water, and Christina was quite reluctant to turn to walk back toward Bath again.

As the wall and trees of Sydney Gardens appeared down the hill before them, nothing could have been further from Christina's mind than Mr Grenfell or his balloon, but then Jane suddenly said something that set alarm bells ringing in her head.

'Christina, did you know there was a labyrinth in the gardens?'

'I thought you loathed mazes,' replied Christina after a moment.

'Just because I got lost in one when I was ten?'

'You howled for hours.'

'I'm a big girl now.'

'Yes, you are, which is why you'll gladly forgo the lure of the Sydney Gardens labyrinth,' Christina said a little tartly, her suspicions well and truly aroused.

'Christina, I only thought it would be a diversion to—'

'To trick me in the Vauxhall so that you can view Mr Grenfell and his odious balloon from close quarters,' Christina finished for her.

Jane pouted. 'I only want to see the labyrinth,' she insisted.

'Oh, of *course*,' replied Christina acidly.

'Don't use your best vitriol on me, for I don't deserve it. No, truly I don't deserve it, which you'd realize full well if you'd glanced down toward Great Pulteney Street a moment ago.'

'And what has Great Pulteney Street got to do with it?'

'Everything. Mr Grenfell rode away down it just now. I saw him.'

'And how could you possibly know it was he?'

'Who else would go riding in trousers?'

Christina stared at her, and then had to laugh. 'I suppose he does rather fit that particular bill.'

'So, you see, it's quite all right if we toddle off to the labyrinth, isn't it?'

'Father still forbade us to go into the Vauxhall.'

'That was before he took out subscriptions. Oh, *please*, Christina, what harm is there in taking a peek at the maze?' Jane was at her most appealing, her big brown eyes wide and soulful.

Christina smiled reluctantly. 'Did I ever tell you you sometimes remind me of a spaniel puppy?'

'I'm of a mind to be miffed,' replied Jane, linking her arm and beginning to walk on down the hill. 'It's settled, then – we'll just make a little detour and go into the labyrinth.'

'Oh, all right, but if you put one foot wrong, Jane Richmond ...'

'I won't, I promise.'

'I've heard your promises before.'

'I mean it this time.'

'You did every other time too,' replied Christina wryly, wondering if she'd just made a very serious mistake.

They approached the entrance of the hotel beneath the lofty portico, which rose on four magnificent Corinthian columns. When their names were ticked off on the relevant ledger, they were permitted through the hotel, where many ladies and gentlemen were enjoying tea. At the rear of the building some handsome double doors opened beneath an outdoor balcony where an orchestra played on special occasions.

They emerged into a wide, rather crowded semicircular area around which stretched a loggia where meals could be enjoyed in private alcoves. A broad walk stretched away up the undulating hillside toward the classical temple, the roof of which they'd seen from the pavement of Sydney Place. The walk was flanked initially by two fine bowling greens, then by trees, shrubberies, flowerbeds, groves, waterfalls, vistas, a sham castle, and, of course, the labyrinth, which was near the temple. The entire hexagonal site was enclosed by the perimeter wall, inside which was a ride where gentlemen, and some ladies, exercised their gleaming mounts. Of William Grenfell's celebrated balloon there was no sign at all.

As the sisters mingled with everyone else on the wide walk, Christina was only too conscious of Jane's frequent surreptitious glances around. At last she felt obliged to remark upon the matter. 'Jane, it seems we're in luck,' she said.

'Luck?'

'Yes, not only is the aeronaut himself absent, his balloon appears to have gone as well.'

'Really? I hadn't noticed,' Jane replied airily.

The labyrinth was a little daunting from the outside, a wall of clipped green hedges from behind which issued the sound of laughter and voices, together with the occasional call for assistance. As Christina and Jane approached the entrance, a young man ushered his rather distressed lady friend out to a nearby bench, offering her his handkerchief as she sobbed. 'Are you all right, Penelope?' he asked anxiously, holding one of her hands.

'I th-thought we'd *never* find our way out, Benjamin,' she declared tearfully. 'We were in there for over an hour!'

'I promise never to take you there again, my love,' he reassured her, kissing her trembling hand. 'Come, I'll take you to the hotel for a restoring dish of tea.'

'Oh, yes, that would be comforting,' she replied, still sniffing.

As they walked away down the hill, Jane halted in her tracks, looking a little doubtfully at the entrance of the labyrinth. 'They were lost in there for an *hour*?'

'So it seems.'

'Suddenly the maze doesn't seem so inviting.'

'I thought you were a big girl now.'

'Don't be beastly.'

'*Moi?*'

'*Toi.*'

Christina grinned, and as one they turned to retrace their steps down the hill. As they did so, their gaze fell almost immediately upon the balloon.

Nearly fully inflated, it billowed above a ten-foot-high scaffolding hung with decorated cloth to conceal what was going on around the base. Hidden from all directions except this one because of the lie of the land, and the density of the surrounding trees and bushes, the balloon rippled from time to time as the breeze moved over the crimson-and-blue gores of rubberized taffeta.

The protective scaffolding was at least sixty feet square, and the cloth hangings were definitely needed to keep out prying eyes, for a crowd of at least fifty people was gathered around what appeared to be the only entrance into the enclosure beyond. This entrance was guarded by a huge black man, who stood with his arms folded, eyeing anyone who dared to come too close.

Jane gazed at the scene, her eyes shining. 'Oh, Christina, isn't it *splendid*?'

'No, it's positively obnoxious,' replied Christina, taking her arm and trying to steer her on her way.

'Can't we go just a *little* closer?' begged Jane, resisting.

'No.'

'But ...'

'Father has forbidden us. And don't try to use the subscriptions as an excuse, for it won't wash.'

'What harm is there in just looking?'

'Where you're concerned, Jane Richmond, probably a great deal of harm! Trouble follows you around.'

'Oh, *please*, Christina,' pleaded Jane urgently.

Christina was about to refuse again, when they both heard a voice they knew well, that of William Grenfell.

'Miss Richmond, Miss Jane, what a pleasure it is to encounter you both again!'

Christina's heart sank as she turned to see him riding up the walk toward them. He wore a pea-green coat, beige satin waistcoat, and brown-and-white-checkered trousers. There was a tall top hat on his head, but as he dismounted he quickly snatched it off to bow as he reached them.

Jane smiled at him. 'Good morning, Mr Grenfell.'

'Miss Jane.' His glance moved warmly over her.

Too warmly, in Christina's opinion. 'Good morning, Mr Grenfell,' she said a little coolly, her manner most uninviting.

His eyes flickered toward her. 'Er, good morning, Miss Richmond.'

Jane tossed her sister a cross look, then smiled at the handsome pilot again. 'I see that the balloon is inflated again, Mr Grenfell. Does that mean you've managed to repair the flap valve?'

'Hopefully.'

'Are you about to make an ascent?'

'No, we're merely preparing for tonight.'

'Tonight?' She looked anxiously at him. 'You aren't *really* intending to go up in the darkness, are you?'

He smiled, obviously flattered by her concern. 'I sincerely hope so to do, Miss Jane.'

'Please, don't.'

'It will be quite safe, I promise you, for it will be a captive ascent.'

'But what if the rope should break again?' she said, showing just a little too much concern.

Christina frowned at her. 'Jane!' she said sharply.

Jane blushed quickly, and fell silent.

William cleared his throat as he sought something else to say. 'Er, would you both like to see the balloon?'

Christina's lips parted to politely decline, but Jane spoke first. 'Oh, could we? That would be *most* interesting.'

Christina was angry now. 'You know we can't possibly do that, Jane,' she said with measured firmness.

'Of course we can,' replied Jane, meeting her eyes defiantly. It was a look that gave full warning; nothing was going to stand in the way of Jane Richmond and the balloon she'd longed to see ever since arriving in Bath.

Christina was in a quandary, for what could she do when Jane was in this mood? Drag her from the Vauxhall? Command her to be obedient? Threaten to leave her to ruin her reputation? No, all these courses were unthinkable, as her minx of a sister knew only too well. There was nothing for it but to consent to the invitation, and do all that was possible to keep Jane from further folly.

Christina exhaled slowly, and then nodded. 'Very well, Jane, we'll look at the balloon, but I promise you that when we get home ...' She allowed the sentence to die away unfinished, for in truth she didn't know what she'd do when they got home, except give Jane a very uncompromising piece of her mind!

Leading his horse, William offered Jane an arm, and with Christina following, they left the walk to go down to the balloon, which loomed higher and higher the closer they came to it.

A boy took the horse, and then the black man stood aside for them to enter the enclosure. There were envious murmurs from the small gathering of onlookers, and those murmurs swiftly became intrigued whispers as Jane was recognized by two gentlemen who'd been present at the ball.

Christina detected the stir caused by this realization, and she endeavored to appear quite unconcerned, as if it was the most natural thing in the world for the future Lady St Clement and her sister to accompany a new gentleman acquaintance to examine a balloon, but in reality she felt like boxing Jane's foolish ears for her. Once again her sister's rashness was going to be the talk of Bath, and this time Robert was here to hear it; Christina had no doubt there'd be many concerned 'friends' anxious to tell him of his future wife's activities in Sydney Gardens.

Inside the enclosure there was quite an astonishing scene as at least ten men went about various tasks connected with the balloon, which swelled magnificently overhead, blotting out the sun. It was fixed above a wooden stage, the entire taffeta globe enmeshed in a rope netting that ended in lines to be attached to the gilded car, which was at present standing separately on the grass nearby. Anchor ropes held the balloon to the staging by a system of pulleys, and two men were operating a strange contraption that evidently produced the inflammable air, for it was placed directly beneath the neck of the globe. On the grass all around, there were casks, bottles, nets, trays, iron stands, and stacks of sandbags. The oars and wings were propped against the staging, as were the furled Union Jacks, while the red pennants that were usually attached to the ropes above the car had been folded neatly in a pile on one of the steps leading up to the staging.

It all looked very complicated and interesting, and Christina and Jane paused to gaze around.

One of the men on the staging called across to William. 'She's ready, Mr Grenfell.'

'Very well. See how it goes.'

There was an immediate increase in activity as the inflammable-air machine was carried quickly down to the grass, and the balloon was raised by using the pulleys and anchor ropes. When it was about ten feet higher than before, some more men carried the golden car up to the staging, fixing it in place by the lines dangling from the net around the globe. When every line had been firmly attached, the

THE WRONG MISS RICHMOND

balloon was eased still further by the pulleys, until it could be felt tugging at the car, anxious to rise into the air. The pulleys were made fast, and the men turned to look at William, who seemed more than well-pleased.

'Well done,' he said. 'You've cut more than a minute off the time.'

They grinned, and returned to their other tasks.

Jane looked curiously at the pilot. 'Forgive me, but why is speed so important? I would have thought that you'd wish to be slow but sure.'

'Ideally, I would, but when it takes a long time not only to inflate the balloon with hydrogen but to then attach the car, crowds can become very restive, even disgruntled. I have no intention of suffering the fate of some of my less-fortunate predecessors, who were practically lynched by impatient crowds.'

'Good heavens, how dreadful.' Jane was appalled.

'Would you like to see in the car?' he asked, anxious to keep her there as long as possible, and knowing that Christina was waiting for a moment to insist upon their return to Johnstone Street.

Jane accepted the invitation without hesitation. 'Oh, yes, I'd *love* to,' she replied, giving Christina another defiant look before slipping her hand over the arm he offered.

Christina remained angrily where she was, silently calling Jane every despicable name under the sun, and according William a curse or two as well. If only she'd held her ground about going to the maze, they'd be safely at home now, sipping tea.

She watched as William assisted Jane up on to the staging, and then into the gilded car. As he followed and began to show her the various ropes and sundry other equipment, one of the pulleys suddenly gave way, causing the balloon to lurch and put all the strain on the remaining pulleys.

Jane gave a frightened cry, reaching out automatically to William, who steadied her and then looked swiftly at his men, but before he could shout orders to them, the other pulleys gave way under the uneven strain. With a jolt the balloon began to rise, the car swaying gently from side to side.

There was instant uproar as the men strove to catch the dangling ropes, but the balloon was eager to be free, seeming to almost leap higher out of reach. Beyond the scaffolding there were cheers as the balloon was perceived to be making an ascent, but the cheers soon turned to cries of alarm as it was realized that this voyage was an accident. Shocked gasps ensued as the balloon rose higher and higher above the scaffolding, revealing the car and its two occupants. Everyone stared at the scandalous sight of Miss Jane Richmond, the future Lady St Clement, standing tearfully in the gallant arms of the dashing young pilot.

Christina was numb with shock, watching in silent horror as the balloon began to drift on the breeze toward the center of Bath. Soon everyone in the gardens could see Jane's plight, for instead of ducking prudently out of sight at the bottom of the car, she remained foolishly in full view, still in William Grenfell's comforting embrace.

Her willful impetuosity had long promised to be her undoing, and now, at this of *all* delicate times in her life, it seemed to have been just that.

13

CHRISTINA GATHERED HER skirts to hurry from the enclosure, Intent upon keeping the balloon in sight as it drifted toward the hotel and Great Pulteney Street. It was all she could think of to do; it was all everyone else could think of as well, for the balloon's unexpected ascent, to say nothing of its exceedingly interesting lady occupant, had riveted the attention of everyone in the Vauxhall. Christina's dismay deepened with each second, for this time there wouldn't be any hope of Jane's folly remaining secret.

The balloon drifted serenely southwestward about fifty feet above the hotel roof, and there was uproar in the area by the loggia as a newly arrived wedding party fell into complete disarray, the guests gaping up into the sky instead of at the hitherto happy couple. Seeing all the attention diverted from her on her great day, the overwrought bride dissolved into floods of tears, but her bridegroom hardly noticed; he was too busy craning his neck to catch the last glimpse of the balloon as it sailed slowly out of sight into Great Pulteney Street.

Christina pushed her way through the turmoil in the hotel lobby. Word of the amazing scene outside had already spread to every room, and all the people who'd been enjoying a sociable cup of tea or coffee now deserted their places to hurry outside into the street. Her way was barred for a time, there was simply too great a crush in the main entrance, and thus she overheard an exchange that gave due warning of how Jane's impropriety was going to be greeted.

A rather vain young gentleman with an affected drawl was speaking to an equally vain and affected young lady at his side. 'I say, Philippa, this is the very thing, you're in with a chance after all.'

'A chance?'

'With St Clement. Don't tell me you can't see that this will as good as finish the Richmond match as far as he's concerned. Dammit, the wench may be a beauty, but she ain't exactly class. Look at her, she's actually *hugging* Grenfell! What sort of conduct is that for Robert Temple's bride?'

The woman called Philippa gazed up at the swaying car beneath the balloon, her eyes sharpening cleverly. 'The creature's quite abandoned, and evidently doesn't care who knows it. You're right, Austin, she has no class at all. I vow that if *I* wished to dally with someone I shouldn't, I wouldn't do it in full view of the world.'

Austin laughed dryly. 'No, my dear, you'd be on the floor of the car with him, well and truly out of sight.'

Christina heard no more, for at last she managed to push outside into the street, where the traffic was in chaos as several carriages attempted to turn in order to pursue the balloon into Bath.

High in the sky, Jane clung, terrified, to William, her eyes tightly closed. She was rigid with shock, deaf to his many pleas that she crouch down out of view in order to protect her reputation. After a while he gave up pleading, for it wasn't having any effect, and anyway, there was so much pleasure to be gained from holding her in his arms. He was ashamed of himself, but couldn't resist, and for a while he was oblivious of the dangers of the unexpected free flight; he was conscious only of the delight of her closeness.

He was brought sharply back to cold awareness by a sudden down-draft that caught the balloon, dragging it sharply earthward. The roofs and chimneys of the north side of Great Pulteney Street swung rapidly closer, and he collected his wits sufficiently to forcibly disentangle himself from Jane's arms. There were a number of sandbags on the floor of the car, and he picked one up, heaving it over the edge and shouting a warning down to the crowded street. The sandbag struck one of the roofs, dislodging several tiles, which fell with it to the pavement, scattering the crowds for a moment.

The balloon continued to descend, although more slowly, and William bent to discard a second sandbag. Jane held on weakly to one of the ropes, her breath catching on a sob as she peeped fearfully over the edge of the car at the scene swaying so alarmingly below.

With the ejection of the second sandbag, which burst in a cloud of sand as it was impaled on a wrought-iron railing, the balloon steadied and then began to climb gently again, still drifting inexorably toward the heart of the city.

William straightened with relief, searching in his pocket for his handkerchief and wiping his brow. He saw Jane's pale anxious face as she continued to cling to the rope, and he reached out reassuringly to touch her arm.

'It's all right, truly it is.'

'Are ... are we going to crash?' she asked tremulously.

'No, of course not,' he replied, although he knew he shouldn't give any such categorical assurances when the truth was that a crash of some sort was a very probable outcome. He had no oars or wings, and he still had grave doubts about the efficiency of the flap valve, which he'd intended to test before attempting another ascent of any sort, whether captive or free, in daylight or at night.

Jane was heartened by his answer, and a small smile appeared on her lips. Suddenly the terrible fear subsided a little, and she began to look around with new eyes. The city was much further below now, the buildings gleaming white in the sun. She could see the river and the abbey, and on the hillside beyond William Street, the curving facades of the Circus and Royal Crescent. The sheer wonder of it all filled her with awed excitement, and she forgot the danger; she also forgot the terrible damage all this was inevitably going to do to her good name.

Her eyes were shining as she looked at William. 'Oh, this is marvelous, as marvelous as I knew it would be.'

Glad to see her at least temporarily restored, he went to stand next to her. 'Your introduction to flight may be unorthodox, but your reaction now is as I expected, for when we met I knew you were a kindred spirit.'

'Did you really?'

'Oh, yes.'

The breeze wafted the balloon, making it revolve slowly for a moment. A sliver of unease returned to Jane, making her instinctively reach out to him. He caught her hand, and after a second's hesitation made so bold as to place his other hand tentatively around her waist. 'Don't worry,' he murmured, 'everything's going to be all right.'

She glanced into his eyes, not moving away as she should. She was exhilarated by the moment, seduced by the sheer wonder of flight, and by the flattering knowledge that the handsome pilot was bewitched by her. She still had no thought for her reputation, or for the effect all this might have upon her prospects with Robert. She did think fleetingly of Christina, however, and looked over the edge at the surge of people and traffic following the balloon along Great Pulteney Street toward Laura Place and Johnstone Street. Was Christina among them? Or had she remained behind in Sydney Gardens?

Christina was hurrying along the pavement toward Laura Place, her heart beating swiftly now because she'd run all the way from the Vauxhall. She'd watched in horror as the balloon had almost descended on to the roof, and now could only hope that William would manage somehow to bring it down safely somewhere.

The open elegance of Laura Place lay ahead now, and Christina could see the windows of number 14A Johnstone Street. Oh, whatever would Father say when today's events came to his ears? He was bound to hear this time, for Jane's latest folly wasn't a private dish of tea in the drawing room, it was very public indeed, and if the balloon continued on its present course, it was a folly that would eventually be witnessed from practically every street and window in Bath! At least Father would be spared actually seeing his daughter's disgrace, for he'd still be at the Pump Room and would be for at least another hour. By the time he emerged, the awful voyage would hopefully be safely over. Hopefully.

Christina halted breathlessly at the beginning of Argyle Street, pressing back against the railings to avoid everyone else as she looked up again at the crimson-and-blue orb in sky. She could see Jane and William in the car, standing far too close together. Oh, Jane, Jane, why can't you at least stand *away* from him? Have you no sense at all?

Her heart pounding now with the effort of running so far, Christina made her way across Pulteney Bridge and up toward Milsom Street. There was mayhem in Bath's most elegant shopping street, for a team of particularly highly strung horses was alarmed by the appearance of the balloon, shying and attempting to bolt. This unsettled other horses, made several dogs begin to bark, and then the surge of pedestrians added to the confusion.

Drifting perceptibly lower again, the balloon floated tranquilly on, its direction taking it now toward the Circus and Royal Crescent. Christina watched in increasing consternation. Was fate intent upon being as unkind as it was possible to be? Was it going to take the balloon and its notorious lady passenger right over Robert Temple's Bath residence? Oh, *please*, no....

But fate had every intention of being that unkind; indeed its purpose seemed to be to actually bring the balloon to grief on the chimneys of Royal Crescent itself, as the two horrified occupants of the car were beginning to realize.

Jane had been so rapt in the wonder of flight that it was some time before she perceived that the rooftops were rather closer than they had been a few minutes before. She glanced at William. 'Aren't we descending?' she asked uneasily.

Looking down, he knew she was right. Quickly he left her side, bending to toss another sandbag over the side, shouting a warning below as he did so. The bag fell with an audible thud on to the cobbled area in the center of the Circus, once again momentarily dispersing the following crowds. The balloon shuddered momentarily, but then continued its very slow shallow descent, drifting inexorably above the roofs of Brook Street toward Royal Crescent.

Jane stared down as the Circus slid away beneath, and then Brook Street. Slowly she looked at William. 'We're still going down, aren't we.' It was a statement of fact rather than a question.

He glanced reluctantly up at the rope that vanished into the neck of the balloon. Was it the flap valve again? Had it opened to allow hydrogen to escape? He reached up, gently pulling the rope. There was no response at all, and he knew then that the valve was indeed open. He tugged at the rope, hoping that by some miracle the motion might close the valve, but he knew it was in vain.

Jane looked at him in dismay. 'Is it broken?'

'I fear so.' He left the rope, moving closer to her again, this time making no pretense about putting his arm around her waist. 'I'll look after you, Jane,' he murmured. 'I'll see that no harm comes to you.'

The majestic sweep of Royal Crescent loomed ever closer on the hillside ahead. She could hear the buzzing excitement of the crowds now, and the clatter of the various pursuing vehicles.

The balloon had been visible for so long, and its route clearly discerned, that many people had already gathered on the sloping grassland in front of the crescent. It seemed to Jane that every soul in the spa had turned out to watch, and at long last the full import of it all began to be borne in on her. The wonder of flight fled, to be replaced by a sinking feeling that had nothing to do with the balloon's unalterable descent toward Bath's most exclusive chimneys. Disaster of more than one kind stared her horridly in the face, and she made it all worse than ever by turning wretchedly into William's arms, hiding her face, but not her person, from the openmouthed stares of those on the ground.

Christina's legs were aching, and her heart was pounding as if it would burst as she pursued the balloon along Brook Street and into Royal Crescent. There she halted, leaning weakly against the railings at the front of the grand curve of houses. The balloon was so low now that it barely cleared the first chimney. The crowds gasped in unison, a shared intake of breath that ended in utter silence as everyone watched in horror.

Christina stared up, very fearful for her sister's safety. If the balloon struck one of the chimneys, the car might turn over, catapulting its occupants to the ground like the sandbags! She could see Jane's frightened face, so very pale and vulnerable, and the firm set of William's jaw as he held her close, evidently helpless to do anything but wait for whatever conclusion fate had decided upon.

Christina's fingers curled convulsively around the iron railings as the car struck the next chimney, dislodging one of the pots, which crashed from the roof to the pavement, shattering into a thousand fragments. The balloon drifted on, and the next chimney was directly in its path.

Everyone was so intent upon what was happening on the roof that not many noticed Robert's fine carriage drawn up in readiness at the curb outside his house. It was waiting to convey him to an appoint-ment at Sheldon House, on the outskirts of the city, and the liveried coachman twisted on the box in order to watch the incredible goings-on overhead.

Robert emerged from his house, pausing in astonishment to gaze at the crowds thronging the usually exclusive and empty slope before the crescent. He wore a fawn coat of quite superb cut, and cream breeches that molded to his hips. A brown beaver top hat was tilted back on his dark hair, and he teased on his gloves, his cane tucked under his arm. He surveyed the sea of upturned faces, and then stepped slowly on to the pavement by the waiting carriage, turning to look up at the roof to see what was causing all the interest. His lips parted momentarily as he saw the balloon, and Jane in William's arms in the car.

As he watched, the car struck the next chimney pot, grating against it for what seemed like an age before swinging free again, rocking to and fro as the balloon drifted onward to the next obstacle, the chimney of Major General Sir Harold Penn-Blagington's residence, immediately next door.

The car struck with a heavy blow this time, and at such an angle that it caught fast, arresting the balloon. For a moment there was a breathless silence; then everyone screamed as the car shifted, sliding down the slope of the roof and dragging the balloon heavily on to the chimney pot, which had cracked in the collision. A jagged gash was torn in the rubberized taffeta, and the hydrogen that had been escaping slowly through the damaged flap valve now found instant freedom. The globe began to deflate visibly, collapsing over the roof like a discarded cloak.

The car continued to slide down the roof, tilting at such an alarming angle that Jane and William were knocked off balance. Jane screamed in terror, and William strove to keep hold of her as they were flung against the side of the car. The world seemed to lurch suddenly, and they were both vaguely aware of the watching crowd's screams as the car tipped very slowly over the low stone balustrade at the edge of the roof.

William closed his eyes, holding Jane tightly. 'I love you,' he whispered in her ear, thinking the words would surely be his last, but then there was a sickening jolt, and the car was suddenly still. The balloon itself was wrapped firmly around the chimney pot, and there was no more slack in the ropes; the car had fallen as far as it could.

Hardly daring to breathe, William opened his eyes again, glancing hesitantly around. To one side there was the terrible drop to the pavement, the sharp iron railings, and the faces of the staring crowd; to the other side, incredibly, there was a window, for the car had come to rest level with the top floor of the house. He found himself staring into the startled eyes of the footman whose room it was. He hugged Jane tightly. 'We're safe! Look, we're safe!'

Timidly she drew back a little from his arms, staring around. A glad sob welled in her throat, and she forgot propriety again, slipping her arms relievedly around him.

William wouldn't have been human had he not responded, but as he did so, something made him glance down at the pavement; he found himself looking directly into Robert's rather pensive eyes, and with a guilty start he hastily disengaged himself from Jane.

But fate hadn't finished with her yet, it had still more spite in store. Assisted by some of his companions, the footman at last succeeded in opening the window, which was very stiff from lack of use. Hands reached out to rescue the two in the car, and William assisted Jane, lifting her by the waist because of the steep angle of the car. As she leaned toward the window, a playful breath of breeze caught her pink lawn skirts, fluttering them gaily above her knees and affording everyone in the crowd a very shocking view of her legs. The more vulgar elements among the onlookers were moved to whistle and applaud, and with a miserable sob Jane escaped from their stares, wriggling hastily through the window.

She was closely followed by William, and the window was then closed immediately, leaving the empty car swinging idly against the side of the house.

14

O N THE PAVEMENT, Christina had watched everything with the
utmost anxiety, not daring to believe Jane was really safe until
the window had closed. Tears were wet on her cheeks as she sought
to compose herself, ready to approach Major General Sir Harold
Penn-Blagington's door, but as she sought her handkerchief in her
reticule, something made her glance along the pavement; Robert
had seen her and was coming over.

'Are you all right, Christina?'

'I ... Yes.' But her lips were trembling, and fresh tears stung her eyes.

'Please don't cry,' he said gently, 'she's quite all right now.'

'I ... I know, it's just ... I've followed the balloon all the way from
Sydney Gardens, and when I saw it getting lower and lower I thought
they'd both be killed.' She blinked the tears furiously away. 'Jane was
just looking at the balloon, and Mr Grenfell asked her if she'd like to
see the inside of the car. The next thing I knew, a pulley broke loose,
and then the balloon began to rise. It ... it was dreadful.' The words
came out in a rush because she was upset, and because she was
dismayed at having to be the one to try to explain to him.

'I'm sure it was.' He glanced toward the door of the major
general's house. 'I think we should go to see them, don't you? My
carriage is at your disposal, so you won't have to walk the gauntlet
of Bath all the way to Johnstone Street.'

'You're very kind.'

'Kindness has nothing to do with it.'

She looked quickly at him. 'You won't think badly of Jane, will
you? She only wanted to see the balloon, she didn't want to do
anything shocking. You do believe me, don't you?'

'Yes, Christina, I believe you. Now, shall we adjourn to my neighbor's house and see what's what?'

She accepted the arm he offered, and they made their way through the crowd toward the major general's door, but as they reached it, they could hear raised voices within.

The door opened suddenly, and the major general himself appeared to personally eject his uninvited guests. He was a very choleric military gentleman, once the scourge of his regiment, and he had a bandaged foot that told of gout as troublesome and painful as Mr Richmond's. He brandished a walking stick as he glowered at a very contrite William, who was still attempting to comfort a weeping Jane.

'Be off with the pair of you, and you, sirrah, will be receiving a bill for the damage to my property.'

'Of course, sir,' replied William. 'I apologize again for the intrusion.'

'From what I hear, sirrah, apologizing is fast becoming a way of life for you!' snapped the other furiously, bristling more and more with each second.

'Maybe this isn't the time to ask, but when would it be convenient to collect the balloon?' ventured William.

'Without delay!' The major general withdrew into the house again, slamming the door.

Jane saw Christina and Robert then, and dissolved into still more tears as William ushered her gently toward them. He looked rather uneasily at Robert. 'Robert, I can explain everything.'

'I'm sure you can, but later will do,' said Robert, only too aware of the intense interest of the watching crowd on the pavement, all of whom now knew their identities.

But William was anxious. 'For Lord's sake, don't misunderstand, Robert. The damned balloon broke free, the flap valve jammed again, and the hydrogen escaped....'

'I don't think I misunderstand at all, William,' replied Robert in an oddly soft tone that made Christina look quickly at him.

William detected something as well, clearing his throat uncomfortably. 'Er, until later, then,' he murmured.

'Please call on me this evening.'

'Very well.'

'And now, I suggest you join us in my carriage. I can convey you as far as Johnstone Street, from where I'm sure you'll wish to go to Sydney Gardens to collect your assistants.'

'Yes. Thank you.'

The people on the pavement parted as Robert escorted Jane to the carriage, closely followed by Christina and William. Jane was still very distressed, sitting quickly in a corner seat and averting her face from her three companions. Christina sat next to her, taking her hand comfortingly, but nothing could offer solace for what had occurred.

The carriage drove off very slowly, the coachman easing the nervous team through the crush of people. Only when the crescent was behind them could the team be brought up to a good pace, their hoofbeats ringing on the cobbles of Brook Street, which had cleared almost miraculously, as the crescent would as well now that the players had removed from the stage.

William sat awkwardly, glancing at Robert from time to time, but Robert's face gave nothing away; his expression was impassive as he gazed out of the carriage window.

Nothing was said all the way back to Johnstone Street, and as the coachman maneuvered the team to a standstill at the curb, Jane didn't wait for either Robert or William to alight first, but forestalled them both by stepping quickly down to the pavement and hurrying tearfully into the house, leaving the front door swinging behind her.

Christina didn't know quite what to do, remaining in her seat for a moment as William climbed out. He turned a little guiltily on the pavement, looking at her. 'I must ask you to forgive me, Miss Richmond.'

She met his eyes, and declined to reply. He'd behaved very badly indeed, egging Jane on because he wished to be with her, and if he thought that her, Christina's, forgiveness would be forthcoming, he was very much mistaken.

He glanced uncomfortably at Robert. 'I will see you tonight, then.'

'You will.'

As William hurried away along the pavement toward Great Pulteney Street, Christina toyed with the strings of her reticule, raising her eyes to Robert's. 'You did mean it when you said you believed me about Jane's blamelessness?'

'Yes, Christina, I meant it.'

'She would never have stepped into that wretched car if she'd known what was about to happen.'

'I'm sure she wouldn't. Christina, please don't look so anxious, for I understand.'

'Do you, my lord?'

'Yes.' He smiled. 'Don't you think it a little formal for you to call me "my lord" when I am familiar enough to call you by your first name? Or is it perhaps that you think I've presumed?'

'Oh, no, of course I don't!' she said quickly, her cheeks coloring.

'Then will you please call me Robert?'

'If … if that is your wish.'

'It most certainly is.'

She smiled, loving him so much that it was anguish not to touch him.

He sat forward, taking her hand suddenly. 'Christina, I don't want you to worry that today's events have in any way changed my mind about the future.'

She had to pause to maintain her calm, for the touch of his hand and the softness of his voice played havoc with her heart. At last she could meet his eyes again. 'I'm so very glad to hear you say that, Robert, because my sister became innocently embroiled in that scrape, and if you'd turned from her because of it …'

'You don't credit me with a great deal of honor, Christina.'

Her flush deepened. 'Please don't think that, for I think you very honorable indeed.'

'I'm pleased to hear it.' He still held her hand, and showed no sign of releasing it. 'When you go in, will you please reassure Jane that I don't misunderstand anything? Tell her that I'm as anxious as she no doubt is to silence any clacking that may arise from today, and that in order to achieve that silence I think it best if we all appear in public as soon as possible. By all, I mean the Richmond family and myself, not William Grenfell.'

'Yes, I agree.'

'Perhaps a sortie to the Theater Royal would be suitable?'

She nodded. 'When would you suggest?'

'Tomorrow night. I'd say tonight, but I think Jane might need a little time to recover.'

'I think you're right, she's very upset indeed.'

'Christina, you'll be sure to convey my best wishes to your father, won't you? I think his mind should be set as much at ease as Jane's.'

'I'll do my best, Robert, but when one is in the parental firing line, nothing is very easy.'

'Is that where you'll be, then? The parental firing line?'

'Almost certainly. I'm the elder sister, and therefore held to be responsible.'

He smiled a little wryly. 'With a sister of Jane's, er, spirit, your position can never have been an easy one.'

'There have been some extremely trying moments,' she admitted, returning his smile.

'Of which this is one of the worst?'

She fell eloquently silent.

He smiled again, drawing her hand to his lips. 'I wonder if Jane has any idea how very fortunate she is to have you?' he murmured.

Her lips parted on a secret frisson of pleasure, and she felt the warmth increase on her already flushed cheeks. She had to look away, for she was sure that there were too many telltale signs in her eyes, and that at any moment he might look properly at her and realize the truth.

He released her hand at last, stepping down to the pavement to assist her. 'Until the theater tomorrow evening,' he said.

'Until then.' Inclining her head, she hurried toward the door of the house, pausing to look back as he entered the carriage once more. As the coachman's whip cracked and the team strained forward, he didn't glance at the house.

She went inside and found the butler waiting. Jane's sobs could be clearly heard, and the butler was anxious. 'Miss Richmond?'

'It's all right, I'll go to her now. Would you have Ellen bring some camomile tea?'

'Yes, madam.'

'I take it my father hasn't returned yet?'

'No, madam.'

'When he does, I rather think he'll wish to see me immediately.'

'Very well, madam.' Looking rather curiously at her, the butler bowed and hurried away toward the kitchens.

Christina discarded her jockey hat, reticule, and gloves and went quickly up to Jane's room.

Jane had flung herself on her bed, her face buried in the coverlet, and she was weeping inconsolably.

Christina hurried to her, sitting on the bed and putting a gentle hand on her shaking shoulder. 'Please don't cry any more, Jane.'

'I w-wish I w-was dead!'

'It's going to be all right. Robert doesn't want to cast you off.'

Jane's breath caught, and she sat up, staring incredulously at her. 'He doesn't?'

'No.'

'Oh, Christina!' Jane flung her arms behind her sister's neck, beginning to sob again.

Christina embraced her, stroking the nape of her neck. 'It's all right, sweetheart, you've somehow emerged with the betrothal still intact.'

'I don't deserve it, do I?'

'No,' replied Christina honestly.

Jane drew back, dabbing her tearstained eyes with her handkerchief. 'I can't believe I behaved as I did. I must have been quite mad.'

'A balloonatic of the highest order,' replied Christina, smiling.

'Most probably.' Jane twisted the handkerchief in her lap. 'I wish it hadn't all gone wrong.'

'With the balloon? It couldn't have been foreseen.'

'I didn't mean the balloon,' said Jane in an odd tone.

'Then what? Oh, you may have damaged your reputation somewhat, but if Robert still intends to marry you, it will be a passing wonder.'

'I didn't mean my reputation, either.'

Christina looked curiously at her. 'I don't understand. Is something else wrong, Jane?'

Jane lowered her glance, her lips parting as if she were about to confide something, but at that moment there was a tap at the door. It was Ellen with the camomile tea. The maid came in and put the tray on the little inlaid table next to the bed, then looked anxiously at her mistress.

'Is there anything you wish me to do, Miss Jane?'

'No, thank you, Ellen.'

The maid bobbed a curtsy and quietly withdrew.

Christina poured the tea and looked at Jane again. 'What were you about to tell me?'

'Nothing,' replied Jane quickly.

'Jane ...'

'Truly, it was nothing. I'm being silly.' Jane managed a smile. 'I think the excitement of the betrothal has made me overwrought.'

'If you're sure ...'

'Quite sure. I'm very sorry about today, Christina. You tried so hard to make me conduct myself properly, but I still threw caution to the winds, and I did it quite willfully.'

'I could have wrung your mulish neck,' answered Christina with feeling.

'I don't blame you. Oh, how am I going to face the world again? I won't dare to step out of the door.'

'You'll dare, because you'll have Robert at your side. He suggests we all go to the theater together tomorrow night, to still the gossip.'

'We?'

'Not precious William, if that's what you're thinking, just you, and Father and I.'

'Oh.'

'I tell you this, Jane: if William Grenfell's dashing nose is bloodied tonight by your future husband, it will be no less than he deserves.'

Jane's eyes widened with dismay. 'Oh, you don't think Robert would do that, do you?'

'I really don't know,' replied Christina, remembering the strange note in Robert's voice when he'd suggested William should call on him that night.

Jane sipped her tea. 'I hope you're wrong, for it wasn't William's fault.'

'No?'

'Of course not, he didn't *know* the pulley would break.'

'No, but he went out of his way to invite you to look at the balloon, and he pressed you to examine the car, even though he knew full well he shouldn't. More than that, he openly put his arms around you. He's behaved very reprehensibly in all this, and so have you, if the truth must be said.'

Jane lowered her cup, her cheeks very pink as she remembered William's whispered confession of love when the balloon had crashed.

Christina got up from the bed, moving to the window to look down toward Laura Place. There was something of a stir in the street. Mr Pitt's chair was returning, and his supporters were in their usual noisy attendance. As the former prime minister alighted, acknowledging the cheers, Christina's glance moved past him to a second chair; her father had returned as well. She watched as the second chair was set down at the curb. Her father alighted, his face very grim indeed, and without so much as a glance at his hero, he stomped into the house.

Christina's heart sank, for there was no doubt that he'd been regaled with the full story of his younger daughter's scandalous exploits.

15

IT WAS VERY still and cold that night, and a mist rose from the river to envelop the surrounding streets of Bath. The mist was only low, not reaching the loftier heights of Royal Crescent, where at nearly ten o'clock William took his leave of Robert.

William had spent a very tense evening in the usually comfortable company of his old friend, waiting all the time for the matter of Jane's presence in the balloon to be introduced into the conversation. Several times he'd attempted to mention it, but on each occasion Robert had skillfully changed the subject. For William the evening had been a terrible suspense, because he was only too aware of his own guilt where Jane was concerned. It wasn't until the moment of departure that Robert at last brought up the matter.

They'd just emerged into the darkness, where a chair was waiting to take William to his lodgings in Queen Square. Robert glanced up at the roof of the major general's house. 'I noticed when I returned from Sheldon House that you'd successfully repossessed your property.'

'Er, yes. Although not without difficulty.'

'I trust the balloon can be swiftly repaired?'

'Not swiftly enough for there to be any further ascents from Sydney Gardens.'

'That is news which I'm sure will be greeted with universal disappointment,' replied Robert, smiling a little as he toyed with the lace at his cuff.

William looked uneasily at him. 'Robert, about today ...'

'What about it?'

'I feel I have to explain Miss Richmond's presence in the balloon.'

'I understand it was an unfortunate accident.'

'Yes, but ...'

Robert smiled again. 'If it was an accident, William, there can't be anything to explain. The Misses Richmond happened to be in Sydney Gardens, where you encountered them. The younger Miss Richmond expressed an interest in the balloon, and while she was examining it with you, the balloon broke loose and there was nothing you could do until the roof on Royal Crescent brought the flight to a halt. Isn't that how it happened?'

'Yes. But ...'

'But what?'

Oh, how William wished the other would stop being so eminently reasonable, for it wasn't making his position any easier.

Robert studied him. 'William, is there something you wish to tell me?' he asked softly.

William looked reluctantly at him. 'I think perhaps there's a confession I should make.'

'No, William, you needn't bare your soul, for I don't think I'm under any illusion. I've known you for a long time, long enough to read you fairly accurately, and your manner today made your interest in my future bride very clear indeed. Tell me, my friend, is the interest returned?'

William stared at him. 'I ...'

'Come now, it's a perfectly sensible question. You are quite obviously taken with her, and all I wish to know is if she views you in the same way.' Robert's gray eyes were calm and clear, and there was still no hint of any simmering anger.

William suddenly wished he could read Robert, Lord St Clement, as well as that gentleman could evidently read *him*. He shifted his position. 'No, Robert, the fault is entirely mine. I've been guilty of allowing my feelings toward her to get the better of both my honor and my loyalty to you. I can only ask you to forgive me.'

'Forgiveness can hardly be granted if the sin is likely to be repeated,' replied Robert, still studying him closely.

'You have my word. In future I will keep well away from the Richmond family.' William lowered his eyes for a moment. 'I envy you, Robert, I envy you with all my heart, for I believe her to be the most wonderful, enchanting, delightful—'

'William, to say that you are smitten would apparently be to put it far too mildly.'

William flushed. 'I've given you my word, and you may be sure that I will keep it, because I intend to leave Bath within a day or so. Robert, I deeply regret having permitted this situation to arise, and if I've damaged my friendship with you on account of it, I'll never forgive myself.'

'Our friendship hasn't been damaged, William, for as I said, I know you very well. You've always been a man of honor, and I know that you wouldn't have welcomed the attraction you undoubtedly feel toward the woman who is to be my wife. I trust you will respect *my* honor now by forgetting that I felt the need to question you concerning *her* feelings for you.'

'That is already forgotten, Robert.'

'Thank you.'

Robert extended his hand. 'I've no doubt we'll meet again soon.'

'Good-bye, Robert.'

'William.'

Robert stood back as his friend entered the chair, which was speedily conveyed away in the direction of Brook Street; then he reentered the house, going up to the drawing room to pour himself a large glass of cognac. Swirling the amber liquid in the large-bowled glass, he moved to the window, opening one of the shutters and gazing down over the dark, open hillside toward the misty lights of Bath in the valley below.

Behind him the sumptuous blue-and-gold room glowed richly in the candlelight. There was Chinese silk on the walls, velvet chairs and sofas, and a costly Axminster carpet on the floor. Gilded picture frames caught the low light, and mirrors reflected the crystal drops of the unlit chandeliers. There was a portrait above the marble mantelpiece of an extremely lovely young woman dressed in the fashions of a quarter of a century before. She had a mass of golden curls, and wore a wide-brimmed hat that was tied beneath her chin with immense green ribbons. Her green eyes were matched not only by these ribbons but also by the shining satin of her tight-waisted gown, and there was a basket brimming with flowers on the table next to her. She was smiling out of the canvas, an entrancing smile that the artist had captured to perfection. It was a portrait of Lady Chevenley, the widowed aunt whose house it was, and who was at present staying at Bellstones.

Robert was oblivious of the room. He continued to gaze out of the window, the cognac swirling in his hand. The glass-domed clock on the mantelpiece ticked slowly, and the fire shifted in the hearth, sending a stream of sparks up into the chimney toward the star-studded sky.

Suddenly Robert came to a decision. Draining his glass, he replaced it by the decanter and then went to sit at a fine writing desk near the door. He took a sheet of cream vellum, dipped a quill in the silver-gilt inkwell, and began to write to Jane.

Several minutes later a running footman set out for Johnstone Street.

Several hours after the letter had been delivered, number 14A was in darkness, except for a solitary light in Jane's bedroom. Everyone else was asleep, but Jane wasn't only awake, she was fully dressed. The candle on her dressing table swayed and smoked as she paced restlessly to and fro, the train of her long-sleeved apricot wool gown dragging on the carpet. Her red hair was brushed loose about her shoulders, and she fidgeted with the white cashmere shawl over her arms, tying and untying the long fringe.

Robert's letter lay on the dressing table by the candlestick, and she paused to pick it up, reading it again, but she put it down immediately when she heard her maid quietly approaching the door.

Ellen came in. 'He's here, miss.'

'In the coach house?'

'Yes, miss.'

'Very well.' Jane glanced at her reflection in the glass, then hurried softly from the room, slipping down silently through the dark house.

Yet another hour passed, and Christina had been sleeping restlessly for some time. At last she awoke. By the light of the night candle she could see the clock on the mantelpiece. It was half-past one. She lay there for a moment, wishing she could turn over and go back to sleep, but knowing that it wouldn't be that easy.

Thoughts milled around in her head, thoughts of Robert, of her love for him, of Jane, of William, and of the disastrous free flight, details of which must have rung through every drawing room in Bath that night. She wished she'd never been persuaded to leave Stroud, that haven of dull calm, where few ripples disturbed her life. Now her world had been rocked by ripples, and would never be the same again.

She stared across the shadowy room toward the fire glowing faintly in the hearth. Sleep had deserted her completely now, and dawn was still hours away. She had to try to sleep, for at least then she could escape from her unhappiness. Maybe a warm drink would help. Flinging back the bedclothes, she got up to put on her wrap; then she lit a fresh candle and shielded the new flame with her hand as she slipped from the room.

On the landing something made her glance toward her sister's door. She noticed straightaway that it was ajar, a fact that surprised her, for Jane always closed her door at night. Puzzled, Christina approached the door, pushing it open still further and peeping inside. Jane's bed was empty, and the coverlet was so neatly turned back that it was obvious that no one had slept in it that night.

Christina went into the room, holding the candle up to look around. 'Jane?' There was only silence. Puzzlement was replaced by alarm, and for a moment she contemplated arousing her father, but then she thought better of it; after all, she herself was about to go down to make a warm drink, and it could be that Jane was doing the selfsame thing.

The candle fluttered as she retraced her steps to the top of the stairs, and her shadow leapt against the wall as she went quickly and quietly down. At the bottom she was about to go to the door leading down to the kitchens when she heard a sound in the dining room. She froze, for it was the unmistakable squeak of someone closing the French windows into the garden. Then she heard a rustling sound as someone hurried toward the door into the hall. Extinguishing the candle, Christina hastened to the drawing room, pressing back out of sight as a shadowy figure emerged from the dining room and came toward the foot of the stairs.

Christina peeped carefully out, and recognized Jane immediately. 'Jane?' she whispered, stepping into view.

Jane gave a startled gasp, whirling guiltily around. Seeing it was only her sister, she exhaled with relief. 'Christina! You gave me a fright!'

'Where on earth have you been?'

'I, er, went out into the garden for a short while, because I had a headache and thought the cold night air might make it go away.'

'And did it?'

'Partly.'

Christina looked at her in the darkness. 'How long were you out there?'

'Only a few minutes. Why?'

'Your bed hasn't been slept in, and you're fully dressed.'

For a moment Jane didn't reply; then she gave a slight laugh. 'How very suspicious you seem to be these days, Christina. Have you been snooping in my room?'

'Not exactly. I was coming down to make myself a warm drink, and I noticed your door was ajar.'

'I fell asleep in the chair by the fire, and my neck must have been at an awful angle, because I woke up with the headache.' Jane pressed her fingertips to her temples, smiling ruefully. 'I still have it, but maybe your warm drink might do the trick.'

Christina didn't know what to think. Jane sounded so believable, and yet there was something that didn't seem quite right. What that something was, Christina couldn't have said, but it was there, lurking on the edge of recognition. She managed a smile. 'A warm drink it is, then. Will you come to the kitchens with me?'

'Of course.'

They went through the door to the basement, going down the short flight of stone steps into the still-warm kitchen, where the smell of the evening's roast beef hung in the air.

Jane sat by the scrubbed wooden table while Christina poured some milk from the jug into a copper pan on the fire in the immense hearth. More copper pans shone on the whitewashed walls, and the low light illuminated a dresser where shelf after shelf of fine crockery and porcelain had been set out with loving care. A sugar loaf and a large ham wrapped in muslin were suspended from the ceiling, together with bunches of sweet-smelling herbs and a long bunch of onions. A door stood open into a dark pantry with marble shelves, and another door led to the washroom and other laundry facilities.

Christina poked the fire until flames leapt into life, their brightness flickering over the room. When the milk was warmed, she poured it into two blue-and-white cups, giving one to Jane and then sitting down at the table as well.

Jane sipped the milk and smiled at her. 'It's been a horridly long day, hasn't it?'

'Thanks to you and Mr Grenfell,' Christina replied dryly.

'I'm really very sorry, Christina. Do you think Father has forgiven me now? I went out of my way to be good at dinner. I tried my very hardest.'

'I'm sure you succeeded, for he was his old smiling self by the time the caramel cream was placed on the table.'

'I nearly died when he told me he'd actually been talking to Mr Pitt when word of my escapade rang through the Pump Room like a wretched bell.' Jane lowered her eyes regretfully.

'I trust you'll have the grace to stay well away from Mr Grenfell from now on. Surely you've learned a little wisdom by now?'

Jane nodded. 'It's academic now, anyway. He's leaving Bath tomorrow or the day after.'

'Is he? How do you know that?'

'He told me.'

'You haven't mentioned it before.'

Jane shrugged a little. 'It didn't occur to me to mention it.'

'Let's hope *everything* about that wretched man fades as completely from your mind,' replied Christina caustically, noticing how her sister was avoiding her eyes.

'You aren't going to lecture me again, are you?'

'Do I need to?'

'No, not anymore. I know I've made promises in the past, but I really mean it this time. I've decided exactly what I want, and I intend to have it.'

Christina studied her in the firelight. 'You seem to have found new heart from somewhere.'

'I have.'

'So, you're ready to look the *monde* in the eye at the theater tomorrow?'

'Yes, except that I'll be looking the *monde* in the eye before then. Robert is taking me for a drive in the morning. He invited me in the letter he sent earlier.' Jane finished her milk and got up. 'And if I'm to look my best for that drive, I'd better hie myself to my bed.'

'I'll be up in a minute or so. I haven't finished my drink yet.'

'All right. Good night.' Jane kissed her on the cheek and then hurried out, the train of her apricot wool dress swishing behind her.

Apricot wool. Alone in the kitchen, Christina suddenly realized what had been nagging away at the back of her mind since encountering Jane at the foot of the stairs. Her sister had been ready with an explanation for still being dressed, and for not having slept in her bed. Anyone could fall asleep in a chair, that was reasonable enough, but a lady whose maid had attended her at bedtime, as Ellen had attended Jane, would have been in her nightgown and wrap, not in an apricot wool day dress. Even if Ellen had gone to her mistress's room and found her already asleep in the chair, the apricot wool remained odd. Jane had worn beige taffeta at dinner, and it had been nearly midnight when she'd retired and Ellen had gone to attend her. If she hadn't changed into her nightclothes then, why hadn't she still been in her evening gown when she went out to the garden? Why go to the trouble of putting on the apricot wool, which inevitably meant changing *again* before going to bed?

Christina ran her fingertips thoughtfully around the rim of her cup. The only reason for changing into the apricot wool that sprang to mind was that Jane had intended all along to go out, and wool was infinitely warmer than taffeta, and infinitely more proper than night-clothes. Yes, Jane had purposely changed to go out, and her skeptical, sorely tried sister doubted very much if her purpose had had anything to do with a headache.

With a sigh, Christina finished the milk. She suddenly found herself thinking of the occasion of her return from the circulating library with Robert. She'd been so convinced she'd seen Jane enter the house in front of her, and yet Jane had denied it. Oh, there'd been an explanation for Ellen being seen putting away the pelisse, but a much more credible explanation was that the maid had moments before relieved her mistress of the pelisse, because said mistress had indeed been out somewhere.

Jane was up to something. But what? Knowing her, that something could be just about anything. And there was no point in confrontation, for glib explanations were evidently second nature to Jane Richmond these days.

16

ROBERT ARRIVED THE following morning as promised in his letter and Jane accompanied him for a drive lasting several hours. Their route deliberately took in a number of fashionable places, so that Jane soon found herself facing Bath's highly intrigued society. She braved it all, finding it less of an ordeal than she'd expected because Robert was there with her, making his support and regard very clear to everyone.

They returned to take tea with Christina and Mr Richmond, and a very agreeable hour was passed in conversation before Robert left. That hour was very hard for Christina, but when it was over she was satisfied that she'd acquitted herself more than adequately. She'd kept a very tight grip on her inner feelings, and had protected herself as much as possible by addressing herself mostly to her father and sister, thus keeping Robert at a distance she found able to cope with.

She did the same that night, when they all sallied forth to the theater. There had been a great deal of whispering as they'd entered their box, and during the intermission many quizzing glasses had been turned upon Jane, but Robert had remained close to her throughout, intimating by his every action and smile that nothing had changed.

Over the next week it was the same, with Christina doing her best to discreetly shun Robert without his realizing it. William Grenfell and his balloon vanished from Sydney Gardens, and from Bath itself, but Jane didn't seem to even remark the fact. The future Lady St Clement positively dazzled everyone with her happiness. She was captivating, even managing to achieve the perfect blend of shyness and humor when she bravely related the tale of the balloon flight to a daunting gathering of dowagers at the Assembly Rooms tearoom. She was so charmingly contrite that she engaged their sympathy, and after that her sins were entirely forgotten; over the years Jane had had a great deal of practice when it came to smoothing over the results of her impetuosity, and with William Grenfell and his balloon removed from the scene, it seemed she was herself again.

Christina watched Jane closely throughout that rather wet week, when the weather changed dramatically, and her fears were gradually allayed. Whatever Jane had been up to, she didn't seem to be up to it any longer, but with William gone, and with the visit to Bellstones looming ever closer, the St Clement match seemed happily secure at last. Christina wasn't looking forward to Bellstones, but knew she couldn't wriggle out of it without causing a great deal of comment, to say nothing of the hurt such an action would cause both Jane and her father. As far as the meantime was concerned, however, she did her utmost to stay out of Robert's way. She was careful to be out when he was due to call, and she invented other engagements in order to escape early from any function at which they were both present. She did it to spare herself needless torment, and to avoid any chance of unwittingly revealing the truth, for there were times when she'd felt Robert's thoughtful gaze upon her, as if he was beginning to suspect something.

Toward the end of the week, when the rain seemed to have been falling forever, and, with four days to go before they all set off for Bellstones, a grand ball was arranged on the spur of the moment at Sheldon House, where the family was overjoyed at the unexpected return from India of one of its best-loved members. Lord and Lady Sheldon were leading lights when it came to hosting grand functions, and there wasn't a soul of consequence who didn't receive, and accept, an invitation. Invitations arrived at Johnstone Street, much to Jane's joy, but Christina determined immediately that she would feel indisposed on the night of the ball, and thus again avoid Robert's company.

She played her role with great guile, seeming to be looking forward to the ball almost as much as Jane, when all the time she had no intention at all of going. Neither Jane nor Mr Richmond suspected anything, and both were greatly concerned on the day of the ball when she complained at breakfast of feeling a little unwell. She retreated to her room at midday, drawing the curtains and lying on the bed, pretending to be asleep when Jane peeped in to see how she was. As the evening arrived, and the others began to dress for the ball, she cried off very apologetically, insisting that she really did feel under the weather and would much prefer a quiet evening to the excitement, crush, and noise of a ball. Jane and Mr Richmond were disappointed, and at eight o'clock they set off by carriage in the rain for Sheldon House, on the road to Bristol. Robert was due to join them there, having accepted a dinner engagement first.

Christina prepared to enjoy her quiet evening as best she could. Wearing her dark-blue dimity gown, her hair brushed comfortably loose, she adjourned to the drawing room with *Gil Blas*, determined to shrug off all her troubles by immersing herself in fictional adventures. The rain was lashing against the window as she sat by the fire and opened the page at her bookmark, but she couldn't concentrate. Her attention wandered, and, as always now, she found herself thinking of Robert.

There was a knock at the front door, but she didn't hear it; she knew nothing until the butler came in rather apologetically.

'Begging your pardon, Miss Richmond, I know you're indisposed, but Lord St Clement has called.'

She stared at him. 'Lord St Clement?'

'Yes, madam.'

But Robert was going on to Sheldon House after his dinner engagement, and as far as he was concerned, all three members of the Richmond family were attending the ball. Why on earth had he called? She closed the book. 'Please show him in.'

'Yes, madam.'

The butler withdrew into the hall again, and she rose nervously from her chair, putting the book on a table.

Robert came in almost immediately, pausing in the doorway to smile at her. 'Good evening, Christina.'

'Good evening, Robert.' How handsome he was, especially in evening clothes.

He came toward her, taking her hand and raising it to his lips. 'I trust you don't mind this intrusion?'

'I confess I'm a little surprised, for by rights there shouldn't be anyone at home tonight, we should all have gone to the ball.'

'I guessed you were here. By chance I saw your father's carriage on its way to Sheldon House, and I noticed that only Jane appeared to be with him.'

'You wished to speak to me?'

'Yes, if it isn't inconvenient.'

'Of course not.'

His gray eyes searched her face. 'The butler said that you were indisposed.'

'I was, but I've recovered.'

'I'm glad to hear it. May we sit down?'

'Oh, forgive me,' she said quickly, turning to gesture to a sofa. 'Shall I have some tea or coffee served? Or would you prefer cognac?'

'Cognac would be eminently satisfactory.'

He sat on the sofa, lounging back to watch her as she went to the little table to pick up the decanter. 'Christina, have I offended you in some way?' he asked for a moment.

'Offended me? What a strange question. Of course you haven't,' she replied, endeavoring with all her might to stop her hand from trembling so that the decanter rattled against the glass.

'Not so very strange, for you *have* been avoiding my company.'

She colored, taking the glass to him. 'You're mistaken, for I'm not avoiding you.'

'No?'

'No.'

He held her eyes. 'I wish I felt reassured, but I'm afraid I don't. I look at you now and see that you are, to say the least, ill-at-ease with me. I'm sad that this is so, for when we first met I felt we had a certain warm rapport, but now there's definitely a wall between us, and you, Christina, are the one who's built it. You say I haven't offended you, which prompts me to conclude that you simply don't like me after all.'

'Oh, no, please don't think that! I like you very much indeed.' Too much, by far too much, that's the whole problem. The reply finished silently in her head.

'Then why are you avoiding me?'

Answers didn't come as easily to her as they did to Jane, and to give herself time to reply she returned to the table to pour herself a glass of sherry. She'd thought she was doing the best thing by staying away from him, but she'd only succeeded in giving him the wrong impression.

Pouring her glass, she turned with a smile. 'This is all quite foolish,' she said, 'for there's absolutely nothing wrong, and if I've somehow conveyed the feeling that there is, then I cannot imagine how. Please believe me, Robert, I haven't been avoiding you, nor do I dislike you. Can we set this misunderstanding aside and begin again?'

He smiled, swirling his glass. 'Setting misunderstandings aside appears to be the hallmark of our relationship, Christina, for I seem to recall once thinking that you were to be my bride.'

She gave a light laugh. 'What a catalog of disasters *that* marriage would undoubtedly have been.'

'Do you think so? Now I'm of a mind to be insulted.'

She was determined to steer the conversation on to a new tack, and sitting down opposite him, she asked him about Bellstones. 'I've been longing to ask you more about Bellstones, Robert. From what you said at dinner the other evening, it seems very beautiful.'

For a moment she thought he'd begun to see through her, for he paused in a way that unsettled her more than ever, but then he nodded. 'It *is* very beautiful, especially at this time of the year, when the park and surrounding moor are in full autumn color.' A gust of wind drove the rain against the window again, and he glanced toward the lowered ruched curtains. 'The Darch will soon be in full spate if they've had all this rain down there as well.'

'The Darch?'

'The river in the valley directly below Bellstones. I think I told you it rises in a lake on the high moor. It's soon in flood after a lengthy spell of rain.' There was a note of longing in his voice as he spoke of his home, a yearning to be there, not in the stifling atmosphere of Bath.

'You love Bellstones very much, don't you?' she said.

'It's the most perfect place on earth, and I long to kick my heels of

London, Bath, Brighton, Cheltenham, and every other place of fashion.'

She was surprised. 'But I thought you were very much a London soul.'

'I was, but I've more than had my fill. I think I decided once and for all when those two tiresome women fought over me on the steps of St George's. It was the last straw.' He gave a quick, apologetic smile. 'Please forgive me for mentioning such a vulgar incident.'

She thought of Jane, who was looking forward so much to the excitement and whirl of London.

He watched her. 'What are you thinking about?'

'Jane,' she replied honestly. 'Does she know you feel this way about London?'

'Yes. I didn't think it right to mislead her.'

Christina was taken aback. Jane knew and yet hadn't mentioned it? Such reticence was entirely out of character in one whose great joy was a bulging social calendar. Realizing her silence was making him curious, she sipped her sherry and then spoke of Bellstones again. 'Can you solve a mystery for me? Why is it called Bellstones?'

He smiled. 'There's a ruined belltower on the moor. It was put there originally by an ancestor of William Grenfell's, a gentleman who greatly feared a Spanish invasion, and who didn't have much faith in a beacon being properly visible on a bright sunny day. He had the tower built and an immense bell installed, and it's said that this bell could be heard all the way to Dartmoor. Anyway, there was a dreadful storm one winter, and the tower collapsed. An ancestor of mine acquired some of the stones and used them in the building of a stableblock for his thoroughbreds. He was soon nicknamed "Old Bellstones", and with the passage of years the house became known as Bellstones, which is, you'll grant, more entertaining than plain Darch House, which was its original name.'

'Much more entertaining.'

'Exmoor abounds in interesting stories.'

'I look forward to hearing them.'

'And I look forward to telling you. You're a very rewarding audience, Christina.'

'Perhaps it's the talent of the raconteur, sir.'

'Perhaps.' He smiled at her.

His smiles had the power to storm her defenses, and she had to look quickly away. A fluttering pulse raced through her, making her shiver.

He sat forward immediately. 'Are you cold?'

'No,' she replied quickly. 'It's nothing. Truly.'

'But you haven't been well today, and I'm being boorish enough to impose my company on you.' He finished his cognac and put the glass down before getting to his feet. 'It's time I took myself to the ball anyway. Jane will no doubt be wondering what's happened to me.'

She got up as well. 'I do hope that I've allayed your fears now?'

'You have.' He took both her hands, looking into her eyes. 'I hated the feeling that I'd somehow managed to alienate you.'

'Be assured that I *do* like you, and I *do* approve of you as my brother-in-law.'

'Then I'm content,' he murmured, hesitating before bending forward to kiss her on the cheek. 'Good night, Christina.'

'Good night, Robert. I trust you enjoy the ball.'

'It would have been much more agreeable if you'd been there.'

'I'm sure Jane will more than make up for my absence,' she replied.

He seemed to become suddenly aware that he still held her hands, and quickly released them before turning to go out. She heard him speak to the butler; then the front door was opened. A draft breathed through the house, moving the curtains; then the door was closed. His carriage drew away a moment later, and then there was silence, except for the patter of the rain on the glass.

Christina raised the hand to her lips, kissing the skin he'd kissed a moment before. Hot tears stung her eyes, and a sob caught in her throat. How long would she have to endure this pain before it became bearable?

17

THERE WAS RAIN for the next four days as well, but on the morning of the departure for Bellstones the sun was shining again. At seven, two carriages set off from Johnstone Street, Christina, Jane, and Mr Richmond traveling with Robert in his coach, the valets and maids following in the Richmond vehicle.

All the rain had swollen the Avon so that it pounded over the weir as the carriages crossed Pulteney Bridge on their way southwest out of Bath toward the market town of Midsomer Norton. It was seventy miles to Bellstones, too far to accomplish in one day on the poor roads of the west country, and it was intended that they would stay overnight at the Red Lion Inn in Bridgwater, which was about halfway. They halted at Wells for luncheon, and then drove on through the long afternoon.

During that day Christina had to call upon all her acting skills, especially when they neared Bridgwater and both her father and Jane fell asleep. Robert sat in the seat opposite, and it was quite impossible to avoid conversation. He was so easy to talk to, and so amusing that at times she knew she was perilously close to allowing her protective mask to slip. She was relieved when they reached Bridgwater, and alighted gladly when they entered the yard of the busy Red Lion Inn. She didn't linger over the fine pheasant dinner, but retired quickly to the shelter of her room, where she hid in the capacious bed, fighting back the hot tears that were always so close now.

The next day they continued on their way to Bellstones, driving west along the coast on the road that led to the fishing port of Minehead. The Bristol Channel was deep blue beneath the clear

October sky, and far out on the water there were several frigates, their sails straining before the freshening breeze. They halted for luncheon at a wayside inn near the village of Williton, taking their time over the meal because the afternoon would be arduous for both travelers and horses as they entered the steeply rolling terrain of Exmoor.

They set off on the final stage, driving further westward along the coast for a mile or so before turning suddenly southwest. Exmoor was soon silhouetted against the skyline ahead, and the road deteriorated, rapidly becoming little more than a track. The hills were steep, plunging down into narrow tree-choked valleys, and the horses were soon tired. At last they descended into a long valley, where the track followed the banks of a swollen river. It was the Darch, the same river that flowed past Bellstones.

The moor rose all around, clearly visible beyond the autumn foliage overhanging the way.

In the shelter of the trees there were secretive herds of red deer, glimpsed only now and then as the two carriages proceeded slowly beside the river.

The open hillsides were still clad in the summer glory of late heather and gorse, clear-cut against the wide heaven, and wild ponies and flocks of sheep could be seen roaming free. Far above, wheeling gracefully in the stream of air sweeping over the high moor, there were merlins and buzzards, birds of prey that flourished in this wild but beautiful part of England.

As Robert had predicted, the Darch was in full spate after all the rain, its waters foaming and splashing over rocks, filling the valley with a thunderous roar. It was a salmon river, one of the finest in the west country, and from time to time a flash of silver gave evidence that the fish were beginning to swim in from the sea to spawn.

The afternoon wore on toward evening, and the light began to change. The track may have been narrow and poor, but it was well-used, because there were straggling villages along the valley. Occasionally they encountered strings of packhorses, the most usual form of transport in Exmoor, but there were some farm carts laden with produce, *en route* for the following day's market at Darchford, the largest of the villages.

A stone bridge spanned the river at Darchford, and there was a tang of woodsmoke from the chimneys of the thatched cottages. It seemed that all the folk of Exmoor had congregated ready for the market, which took place on the wide village green, and as the carriages drove over the bridge, the sound of fiddle music carried clearly on the breeze that rustled through the autumn leaves.

Jane had been asleep for some time. Traveling in a carriage frequently affected her in this way, and she didn't stir as they drove through Darchford, nor did she look up when Robert pointed out another track and told them that one mile away along it was Grenfell Hall, William's family home. Christina glanced unhappily along the other track as it wound away along the bottom of a hill, soon vanishing among the trees. William Grenfell's residence was a little too close for comfort.

Shadows were lengthening now as the sun began to set. The Darch still frothed noisily beside the track, its waters sometimes threatening to spill over the bank, and soon there was a new sound, a deep thundering that told of rapids. Leaning closer to the glass, Christina gazed ahead, and sure enough, she saw the pounding white water as the river plunged down a drop of about fifteen feet. The track climbed beside the rapids, and as the carriage breasted the slope, Christina saw how wide the river was beyond, wide enough to encompass a small islet green with shrubs and low trees. Upstream of this islet, where the river narrowed again, a five-arched stone bridge spanned the water, carrying the track to the lodge and armorial gates of Bellstones, which was hidden beyond a thick screen of tall trees.

Followed by the green Richmond coach, Robert's carriage crossed the bridge, the coachmen easing their tired teams with great care, for although the horses were weary, they were still easily unnerved, as was swiftly evidenced when a broken branch, carried downstream on the water, struck the bridge. The sound rang loudly above the thunder of the river, and the Richmond team shied, tossing their heads and fighting the bit until the coachman managed to impose his will on them once more.

The noise of the branch against the bridge woke Jane with a start, and she sat up sharply, obviously disoriented for a moment. Robert smiled, putting his hand reassuringly over hers. The lodgekeeper had seen the carriages approaching, and flung open the gates in readiness, doffing his hat respectfully as they passed.

As they entered Bellstones, the trees peeled back and the drive swept up through a gracious park toward the early-Tudor splendor of the great house. Set between the valley and the high moor beyond, it was a breathtaking sight, a rambling three-story mansion with gables, turrets, battlements, and towers. Mullioned windows caught the dying blaze of the setting sun, and a gilded weathercock on the stableblock that had been built of stones from the warning bell tower high on the moor, swung gently to and fro as the breeze blustered playfully around it.

The main entrance of the house was beneath an arched stone porch topped by carved stone lions, which heraldic beast Christina was to learn was the Temple family emblem. The closer the carriages drew, the more clearly she could make out details on the house. There were more stone lions on the roof, and gargoyles with fearsome faces jutting by the eaves. The chimneys were spiral, and there were many of them, for the Tudors didn't like to be cold, especially in this bleak area of winter winds, rain, and snow.

There was a shallow sheltered combe leading down from the south of the house, extending to the trees in the valley below. Terraced gardens were laid out down the combe, each one different, and each one immaculately tended.

The carriages bowled the final yards to the entrance porch, and the studded double doors opened as a butler emerged to welcome them. He was a tall, well-built man in his late forties, with the ruddy complexion of one who spent many hours in the open air. His gray-streaked hair was worn long, and tied back with a dark-blue ribbon that went with the blue of his plain, serviceable coat. He looked as much a steward as a butler, and Christina was to discover that he did indeed perform both duties. His name was Campion, and he was held in justifiably high esteem by his master.

The carriage swayed to a standstill, and Robert alighted. 'Is all well, Campion?'

'It is, my lord.'

'My aunt included?'

'Her ladyship is very well indeed, my lord. She isn't at home at the moment, but is paying a call upon Mr and Mrs Grenfell. I believe Mrs Grenfell is a little unwell, and her ladyship took some peaches from the greenhouse.'

'Will she be returning for dinner?'

'Yes, my lord. She was very clear upon the point.' Campion's glance moved toward the carriages. 'I trust you had an agreeable journey, my lord?'

'Excellent, thank you.' Robert turned quickly, assisting Mr Richmond down, for long journeys and gout did not blend easily together.

''Pon my soul, I'm not getting any younger, that's plain enough to feel,' grumbled Mr Richmond, rubbing his stiff back and placing his foot down very gingerly.

'I'm sure a rest will soon restore you, sir,' said Robert, turning then to assist Christina and Jane.

Christina glanced around at everything. She took in first the magnificence of the old house, and then the glory of the Exmoor scenery, caught in the gold and crimson of the sunset. From this elevated position on the hillside there was so much to see, from the curls of smoke rising from the cottages of Darchford, to the wild openness of the high moors rolling away all around. Looking down through the park toward the lodge, she could see the gates quite clearly, and beyond them the bridge over the Darch. The sunset burnished the autumn foliage so that the valley was bright with warm colors, from the palest of rose to the deepest of copper. There was something magical about it all, an enchantment that wove around her in those brief moments; she understood why this place meant so very much to Robert, and why the diversions of London no longer held any charm.

Robert was presenting Campion to Jane, and Mr Richmond came to stand next to Christina, savoring the view with her. Suddenly he stiffened, staring at something on the far horizon.

'Good God above,' he breathed in disbelief.

'What is it, Father?'

'Over there. D'you see?' He pointed.

She followed his finger, and her heart sank with dismay as she saw something she recognized only too well, the crimson-and-blue orb of William Grenfell's balloon. It floated above the moor, small but bright in the rays of the sun.

Mr Richmond shook with anger. 'The man's impudence knows no bounds! He obviously intends to pursue Jane here as well!'

'Hush, Father,' replied Christina in an undertone, glancing uneasily toward Jane and Robert as they spoke to the butler.

'The fellow should be clapped in irons!'

'Father, he has every right to be here, he *lives* here!'

Robert offered Jane his arm to proceed into the house, and as they vanished into the shadows of the porch, Christina looked urgently at her father.

'There's nothing we can do about Mr Grenfell, Father. It would be better to appear uninterested in him than to make our displeasure known.'

He nodded, drawing her hand through his arm and patting her fingers. 'You're right, my dear, as you usually are, but I won't be able to relax until Jane is safely betrothed to Robert.'

'She will be, and then Mr Grenfell will cease to matter, if, indeed, he matters anyway. After all, she hardly noticed he'd left Bath.'

'The fellow's besotted with her – of *course* he matters. Love is a very powerful emotion, as even I know.'

'*Even* you?' She smiled. 'I'll vow you were a real breaker of hearts when you were younger.'

'On the contrary, my dear, for mine was the heart that was broken.'

'Alicia Partington?' she asked, remembering his words in the drawing room at Johnstone Street.

'Ah, sweet Alicia,' he murmured, a faraway look in his eyes. 'She was the loveliest creature in all London, but she possessed a fickle and cruel heart. No doubt I was better off without her.'

'Well, you'll never know that for sure, will you?'

'No. Anyway, it's time for us to go inside.'

He turned to escort her to the porch, and Christina glanced back at the balloon, still clearly visible just above the horizon, close to where Grenfell Hall must lie. William's presence was going to cause trouble of one sort or another, her every instinct told her as much, for to be sure, things had begun to go wrong from the moment that same balloon had been espied above the rooftops of Bath.

18

THE ENTRANCE HALL was a lofty place, its dark-paneled walls hung with fine Flemish tapestries. A grand staircase with carved wooden lion newel posts rose at the far end of the stone-flagged floor, dividing at a half-landing to reach the great open gallery that surrounded the entire hall. There was a huge stone fireplace where long flames crackled around fresh logs, and in the recesses on either side of the chimney breast stood suits of armor of considerable age. A number of doors opened off the hall and gallery, all of them heavily carved and studded, and each one was flanked by rich green velvet curtains. The setting sun shone through high stained-glass windows, casting spangled lights over the gallery and staircase, and there was a timelessness about it all that captured Christina's imagination. It was possible to conjure Queen Elizabeth into life again, and see her descending to the hall in her jewel-adorned gown, perhaps pausing at the bottom with a pale hand on one of the lion newel posts.

A line of servants was waiting to one side of the main entrance, and Robert was introducing them all to Jane. When he then proceeded to introduce Christina and Mr Richmond, it soon became apparent that Christina's presence was causing some consternation, for the housekeeper discreetly whispered something to Campion, who immediately turned apologetically to Robert.

'My lord, I fear there's been a misunderstanding.'

'Misunderstanding?'

'Yes, my lord. The housekeeper did not realize that there would be two Misses Richmond, and as a consequence, only the queen's chamber has been made ready.'

Robert looked at the housekeeper. 'Is this true, Mrs Tremayne?'

The woman bobbed a hasty curtsy. She was short and rather round, with a handsome country face, and she was very tidy and precise in dark-brown taffeta. 'Yes, my lord, I'm afraid it is. When your letter arrived informing me that guests were to be expected, I fear I misread your writing, thinking you'd made a mistake when you wrote "Mr Richmond and his daughters". I thought it must really mean "daughter", and I've made arrangements accordingly.' She looked more than a little flustered, for she knew the fault was entirely hers.

Robert smiled a little. 'Don't distress yourself, Mrs Tremayne, for I can understand the error.'

'Thank you, my lord.'

'I think perhaps Miss Christina would appreciate the garden room. Can you see that it's made ready without delay?'

'Yes, my lord.' Nodding sharply at some of the maids, the woman hurried away toward the staircase, her skirts rustling and her bunch of keys chinking. The maids scuttled after her, striving to be out of earshot before beginning to whisper together.

Robert turned to Christina. 'Your unexpected appearance on the scene has caused a little upset, I fear, and the fact that your room has yet to be prepared makes my original plan somewhat awkward. I was going to suggest we all adjourn to our various chambers to refresh ourselves after the journey, and then take a welcome dish of tea together in the great parlor.'

Christina was anxious not to be the cause of any difficulty. 'I'm sure we can still do that, for I can accompany Jane to her room.'

Jane nodded immediately. 'Oh, yes, of course.'

Robert looked at them both. 'If you're quite sure...?'

'Quite sure,' they replied together, smiling because they'd spoken in unison.

'Then you will both be shown directly to the queen's chamber, and when the garden room is ready, word will be brought to you. That is the door of the great parlor' – he pointed – 'and shall we say tea in half an hour's time? I'm sure the garden room will take only a little time, for Mrs Tremayne is always careful to keep everything aired.'

Mr Richmond nodded. 'Half an hour? Excellent. But, I say, sir, when will dinner be served? I vow it seems an age since we had luncheon.'

Robert smiled. 'Dinner is always at half-past eight.' He glanced at his gold fob watch. 'That's in an hour and a half, and since it will be the best Exmoor venison, I promise you'll find it well worth waiting for.'

'Venison, eh? Couldn't be better.' Mr Richmond beamed with approval, the tiresome matter of William Grenfell evidently forgotten for the moment.

Robert beckoned to two waiting footmen. 'Please show the ladies to the queen's chamber, and Mr Richmond to whichever room has been prepared for him.'

Mr Richmond followed his footman up the staircase, and Christina accompanied Jane behind the other footman.

The queen's chamber was at the front of the house, directly over the main entrance, with the same wonderful view that Christina had admired on alighting from the carriage. It was a very regal room, with a great four-poster bed that Queen Elizabeth herself had once slept in. Adorned with Tudor emblems and the initials 'ER', and rich with scarlet-and-gold damask, it was impressive enough to stop Jane's breath as she entered.

The setting sun was shining directly in through the west-facing windows, but the footman lit a number of candles before withdrawing.

As the door closed behind him, Christina turned to face her sister. 'Did you know William Grenfell was here in Exmoor?' she demanded without preamble.

Jane looked at her in hurt surprise. 'No, and I'm offended you should ask.'

'Your recent exploits have left me justifiably suspicious.'

'So I've begun to realize.'

'Do you blame me? You haven't exactly inspired confidence, and there have been one or two rather odd occurrences—'

'Oh, no, not the yellow pelisse *again*! I've told you all about that, Christina.' Jane unpinned her hat and tossed it crossly on to the bed.

'Yes, you've told me all about it, and you had an equally ready explanation for having gone out into the garden in the middle of the night, but I find it curious that you bothered to change into the apricot wool first.' There, she'd put her doubt into words at last.

Jane stared at her. 'So *that's* what's been on your mind these past few days, is it?'

'Yes. I suppose you're going to airily explain it away, just as you did the yellow pelisse?'

Jane drew a long breath, hesitating before speaking. 'There is an explanation, but you probably wouldn't believe me if I told you.'

'Try me.'

'Very well. I decided to undress myself that night, and so I sent Ellen away, but instead of getting on with changing, I sat in the chair for a while. I had my bottle of scent in my hand, the essence of roses Aunt Brooks sent to me, and the stopper can't have been in properly, because the scent spilled all over me while I slept. When I woke up I was simply reeking of it, and I had a dreadful headache. I knew I had to get some fresh air, and I was about to change into my night things, because my evening gown smelled so of the scent, when I realized it would be very cold outside. So I changed into the first warm dress that came to hand, the apricot wool.'

It was plausible enough, and Christina might have believed it, except for one glaring detail. 'If you'd spilt scent all over yourself, and then slept for several hours, the whole room would have smelled of roses. When I looked in, I didn't notice anything.'

'Well, it *did* smell of roses.' Jane met her eyes squarely.

Christina simply didn't believe the story, reasonable as it was, and with that disbelief came strong doubts about the forthcoming betrothal. 'Jane, are you absolutely sure that you wish to marry Robert?' she asked quietly.

Jane nodded. 'Absolutely sure.'

There wasn't time to say any more, for the housekeeper came to say that the garden room was ready, and to personally escort Christina to it along the gallery and down a passage.

It was a charming room, facing south over the combe and terraced gardens. Like the rest of the house, it had paneled walls hung with tapestries, and there was a collection of Tudor miniatures on the wall opposite the mullioned bay window. The last of the sunset cast a very faint light over everything, a light that was added to by the candles that had been lit in readiness, and by the new fire. The four-poster bed was smaller than Jane's, and hung with pale-green brocade. The same brocade had been used to cover the chairs by the fire, and the window seat that filled the bay. There was an immense wardrobe, big enough to step into, and Jenny was already unpacking her clothes.

A kettle simmered on the fire, and the maid hurried to it the moment her mistress entered. There was a fine French washstand in a corner behind a screen, and soon Christina had been relieved of her pelisse, bonnet, and gloves. All journeys, no matter how comfortable and luxurious the carriage, made one feel so stale and untidy, and it was good to rinse her face in warm water. Within a few minutes she was refreshed and seated at the dressing table in the corner, while Jenny unpinned and recombed her long hair. Her cream sprigged-muslin gown still felt comfortable, and looked well in spite of the journey, and she elected to continue wearing it until it was time to change for dinner.

Jenny put down the comb and pins. 'Which gown shall I put out for dinner, Miss Christina?'

'The lilac satin, I think, provided it isn't too crumpled.'

'I'll see it's ready, miss. Will you wear the amethysts with it?'

'No, my mother's pearls.'

'But, miss, you still haven't had the clasp repaired.'

'It was all right at the ball, and to be honest, I really don't think there's anything wrong with it. I'll have the Stroud jeweler look at it when we go home.'

'Yes, miss.'

'Now, then, I can find my own way down to the great parlor for tea, but I'm sure you must be gasping for a cup yourself, so you can take yourself down to the kitchens if you wish.'

'Oh, thank you, miss,' replied the maid gratefully. 'I'll be sure to finish putting everything away before you need to dress for dinner.'

Jenny hurried out, and after a moment Christina got up to go to the window. She looked out over the shadowy gardens, which were almost in darkness now that the sunset was little more than a dull stain of color on the western horizon. A fountain played on the third terrace down from the house, and in the valley beyond, the trees marking the Darch's way were thick and mysterious. Her gaze moved along the valley toward the village of Darchford, visible only as two or three lights in cottage windows. Suddenly she noticed two other lights as a carriage crossed the bridge and drove through the lodge gates. It must be Lady Chevenley returning from her visit to Grenfell Hall.

Christina remained at the window for several minutes after the carriage lamps had passed out of sight around the front of the house; then she turned to look at the clock on the mantelpiece. More than half an hour had passed, and the promised dish of tea would be being served in the great parlor. Dismayed to think she was going to be late, she picked up the shawl that Jenny had put out for her, and hurried from the room. She wasn't the only one to be late, because her father was only just descending the staircase ahead of her, and had reached the bottom to cross the hall by the time she began to go down as well. As she hurried across the hall behind him, she heard his startled exclamation from just inside the great parlor.

'Good God above! It can't possibly be …'

'Yes, Hal,' replied a woman's amused voice, 'I am Lady Chevenley.'

Christina halted in astonishment, listening.

Her father spoke again. 'Alicia. Alicia Partington, after all these years …' Taken as much by surprise as he, Christina moved hesitantly closer to the door. Should she go in? She was undecided, for it didn't seem right to intrude. She was almost certain her father and Lady Chevenley were alone, because surely there'd have been some reaction from Jane or Robert, had they been present.

Mr Richmond and Lady Chevenley were indeed alone, for Jane was still in her room, and, unknown to Christina, Robert was at that very moment descending the staircase behind her.

He paused at the bottom, looking curiously at her rather furtive figure by the door of the great parlor; then he came quietly over, making her jump by putting his hands suddenly on her shoulders. 'Are you much given to ear-wigging at doors, madam?' he asked softly, laughing as she stifled a gasp.

Recovering a little, and blushing at having been caught in the act, she quickly put a finger to her lips, pointing toward the door. 'I really don't think we should go in just yet,' she whispered. 'Did you know that your aunt was once my father's great love?'

He stared at her. 'No, I didn't.' He said nothing more, for Lady Chevenley was speaking again in the parlor.

'Has the cat got your tongue, Hal Richmond?'

'I ... I don't know what to say. I had no idea you were Robert's aunt.'

'I didn't think you did, and it amused me greatly to keep silent about our acquaintance. I've been waiting for this moment, just to see the look on your face, and I must say, it was worth waiting for.' She chuckled.

Mr Richmond began to recover from his initial shock. 'I don't find it at all amusing, madam,' he said rather stiffly.

'Madam? Come now, I seem to recall once being your adored Alicia.'

'That was before ...' He broke off, clearing his throat.

'Before the advent of Vincenzo Lunardi? Yes, I suppose it was,' she replied.

Christina and Robert recognized the name, for Vincenzo Lunardi had been the first man to ascend in a balloon in England.

Mr Richmond was a little cool. 'I don't wish to discuss it.'

'I seem to recall that that was your attitude at the time,' mused Lady Chevenley with a sigh. There was a pause, during which she was evidently perusing her former lover from head to toe. 'I often wondered how you'd turned out, Hal, and it pleases me to still be able to see the slender, dashing young blade I remember.'

'If you're fishing for compliments, which my past experience tells me you most probably are, I'll oblige your vanity by replying that you haven't changed a great deal either, you're still as lovely as ever.'

'Thank you, Hal. You could have said it a little more gallantly, but at least you've said it. Now, then, when was it that we last saw each other?'

'The fifteenth of September, 1784, in Chelsea,' he replied promptly.

'How gratifyingly instant and accurate you are, Hal.'

'I'm hardly likely to forget the day you first clapped eyes on that damned flying Italian.'

'Ah, dear Vincenzo, he was *so* adorable. I vow half of England gathered that day to watch, and he gave them *such* a spectacle to behold.'

'The popinjay in him made him a natural for Astley's,' Mr Richmond said scathingly.

'He wasn't a popinjay, he was utterly charming.'

'The practiced charm of the philanderer.'

'Hal, are you suggesting that I succumbed to his advances?'

'No, of course not, for you were ever the lady, but *he* wasn't a gentleman, and what he had in mind for you was very clear indeed.'

She chuckled. 'Yes, I suppose it was. I confess to having been rather flattered.'

'You made a positive meal of it,' replied Mr Richmond, still deeply piqued by those long-gone events.

'If I did, Hal, you had only yourself to blame.'

'I fail to see ...'

'That always was your trouble, you *always* failed to see. I adored you, but you were infuriatingly complacent. It didn't matter to me that you were only moderately wealthy, I loved you, and I wanted to marry you, but *you* dilly-dallied without coming to the point of asking me. I thought I'd make you jealous, and so I encouraged Vincenzo to lay siege to me, but it went hopelessly wrong that day in Chelsea, didn't it? My, what a dash you cut at first, and how splendidly you rode that brute of a Hanoverian. I confess I thought you ten times as attractive as poor Vincenzo.'

'I don't wish to be reminded of anything that happened that day.'

'No, I can quite understand that,' replied Lady Chevenley, her voice breaking suddenly on an irrepressible snort of laughter. 'Oh, dear, if you hadn't chosen that particular mount, if they hadn't fired those cannon when the balloon began its ascent, and if that pile of, er, manure hadn't happened to be just where it was ...' It was too much, and she dissolved into mirth.

Mr Richmond was far from amused. 'Apparently you still find it as entertaining now as you did then.'

'I couldn't help smiling when you were tipped into the mire,' she admitted weakly, struggling to stem the laughter.

'Smiling? You guffawed so much you practically fell out of your carriage!' he snapped.

'Guffawed? Hal Richmond, I've never been so unladylike as to guffaw in my life.'

'You don't think so?' he responded acidly.

'I know so. I also know that you still refuse to see my actions that day for what they really were.'

'I saw that you preferred that Italian showman to me, and I removed myself from London forthwith.'

'Yes, you did. And you returned all my letters,' she added.

'I wished to have nothing more to do with you.'

'Yes, well, I was miffed enough with you to wish to have nothing more to do with *you*, as well. I took myself off to relatives in Madras, met Chevenley, and was reasonably happy with him until his death eight years ago. But you, I gather, remained a widower.'

'I did not, as you must know full well. I married Georgiana Vesey, almost immediately after leaving London, Jane's mother, but she, alas, again made me a widower within the year.'

There was a surprised silence, and then Lady Chevenley spoke again. 'You married twice? So *that* explains my muddle.'

'Muddle?'

'Yes, when Robert first told me of his intention to marry your daughter, he said she was the child of your marriage to Georgiana Vesey, but I seemed to remember you speaking to me of your late wife Jeanne, or Joan, or some such name.'

'Joan. Joan Stapleton. She was a clergyman's daughter.'

'That's right. Well, Robert was most insistent that your wife's name was Georgiana, and I simply thought my memory had played me false. The fact that your daughter's name was Jane didn't mean anything to me one way or the other, for I couldn't remember the name of your child.' She paused. 'Hal, am I to understand that you have two daughters?'

'Yes. My elder daughter is Christina, and Joan was her mother. Jane is the daughter of Georgiana.'

'Oh.'

'Is something wrong?'

'Er, no. At least, I don't think so.' Lady Chevenley then adopted a brisker tone. 'Now, then, this tea is getting cold, and since the others show no sign yet of joining us, I suggest you sit next to me on the settle, and I'll pour.'

Outside, Christina and Robert drew back from the door, moving far enough away to be able to talk without being heard. Christina was a little bemused, for it was astonishing to learn that Lady Chevenley was her father's beloved Alicia; it was also strange to hear the story of the day in London when the loathing for balloons and balloonists had apparently been born.

Robert smiled, glancing back at the parlor door. 'Well, we may not have known about my aunt's part in your father's past, but at least his instant dislike for poor William is now amply explained.'

'Yes,' she replied, thinking that her father would have disliked William even if he hadn't had any connection with balloons, for William had made his liking for Jane far too plain.

'Shall we go in?' asked Robert.

'Yes, but I think we should pretend we know nothing, don't you?' She looked at him. 'Robert, why is my presence causing such consternation?'

'Consternation? Oh, hardly that.'

'Your aunt seemed, well, almost uneasy when she learned about me.'

'I'm sure you're wrong. To tell the truth, my aunt prides herself on her memory, and I think she's a little put out to realize she hadn't remembered as clearly as she thought where your father's first marriage was concerned. Come now, let's face them.' He offered her his arm, and together they entered the great parlor.

The vast room was very splendid indeed, with a lofty hammer-beam roof and cartwheel chandeliers of considerable age. The glow of candles and firelight was almost lost in such a large chamber, but the two on the settle next to the fireplace were picked out very clearly indeed.

Alicia, Lady Chevenley, was a very striking woman, her long graying hair powdered and curled in an old-fashioned but very becoming style. She wore a dark-rose dimity gown, and there were opals at her throat and in her ears. She surveyed Christina.

'Ah, there you are at last, my dear. Welcome to Bellstones.'

'Thank you, Lady Chevenley.' Christina gave a respectful curtsy.

'You'll no doubt be astonished to learn that your father and I are old friends.'

'Indeed?' Christina trusted she looked suitably surprised.

'Yes, although when last we met, which was a disgracefully long time ago, I was still unmarried. Tell me, my dear, did you have an arduous journey from Bath?'

'Not at all, it was most agreeable.'

Lady Chevenley smiled. 'You're very pretty, my dear, and now that I've met you, I'm quite sure Robert has chosen well, for you'll be a great asset, both to him and to Bellstones.'

Christina was acutely embarrassed to again be mistaken for Jane. 'Oh, my lady, I ... I think—'

Robert intervened hastily. 'Aunt, I fear you're making an error. This isn't Miss Jane Richmond, it's her elder sister, Christina.'

Lady Chevenley seemed stunned, staring at him for a long moment before managing a smile. 'Oh, dear. When you came in together, I just thought – Robert, why didn't you inform me of the situation?'

'The omission wasn't intentional, believe me.'

His aunt searched his face for a moment, and then nodded. 'No, I'm sure it wasn't,' she murmured.

At that moment, Jane herself came into the parlor, her frilled white lawn gown fluttering as she moved. A pink-and-white shawl dragged on the floor behind her, and the single long curl from the knot in her hair bounced. There was a pretty flush on her cheeks, and her brown eyes were meltingly apologetic as she hurried toward them, sinking into a becoming curtsy before Lady Chevenley.

'I'm so very sorry I'm late, I truly didn't mean to be. The hem on my other gown had come undone, and there wasn't time to sew it up again.' She raised her big eyes to Lady Chevenley. 'Please forgive me.'

'You're forgiven, of course, my dear. Stand up, now, and let's have a look at you.' As Jane obeyed, Lady Chevenley studied her carefully, before nodding. 'Charming. Quite charming,' she murmured, her glance moving momentarily toward Robert. 'Well, this surfeit of young ladies has at least solved a problem for me.'

Robert raised an eyebrow. 'A problem? For you?'

'Merely a matter of numbers at the dinner table tonight. I suppose you know I've been visiting the Grenfells?'

'Yes.'

'It was my intention to invite Mr and Mrs Grenfell to dine with us, but she really is too indisposed, and, as you know, they never go out unless both are able to. I was surprised to find William at home on a visit.' She turned suddenly to Mr Richmond. 'I understand you made his acquaintance in Bath?'

'Yes, that's correct.' Mr Richmond's lips twitched.

'He spoke so glowingly of you that I was prompted to invite him to join us this evening.'

Mr Richmond looked at her with a total lack of enthusiasm, and said nothing.

A little taken aback at this response, Lady Chevenley turned to look at the others. Jane lowered her glance, fidgeting with her shawl, and Christina found the fire totally absorbing. Lady Chevenley engaged her nephew's gaze, then. 'Five would have been a disagreeable number at table, don't you agree? Six is so much better.'

'Indeed so,' he murmured.

Lady Chevenley glanced thoughtfully around again, for it would have taken a very dull intelligence indeed not to have detected the strained atmosphere that had entered the proceedings the moment William Grenfell's name had come up.

19

I T WAS A quarter to eight, and Christina hurried along the gallery to the queen's chamber to speak to Jane before they went down to dinner. She was wearing the lilac satin gown with the long tiffany gauze sleeves, and her hair was twisted up into a shining knot at the back of her head, with ribbons fluttering down to touch the nape of her neck. Her mother's pearl choker necklace was at her throat, although much against Jenny's advice. The clasp had been difficult to do up, but Christina had been determined to wear it because it was her favorite item of jewelry.

She reached her sister's door. 'Jane? May I come in?'

'Yes.'

Jane was seated at her candlelit dressing table. She looked very lovely in dark-green velvet, her red hair worn a *l'Egyptienne*, and she was just putting on her emerald earrings.

Her eyes met Christina's in the mirror. 'I know what you're going to say, but you don't need to. I'll conduct myself properly tonight.'

'William Grenfell means trouble, Jane.'

Jane rose, and turned to face her properly. 'Christina, I *didn't* know he was here, no matter what you may think, and I'm not at all happy that he's going to be a guest at dinner tonight. I hoped that when he left Bath that that would be the last I'd see of him. I like him very much, Christina, and I know how much he likes me, but it's Robert that I'm going to marry.'

'Lady Chevenley suspects something, you realize that, don't you?'

Jane bit her lip. 'Well, I suppose William *might* have said something to her.'

'Something? Like what, for instance?' asked Christina sharply. 'Jane, what is there for him to tell her? And I'm not just referring to the invitation to tea or the unplanned flight in the balloon.'

Jane looked away guiltily.

Christina stared at her in growing dismay. 'I think you'd better tell me what's been going on,' she said firmly.

'You ... you won't approve.'

'I still need to know.'

'You were right when you thought you saw me returning to the house in the yellow gown and pelisse, for I'd slipped away secretly to Sydney Gardens to watch the balloon. William saw me as the balloon descended, and he called out to me, but I was afraid to speak to him and so I ran back to Johnstone Street.'

'Oh, Jane, when I *think* of the times you've fibbed to me about that wretched pelisse!'

'And about going out into the garden at night.' Jane forced herself to meet Christina's eyes. 'I really went out to meet William in the coach house.'

Christina couldn't believe her ears. 'You ... you what?' she asked faintly.

'I know I shouldn't have, but I was so confused. I liked him so much, and I enjoyed his company. I ... I didn't want to make a mistake by marrying Robert if it was William I really loved.'

Christina closed her eyes. How *could* Jane have been so foolish? 'You've really excelled yourself in indiscretion, you realize that, don't you? Can William be trusted to be honorably silent about it?'

'I ... I think so.'

'You'd better *know* so, Jane.'

'He loves me, Christina.'

'Enough to fight for you, no matter what?'

'He promised me he wouldn't, and I really think he meant it. He wouldn't have hinted anything to Lady Chevenley, I'm sure. Besides, he didn't only promise me, he promised Robert as well.'

Christina stared at her again. '*Robert* knows about all this?'

'No, of course not, he only knows that William loves me. William called on him at Royal Crescent, as you know, and Robert perceived how William felt about me. William gave him his word he wouldn't pursue me, and met me in the coach house that night to tell me he was leaving Bath, and why.'

Christina looked resignedly at her. 'I really don't understand how you could have been so utterly foolish, Jane.'

Jane bit her lip once more, picking up her hairbrush and running her fingertips over the bristles. 'I thought it was all over. Oh, I knew that one day I'd meet William again, because Grenfell Hall is so near here, but I thought it would be some time away, and that he'd have forgotten me. At least, perhaps not forgotten, but just put me in the past, if you know what I mean. Then, when Lady Chevenley said he was going to dine with us tonight ... I don't know what to do, Christina. It's Robert I want, but if William should ...'

'We'll have to hope he doesn't. There's nothing else we can do.'

'I can't blame anyone but myself, can I?'

'No.'

'I'm sorry, Christina.' Jane's voice was small.

'So you should be, for this could possibly end very embarrassingly for the Richmond family, and if it does, Father will be a long time forgiving you.' Christina realized she was being a little harsh, and smiled. 'Come on, wretch, we'd better go down to this dinner.'

Looking miserable, Jane picked up the cloth-of-gold shawl she always wore with the green velvet gown. 'I really am sorry,' she said again. 'I wouldn't have told you, indeed I meant to keep quiet, but I suddenly just couldn't, I *had* to confide in you.'

'Well, we're allies, now, although I have to confess that I can't understand your even glancing at another man when you have Robert. If he was mine, I'd be the happiest woman on earth.'

'Perhaps he should be yours, you deserve him more than I do. I don't deserve anything after all I've done recently.'

They left the room and walked to the head of the staircase, but then Christina realized she'd left her own shawl in her room. 'You go on down, Jane. I'll follow in a moment.' Turning, she hurried away along the gallery.

The only light in the garden room came from the fire, which flickered brightly in the hearth. Christina went to the bed to pick up the shawl, but a movement by the window made her freeze. 'Who's there?' she whispered nervously.

'It's only me, Christina.' Robert turned to face her, the pin in his neckcloth flashing in the firelight. He was dressed for dinner and had been standing looking out of the window. 'You startled me,' she said, laughing a little. 'Do you often lurk in ladies' bedrooms?'

'There are those who are convinced it's my favorite pastime, but on this occasion I'm here because of this particular room. It used to be mine, before I succeeded to my father's title and was expected to occupy the rather grand King Charles suite in the north wing, but this is still my favorite room. Forgive me if I frightened you, but I didn't expect you to return and catch me stealing a secret moment.'

'If you wish to be alone, I won't be a moment. I only came for my shawl.'

'No, no, please don't rush off, you'll make me feel guilty.' He glanced out of the window again. 'I don't think there's a finer view than this in the whole of England,' he murmured.

She went to stand next to him. An early-autumn moon had risen outside, casting a silver light over everything. The high moors were very clear, she could even see some ponies moving among the heather, while closer to the house, the fountain danced like diamonds in the terraced gardens.

He smiled at her. 'I used to sit in this window seat when I was a boy, just gazing at this view, knowing that one day it would be mine. I remember thinking myself the most fortunate and privileged being in all the world.'

'I'd have felt the same.' She glanced at him. 'If this is still your favorite room, why don't you use it?'

'Tradition decrees that each Lord St Clement must occupy the King Charles suite.'

'How many monarchs have slept here?'

'We've been honored by Queen Elizabeth, Charles the First, Queen Anne, and our present king, when he first came to the throne.' He smiled a little. 'All the best royal heads have rested here, although, of course, that might seem an unfortunate turn of phrase where poor Charles is concerned.'

'It might indeed.'

'What do you think of Bellstones, Christina?' he asked suddenly.

'I like it very much indeed.'

'Does Jane like it as much?'

'I'm sure she does, but we haven't really discussed it.' She felt a little uncomfortable mentioning Jane to him so soon after the revealing interview with her sister.

He was silent for a moment. 'You and she are poles apart in many ways, aren't you?'

'Yes, I suppose we are. She's very definitely a sparkling Vesey, whereas I'm a much more staid Stapleton.'

'Champagne and water?'

'An appropriate comparison,' she admitted.

'On the contrary, it's an entirely *in*appropriate comparison. I have the notion that you regard water as something dull and unexciting, whereas I am inclined to view it as something vital and essential.'

She smiled a little wryly. 'I'm hardly that, sir, but you're very flattering and diplomatic to suggest I am.'

'Diplomacy is an art I've had to perfect very recently,' he replied, with more than a hint of self-mockery.

She looked curiously at him. 'Why do you say it like that?'

He smiled ruefully. 'Take no notice, Christina, for I'm selfishly indulging in the low pastime of cynicism.'

For a moment she didn't know what to say, for a change had come over him. 'Can I help at all?' she asked at last.

The offer seemed to amuse him. 'A quaint thought, under the circumstances,' he murmured.

She searched his face. 'More self-indulgent cynicism?'

'I fear so.' He smiled again. 'Forgive me, I have no right to burden you with my moods.'

'If you're going to marry my sister, you have every right.'

'What do you really think of this match, Christina?' he asked softly, holding her gaze.

'I ... I've already said ...'

'Have you?'

'Yes.' She had to look away.

He put his hand to her cheek, making her look at him again. 'Are you, in your heart of hearts, as overjoyed about it as you say?'

She stared at him, a tumult of emotion coursing through her. She was perilously close to blurting out the truth, perilously close to reaching out to him. His fingers were so soft and warm against her cheek, and his eyes were very clear and gray; she loved him so much it was all she could do to keep a hold on her emotions. Somehow she managed a smile. 'Of course I'm as overjoyed as I say,' she said.

For a long moment he continued to hold her gaze; then he took his hand away. 'Then I must believe you.'

Swallowing, she looked out of the window again, in time to see the lamps of a carriage shining through the moonlight from the direction of the lodge. 'I … I think Mr Grenfell is arriving,' she said, aware that her voice sounded lame.

'Then let us go down to greet him,' he murmured, offering her his arm.

Turning to pick up her shawl, she accepted the arm, and they proceeded from the room, but as they descended the staircase she was still finding it difficult to appear calm and unruffled.

At the bottom of the staircase he halted suddenly, turning her to face him. 'I know I've upset you, Christina, and for that I beg you to forgive me. I don't want to harp on about your attitude to the match, it's just that …'

'Yes?'

'It's just that your answers matter so very much, indeed they matter far more than they should.' He looked into her eyes.

She didn't know what he wanted her to say, and then the need to reply was removed because William's carriage was heard on the gravel outside.

Robert glanced at the door almost in irritation, then continued to escort her toward the great parlor, where Jane, Lady Chevenley, and Mr Richmond were waiting.

20

THE DINING ROOM was vast and baronial, and the six diners sat at one end of the long polished oak table that ranged down the center of the stone-flagged floor. All around there were shadows, except for the flicker of the two fires, one at at either end of the room. Tapestries were dimly revealed against richly paneled walls, suits of armor stood guard in the corners, and a bright array of gold plate shone on a huge Elizabethan sideboard that had legs of carved lions. A tall oriel window gave on to the view behind the house, in daytime a splendid panorama of the high moors, but now all was in darkness, except for the faint glimmer of stars.

The Exmoor venison had been quite superb. It had been preceded by a deliciously light cream of celery soup, and followed by a pineapple ice cream worthy of the great Gunter himself. Now the footmen removed the tablecloth, leaving the silver-gilt epergne, some small cut-crystal glasses, and a decanter of amber liqueur. The epergne tumbled with nuts, grapes, and nectarines, and the decanter clinked softly against the glasses as Robert poured the liqueur; it should have been the perfect end to the meal, but Christina hadn't enjoyed anything.

She had so much on her mind, from Jane's revelations concerning secret meetings with William Grenfell, to her own barely controlled response when Robert had put his hand to her cheek. She knew how very close she'd come to telling him how she felt, and didn't know now how she'd managed to hold back. As a consequence she'd sat unhappily through dinner, aware of all the undercurrents caused by William's presence, and aware, too, that she was beginning to think of possible ways she could leave Bellstones and return to the untroubled haven of Richmond House. But how could she do it without causing a very unwelcome stir? The answer was that she couldn't, for there wasn't an excuse in existence which her father and Jane would understand and accept. She stared at the epergne, her glass of liqueur untouched.

'A penny for your thoughts, Christina,' said Robert, watching her. She looked up quickly, flushing. 'They aren't worth a penny.'

'A halfpenny?'

'Not really.'

'A farthing, maybe?'

'Not even a farthing,' she replied, managing a smile.

He smiled as well. 'Well, whatever their worth, they're evidently very absorbing indeed.'

Mr Richmond grunted. 'She's probably wishing she was in her room with her nose in that disreputable tome he takes everywhere with her.'

She looked at him. '*Gil Blas* is hardly disreputable, Father. Why, it happens to be the blessed Mr Pitt's favorite book.'

William spoke up. 'It's my favorite as well, indeed Le Sage is almost the only point upon which Pitt and I are in agreement.'

Mr Richmond glowered at him, and fell silent.

An awkwardness immediately descended on the small gathering, and William lowered his eyes to the table. He looked as elegant and distinguished as he had on the night of the ball; indeed, he was perfectly turned out, from his sober dark-blue velvet coat and cream silk breeches to the sapphire pin on the knot of his stiffly starched cravat. There was no suggestion of the more outlandish extremes of high fashion, and there hadn't been anything improper in his demeanor throughout. He'd been the perfect gentleman; Jane hadn't been particularly singled out, nor had he glanced at her too often or too long. But no matter how William conducted himself now, Mr Richmond wasn't about to forget his conduct in the past, and couldn't conceal the hostility the pilot had aroused from the outset of their acquaintance. Under such circumstances it was inevitable that the meal hadn't been an entirely comfortable experience for anyone concerned.

Mr Richmond and William had so far crossed verbal swords several times on the topic of politics, and then on a discussion concerning, of all things, the growing of climbing roses. Now *The Adventures of Gil Blas* threatened to provoke another display of controlled acrimony, unless someone could divert the conversation.

Lady Chevenley acted with discreet speed, but unfortunately chose another awkward topic. 'Tell me, William, do you intend to make many ascents in your balloon now you're home?'

'Er, yes, as many as I can. Indeed, I hope to make a number of free flights, and a night flight.'

'Do you really? How very exciting. But isn't that a little too dangerous?'

'Not in the right conditions and when all precautions have been properly taken.' William's glance moved fleetingly toward Jane.

'And what, exactly, are the right conditions?' inquired her ladyship.

'Fair weather, without much of a breeze.'

'Like today?'

'Today was a little windy, which is why I made only a captive ascent.'

'I see. Do you know, I find it all immensely interesting, but then, I've always been intrigued by the notion of flight.' Lady Chevenley was belatedly realizing that in her haste to divert the conversation, she'd chosen a subject even more contentious than *Gil Blas*. She looked uneasily at Mr Richmond's dark expression, and then gave a stifled sigh, which she attempted to conceal by dabbing her napkin to her lips. She looked very lovely in a white silk undergown and fawn lace tunic dress.

Mr Richmond wasn't about to let the matter of balloons pass him by without comment. 'It's against all the laws of nature for man to emulate birds, Alicia,' he declared, sitting back and sipping his liqueur while he looked down the table at the pilot.

Lady Chevenley felt obliged to respond. 'Hal, it's also against the laws of nature for man to travel at speed across the countryside, but he does so by means of the horse.'

'Horses are not made of rubberized taffeta or filled with inflammable air.'

'Why, I do believe you haven't the courage to make even a daytime ascent, Hal,' she replied provocatively.

'Nonsense.'

'*Do* you have the courage, then?'

'Of course.'

'Oh, good. You see, earlier today I discussed the matter with William, and he's very kindly offered to take us all up on the next fine day. Haven't you, William?'

'Yes, Lady Chevenley, I'd be only too delighted.' William's glance slid toward Mr Richmond. 'Would you care to take me up on the invitation, sir?'

'I have no desire to be another Icarus, Mr Grenfell.'

'Nor have I, but we'll be Daedalus instead.'

'I'm content to have my feet firmly on the ground.'

'But how will you know the truth about flight if you do not attempt it?' pressed William a little wickedly.

'I think I know the truth, my boy.'

'In other words, you're prepared to criticize without really experiencing it?' William raised his glass to his lips, holding the other's gaze.

There was silence, with all eyes on Mr Richmond, who really had brought this upon himself. Robert seemed amused, lounging back in his chair, his hand to his mouth. Jane was of two minds, being vaguely discomfited by the whole thing, and at the same time knowing a certain satisfaction that William was at last striking back after being picked on all evening. Christina sympathized with her father to a certain extent, and gave William a cool glance. She was very suspicious indeed of his perfect behavior tonight. Only once throughout the meal had she intercepted him in a glance at Jane that was anything other than correct, and that glance had been far too warm. He was still very attracted to her, and the strength of that attraction could yet override his promises both to Jane herself and to Robert.

Lady Chevenley couldn't resist twitting Mr Richmond a little further. 'Come now, Hal, you must say yea or nay to the challenge.'

Mr Richmond glowered, but knew he was cornered. 'Oh, very well,' he said huffily. 'I will accept the invitation, but it won't change my mind in the slightest.'

Lady Chevenley clapped her hands. 'Excellent! So, we're *all* going to make an ascent!'

Jane smiled, but Christina hastened to decline. 'I, er, think I must cry off, for the thought of going up in a balloon fills me with horror.'

Jane was dismayed. 'Oh, Christina, you can't …'

Lady Chevenley was anxious to persuade her to change her mind. 'But, my dear Christina, I'm sure you'll enjoy it. You must come with us, otherwise you'll be all on your own.'

Robert sat forward. 'Not entirely on her own, for I will be with her. I share her views about balloons, and intend to keep my feet firmly on the ground.' He raised his glass to Christina, smiling.

Lady Chevenley sighed. 'Oh, well, I suppose you're both entitled to do as you wish.'

'We are indeed, Aunt,' he murmured.

Mr Richmond drew a long, disgruntled breath. 'How is it,' he muttered, 'that everyone at this table is doing what they *wish* to do, except me? I don't want to go up in that thrice-cursed contraption, but somehow I am!'

Lady Chevenley chuckled. 'You talked yourself into a fix, my dear.' Then, to prevent further discussion on the matter, she folded her napkin and rose to her feet. 'I've had enough of this drafty hall. Shall we adjourn to the great parlor?'

Robert got up immediately to draw her chair away, and soon made it plain that he had no intention of lingering over the port with two gentlemen as abrasive as William and Mr Richmond. 'We'll *all* adjourn to the great parlor,' he said firmly, offering his aunt an arm.

Mr Richmond rose quickly, moving to Jane's chair before William could, and so William turned to attend to Christina instead.

They followed the other two couples into the hallway and across to the great parlor, but before going in, Christina halted. 'May I have a word with you, Mr Grenfell?'

'By all means.'

'I'll come straight to the point. What are your intentions toward my sister?'

He gave a light laugh. 'That is indeed what I call coming straight to the point. Are you asking the question because you find some fault in my conduct tonight?'

'Your conduct has been almost exemplary, Mr Grenfell, but I have to tell you that I saw how you looked at Jane tonight, and I don't think I misinterpreted anything.'

'Robert's ring isn't on her finger yet,' he said quietly.

She was amazed at his audacity. 'So, you admit you intend...?'

'To win her if I can? Yes.'

'Then it ill becomes you to come to this house, sir, for you're no friend of its master,' she breathed, her anger rising.

'And are you a friend of Jane's?' he inquired softly.

'What do you mean?'

'It means that you aren't the only one to interpret looks. You're far from being indifferent to Robert – indeed I'd say you and I are in very much the same boat: we both love someone we shouldn't.'

Guilty color flooded into her cheeks. 'You're wrong, sir.'

'No, I'm not. Miss Richmond, I would have thought that you, of all people, would understand how I feel.'

She looked away, thoroughly disquieted at being discovered in spite of her efforts. 'Perhaps I do, sir, but there's one great difference between your situation and mine.'

'Is there?'

'Yes. I have no intention at all of causing trouble because of my love. In fact I'm striving to keep it a secret from all concerned, but you ... Well, I have no such faith in your intentions, sir, for even though you know that Jane loves Robert, you still accepted the invitation here tonight, and you don't hesitate to confess to me that you regard her as still available until she wears your friend's ring.'

He lowered his glance for a moment. 'I haven't told you out of uncaring arrogance. I told you out of honesty. You say she's in love with him, but I've yet to be convinced. I promised to keep my distance, and when I accepted Lady Chevenley's kind invitation, I fully intended to keep my word; but when I actually saw Jane again, when I spoke to her and was exposed to her enchanting personality, I knew I couldn't stand by my promise. I love her, Miss Richmond, and I have to fight to win her if I possibly can.'

'Have you no honor, sir? I think it *despicable* of you to come to this house and blatantly declare your intention to steal my sister if you can!' Christina was upset, for every word he uttered confirmed the fear she'd felt on arriving at Bellstones and seeing the balloon on the horizon: William Grenfell's presence was going to cause trouble.

He paused for a moment, looking quizzically at her. 'Do you dislike me, Miss Richmond?' he asked suddenly.

She thought about her reply. 'No,' she said at last, 'but I *do* disapprove of your actions.'

'And if you heard from Jane herself that she wanted me, not Robert?'

Jane's words echoed in Christina's head. *I didn't want to make a mistake by marrying Robert if it was William I really loved.*

'Miss Richmond?'

She looked at him. 'If Jane told me she loved you, sir, that would, of course, be an entirely different matter. But she hasn't told me any such thing,' she added.

He smiled a little. 'You're a very rare woman, Christina Richmond, for your thoughts are indeed entirely of Jane's happiness, and it hasn't occurred to you to encourage my suit in order to secure Robert's freedom.'

She was deeply affronted. 'I'm offended that you should even consider me capable of such duplicity.'

'Perhaps I should be equally offended that you should criticize my regard for Jane. I really and truly love her, Miss Richmond, so much so that I cannot turn my back upon the feeling. The difference between us is that you have found the strength to look away, whereas I have not.' He took her hand, raising it suddenly to his lips. 'If there was any justice in this world, then you would win your heart's desire, and I would win mine.' He smiled disarmingly.

She had to smile reluctantly in return. 'I still disapprove, sir,' she said quietly.

'I know, but at least I am comforted that you don't dislike me personally. Please rest assured that your secret is safe with me, but now I suggest we join the others, or our absence will be remarked.'

He drew her hand over his arm, and they proceeded toward the great parlor.

21

FOR THE NEXT two hours they amused themselves playing cards, but then the conversation turned to music, and Lady Chevenley discovered that Jane was a very accomplished pianist. It was immediately agreed that they would adjourn to the music room across the hall to hear her play the harpsichord.

The music room was a little cooler than the great parlor, and shadows leapt wildly over the paneled walls as the dinner party entered with candles. Jane took her seat at the beautiful gilded harpsichord, while Robert and William sifted through the pile of music sheets on a nearby table. Mr Richmond positioned himself at Jane's shoulder, ostensibly so that he could turn the pages for her, but really so that he could keep William well away from her.

Lady Chevenley sat with Christina on a sofa, and when settled, looked inquiringly across at her nephew. 'What are you selecting, Robert?'

'I thought you'd like to hear "Greensleeves," Aunt,' he replied, smiling at her.

'Oh, excellent. It's so very appropriate for this house. Its author, King Henry the Eighth, may not actually have graced Bellstones with his presence, but his daughter did, and so things Tudor are quite perfect here.'

William found the relevant sheet, placing it in front of Jane, and Mr Richmond immediately edged closer, forcing William to step back out of the way.

Jane began to play. The plain, beautiful notes rang through the room, and Christina closed her eyes, imagining Bellstones in the sixteenth century. She could see ladies in velvet gowns, with little lapdogs in their sleeves, rush-strewn floors perfumed with mead-owsweet, and gentlemen in rich brocades.

As the last notes died away, they all clapped appreciatively, and Jane blushed prettily. 'What shall I play next?' she asked.

Lady Chevenley thought for a moment. 'Is Mr Cotton's "Early Thoughts of Marriage" there, by any chance?' she asked Robert.

He went through the pile of music sheets again, and soon found what he was looking for.

Lady Chevenley smiled at Jane. 'I'm sure you sing as beautifully as you play, my dear, and the words are very, er, telling.'

'I ... I don't know it terribly well, so you will bear with me, won't you?' asked Jane apologetically, studying the sheet.

'Of course, my dear,' Lady Chevenley reassured her, sitting back comfortably again.

As Jane began to play again, William annoyed Mr Richmond intensely by leaning on the harpsichord to watch her. Robert didn't seem to notice anything.

Jane's voice was sweet and clear:

'Attend, my fair, to wisdom's choice,
A married life, to speak the best,
Is all a lottery contest.
But if my fair one will be wise,
I will ensure my girl a prize,
Though not a prize to match thy worth,
Perhaps thy equal's not on earth.

The song continued, but Christina didn't hear it. The words were, as Lady Chevenley so innocently remarked, very telling. It was indeed all a lottery contest, with fate decreeing that she and William should be the losers. She glanced toward Robert, and found that he was looking at her, almost as if he too was affected by the words.

She quickly lowered her glance, hardly noticing when Jane finished the song, and the others applauded again. Mr Richmond asked Jane to play 'The Happy Nightingale', one of his favorites, and Lady Chevenley leaned closer to Christina.

'I do so like "Early Thoughts on Marriage," for it offers such sensible advice. Don't you agree?' The older woman shivered suddenly. 'Dear me, I appear to have left my shawl in the parlor. Christina, my dear, would you be so kind as to fetch it for me?'

'Of course.' Christina got up gladly, for it was almost as if Lady Chevenley knew the truth.

But as she reached the door, Robert picked up a candlestick. 'I'll accompany you, Christina.'

'There's no need, truly,' she said quickly.

'I'm too much the gentleman to allow you to go alone,' he replied, smiling as he walked toward her.

She could only smile reluctantly in return. They crossed the hall to the parlor, where the leaping flames in the hearth warmed the air, sweetening it with the scent of roses from the open potpourri jars standing by the fender.

Christina retrieved Lady Chevenley's shawl from the chair where it had been left, and then turned immediately to hurry out again, but Robert barred her way.

'You've been very quiet tonight, Christina.'

'Oh?'

'You hardly joined in the conversation at the dinner table, and you weren't exactly the life and soul of the card party, were you?'

'I don't have a very gregarious disposition, I'm afraid.'

'Is it that? Or is there something else on your mind?' he inquired quietly.

Her fingers crept nervously to toy with her pearl necklace, but as she touched it the clasp gave way, and the necklace fell to the floor.

'Allow me,' he said quickly, bending to pick it up. He inspected the clasp. 'It seems to be all right.'

'Yes, but I think there's something wrong with it. I'm going to send it to the jeweler in Stroud when we return.' She tried to sound matter-of-fact, but her voice was trembling because she was so disturbed by him.

'I'll put it on for you, and make sure it's fastened properly,' he said, moving behind her and placing the necklace around her neck.

She couldn't entirely disguise the shiver of pleasure that passed through her the moment he touched her. Subtle emotions she wished to suppress rose inexorably to the surface, and she closed her eyes, trying desperately to conceal the effect he was having upon her.

She didn't succeed. The necklace was fastened and secure, but he didn't take his hands away. Her skin was warm beneath his fingers as he moved them softly over her naked shoulders.

Her heart almost stopped at the caress. She knew she should pull away, but she couldn't, she was trapped by her overwhelming love for him. Her breath escaped on a long, telltale sigh.

'Christina?' he whispered, turning her toward him and cupping her face in his hands. 'Christina, I—'

A savage shame swung through her as she realized she'd given herself away, and at last she found the strength to pull sharply away. 'No! Please!'

'Christina—'

'Don't say anything, I beg of you!' Distraught with guilt, she pressed her shaking hands to her cheeks. 'I … I'm sorry, I didn't want you to know anything. I can't possibly go back to the others now.' Choking back a sob, she gathered her skirts, dropping Lady Chevenley's shawl as she hurried agitatedly past him and out into the entrance hall.

'Christina, come back!'

She didn't look back, but fled blindly up the staircase, too guilty and distressed to think of anything but the safety of her room.

He crossed the hall behind her, but as he was about to follow up the staircase, the music-room door opened and Mr Richmond came out.

'Ah, there you are, Robert, my boy. We were wondering what had happened to you.' He glanced around. 'Where's Christina?'

Robert hesitated, and then turned toward him. 'She, er, has a headache, I'm afraid.'

'A headache? Oh, dear, should I send Jane to her?'

'No, I don't think that will be necessary,' replied Robert, glancing up at the empty gallery.

'Are you coming back to join us?' asked Mr Richmond.

'Yes. Of course.' Picking up the shawl, Robert reluctantly accompanied him into the music room.

*

In the garden room, in the shelter of darkness, for there were no candles, and the fire had been banked up for the night, Christina lay weeping silently on the bed. The worst had happened. By relaxing her guard and giving in, so briefly, to the powerful feelings that had beset her from the moment she'd seen him, she'd ruined everything. How could she face him again now? And what if her father or Jane should discover?

About an hour later she heard William's carriage drive away; then Jenny came to her door. Light from the passage flooded into the dark room as the maid entered. 'Do you require me, Miss Christina?' she asked, knowing something was very wrong.

'No. Thank you.'

'Are you quite sure, miss?'

'Quite sure.'

'Yes, miss.' The maid began to withdraw.

'Jenny?'

'Miss?'

'Please tell my father and sister that I'm asleep and not to be disturbed.'

'Yes, miss.'

The door closed softly, and darkness engulfed the room again.

She heard the others retire, and after a while Campion performed his nightly duty of extinguishing most of the lights, leaving only a single candle in the passage outside.

The house had been silent for some time when Robert came to her door. 'Christina? I have to talk to you,' he whispered.

She lay in silence, staring up at the shadows of the bed hangings.

'Please, Christina. It's important.'

Still she didn't reply.

Lady Chevenley's room was nearby, and evidently she wasn't asleep, for she heard the urgent whispering and came to her door. 'Robert? Is that you?'

'Damn!' he exclaimed under his breath, then lightened his voice to reply to his aunt, 'Yes, it's me.'

'Whatever are you doing?'

'Er, nothing. I thought I heard a noise.'

'A noise? What sort of noise?' she asked, a note of alarm entering her voice.

'Oh, just a noise. It probably wasn't anything. Christina appears to have slept through it, anyway.'

'Which is something of a miracle, considering what's going on outside her door. Well, if you're sure the noise wasn't anything to worry about, I think we should retire to our beds, don't you?'

'Yes, Aunt. Good night.'

'Good night, Robert.'

Christina heard his footsteps retreating, and then Lady Chevenley's door closed. Silence returned to the house, and for a long while she continued to stare up at the bed hangings; then she hid her face in her pillow again.

22

SHE FELL ASLEEP at last, but was awakened in the small hours when the fire shifted suddenly in the hearth. She sat up, wishing that all that had happened earlier had been only a bad dream; but it wasn't, it was all too real.

Feeling dreadful, she got off the bed, her gown crumpled and spoiled. Her hair had tumbled loose from its knot, and the satin ribbons fluttered sadly against her bare shoulders. She went to the window, holding the curtain aside to look out. The moon was still up, drenching the combe and terraced gardens with its chill silver light. She stared down at the fountain. The last time she'd looked at that dancing water, she hadn't yet made the ultimate mistake of revealing her heart. She'd still been safe then, still able to look her father and sister in the eyes, still able to smile at Robert. All that had gone now.

Suddenly the room felt confining. On impulse she went to the wardrobe and took out her fur-lined cloak, swinging it over her shoulders. The door into the passage creaked a little as she opened it, but although she listened carefully, she didn't hear anyone else stirring. The solitary candle swayed a little as she hurried past toward the gallery and the staircase.

She emerged from the house into the night. The air was cold, and she drew her cloak close as she moved past the front of the house toward the gardens.

The topmost terrace was paved and surrounded by a stone balustrade on lion supports. There were several statues of mythical creatures – a unicorn, a phoenix, and a centaur – and they seemed almost alive in the pale moonlight as she crossed to the wide flight of stone steps leading down to the next garden.

The second terrace was a place of formal flowerbeds, each one surrounded by a low, precisely clipped hedge, and all the paths converged on a small white marble rotunda in the center. She made her way past the rotunda, where a statue of the god Pan stood in the shadows, and approached the steps leading down to the next terrace, the one where the fountain played in the pool in the middle of the lawn.

Here her steps slowed a little. She walked along a path edged by tall autumn flowers, chrysanthemums, Michaelmas daisies, and goldenrod, and the train of her gown dragged through the fallen leaves of an ancient mulberry tree. The sharp smell of autumn was all around, and she could hear the fountain playing, the water tinkling with the brittleness of approaching winter.

She didn't see the little wooden summerhouse until she was almost upon it. Overhung with weeping willows, and built on a little stone dais, it had a pagoda roof and a doorless entrance that faced across the lawn toward the fountain. The willows stirred in the faint night breeze, and in the shadows inside the pagoda she could see an elegant little wrought-iron seat. She was drawn toward it, stepping up on to the dais and entering the little building that must be so delightful and cool on a hot summer's day.

She sat down, gazing across the moonlit lawns toward the fountain. Sounds other than the water carried to her. She could hear an owl hooting somewhere behind the house, and horses in the stableblock. In the distance, much deeper and less distinct, she could hear the roar of the Darch as it swept past the bridge by the lodge, and the thunder of the rapids downstream.

Her thoughts turned to Robert, and all that had gone wrong. Somehow she had to leave Bellstones, but try as she would, she couldn't think of a reason that would suffice under the circumstances. How could she explain to her father, or to Jane, that she had to return to Stroud before the betrothal?

Her train of thought was broken abruptly by the distinct sound of a wicket gate opening further along the garden, in the high perimeter wall that separated the terraces from the leafy combe beyond. Wondering who could be out and about at such an hour, she rose to her feet, peeping cautiously out of the summerhouse. She could see the wicket gate in the wall, and hurrying in her direction from it, a woman's hooded cloaked figure.

Christina drew back quickly out of sight, pressing back into the shadows as light footsteps approached along the path. The woman came right to the summerhouse, pausing on the path by it to look back toward the wicket gate. She pushed back her hood and Christina was startled to recognize Jane. For the space of a heartbeat Christina could have spoken, but something kept her silent, and then Jane pulled her hood forward again, turning to hurry on toward the house.

Slowly Christina moved to the entrance of the summerhouse. The cloaked figure vanished swiftly up the steps to the next terrace. Christina was about to follow her when she distinctly heard the wicket gate again. With a gasp she retreated into the shadows of the summerhouse once more, peeping very carefully toward the wall. Another cloaked figure had entered the garden from the combe. It was a man this time, tall and top-hatted, and he was walking slowly toward the summerhouse.

Her heart began to pound as the steps came inexorably closer, but then, abruptly, she couldn't hear them anymore. Hesitantly she looked out. The path was empty. Puzzled, she glanced all around, and then she saw him by the fountain. She'd ceased to hear his steps because he'd left the path to cross the soft grass.

He stood with one boot resting on the low stone surround of the ornamental pond, and he'd removed his top hat and was swinging it idly in his hand. She could see him quite clearly in the moonlight; it was Robert.

Christina stared at him, taken a little aback, for somehow, in her heart of hearts, she'd expected to see William Grenfell. Or was that wishful thinking? Did she *want* it to be William because that would, as William himself had said, leave Robert free? But it was Robert, and only one conclusion could be drawn from seeing him return a minute after Jane through the same wicket gate: they'd had a secret assignation, a lovers' tryst. So, William was to share her fate after all, and know the deep misery of unrequited love.

She had to remain in the summerhouse until Robert left, but he showed no inclination to move, gazing at the fountain as it splashed into the pond. At last he put his hat on again, adjusting his cloak as he walked away across the grass.

She waited for several minutes before emerging from the summer-house, hurrying back along the path toward the house. She was afraid Robert might have locked the front door on his way in, but to her relief, it opened at her touch. The entrance hall was deserted, and there wasn't a sound. Her skirts rustled as she hurried softly up the staircase and along the gallery.

At last she reached her room, closing the door thankfully and leaning back on it. The slight draft she'd caused on entering made the fire shift again, and a shower of brilliant sparks flew up the chimney. In the mirror on the dressing table she could see her reflection. Her hair was tangled, the lilac satin ribbons still clinging to their loosened pins, and as she untied her cloak, she saw how creased her lovely gown was. She was a very sorry sight, a different creature entirely from the neat, composed, contentedly undisturbed person she'd been on leaving Stroud what now seemed a lifetime ago.

With a heavy heart she went to the wardrobe, taking off her cloak and replacing it on its hanger. She managed to unhook the gown, stepping out of it and draping it over the back of a chair, for it would need a great deal of attention to remove the creases. The ribbons looked sad as she placed them on the dressing table, and the pins chinked into their dish. Her hair crackled when the brush was drawn through it, and her nightgown felt cold as she slipped it on. She turned the coverlet back on the bed and crept between the sheets, curling up tightly into a ball.

She hadn't removed the pearl necklace. Her fingers crept to touch it, and she remembered the moment he'd placed it around her neck. It had been a bewitching moment, breathless and more seductive than anything she'd ever known before. Her defenses had been stormed by stealth, and her resistance brushed aside with a caress, leaving her totally vulnerable to the heartbreak and pain she'd striven so to avoid.

Tears pricked her tired eyes again. 'Oh, Robert,' she whispered in the darkness, 'I love you so very much.'

23

THE RAVAGES OF the night were only too visible on Christina's face when she woke up in the morning. Her eyes were red and tired, and her face was pale and drawn as Jenny came in with the customary tray of tea.

The maid halted in dismay. 'Oh, Miss Christina …'

'Do I look that bad?' Christina replied resignedly, knowing full well that she did.

'I'm afraid you do, miss.' Jenny put the tray down on the table next to the bed. 'My mother always used to say that cold stewed apple was good on sore eyes. There's some in the kitchen. Shall I bring it?'

'It sounds revolting, but I'll try anything.' Christina sat up wearily, pushing a stray lock of hair back from her face.

'I'll go for it straightaway, miss.' The maid hurried out again.

The cold apple did help; it soothed the salt soreness and restored a little of the lost brightness to Christina's lackluster eyes. With the further judicious assistance of a little rouge, the careful pinning and curling of her hair, and the choice of a carefree pink muslin gown sprinkled with white spots, she knew the best that was possible had been achieved. All she had to do now was screw herself up to the necessary pitch to face everyone at the breakfast table. *All* she had to do? It was the worst part of all.

Outside, it was another beautiful autumn day. The Darch valley was ablaze with color, and the heights of Exmoor stood out clearly against the brilliant blue sky. It was all so lovely and free; so at odds with the way she felt. With a sigh she picked up her shawl, draping it slowly over her arms; then she took a deep breath before leaving the room.

Almost immediately she encountered Jane, and by the brightness of the smile she received, she knew that Robert hadn't mentioned anything about the previous night. Jane looked radiant, and needed no artifice to assist her in her loveliness. She wore a green-and-white-striped lawn gown, long-sleeved and frilled, and several bouncy ringlets fell from the knot at the back of her head. Her shawl, as always, was trailing carelessly along the floor behind her, and there was gaiety in her voice as she greeted Christina.

'Good morning – isn't it a *lovely* morning?'

'Yes, it is.'

Jane searched her face. 'I won't ask if you slept well.'

'And here was I, thinking I'd made a fair fist of looking good.'

'I'm your sister, I know you too well.'

You don't know me at all, thought Christina, looking quickly away.

Jane touched her arm. 'Do you still have a headache? I was quite concerned last night when you didn't rejoin us, but Jenny said you were asleep and ...'

'I ended up awake most of the night. There was an owl, it kept hooting on the eaves right outside my window.' It was all Christina could think of on the spur of the moment to explain her ragged appearance.

'With all the owls we have at home, I would have thought you'd be used to it,' Jane said in some surprise.

'Those are well-bred Gloucestershire owls; these are rather less well-bred Somerset owls.'

'Please, it's my future lord and master's county you speak of so disparagingly,' replied Jane with mock haughtiness, taking her arm as they went down the staircase.

Christina glanced at her. 'Did *you* sleep well?' she asked after a moment.

'Excellently. I don't think I moved in my bed from the moment I closed my eyes.'

'Which was when, exactly?'

'Whatever do you mean?' Jane asked with a laugh.

'I saw you after your assignation with Robert.'

'My what?' Jane came to an abrupt halt, staring at her.

'Your assignation with Robert. I was in the garden last night, in the little summerhouse, and I saw you sneaking back to the house.'

Jane seemed almost uneasy. 'But why didn't you speak to me?'

'I don't really know. You came along the path, paused for a moment with your hood back, and then hurried on tip to the next terrace. It was over in a moment, and when I saw Robert as well ...'

'You did? Where?'

Christina was a little surprised at the question. 'Why, following you, of course. He came in through the same wicket gate. You *had* been meeting, hadn't you?'

'Yes, of course.' Jane gave a light, rather embarrassed laugh. 'I ... I thought we'd been completely discreet.'

'I'm sure you were. *I'm* hardly likely to say anything.' Christina looked curiously at her. 'Why are you looking so worried? It's surely the most natural thing in the world for you and Robert to wish to be alone.'

'Yes, I suppose it is.'

'Am I to understand from this that you and Robert now have a love match?'

Jane hesitated, and then looked shyly at her. 'Yes, Christina, I love him so much I'm all at sixes and sevens.'

Christina's heart tightened with conflicting emotions: joy for her sister, anguish for herself. She managed a smile. 'I'm very, very happy for you.'

'Christina, I ...'

No more was said, for at that moment Lady Chevenley appeared at the top of the staircase behind them, looking splendid in crisp lemon cotton. 'Good morning, my dears, I trust you both slept well?'

'I did,' replied Jane, 'but I'm afraid Christina was less fortunate.'

Lady Chevenley swept down toward them, eyeing Christina. 'You do look a little wan, but I'm sure our good Exmoor air will soon put you right.'

'I hope so.'

Jane smiled. 'Good Exmoor owls have a great deal to answer for, Lady Chevenley.'

'Owls? Whatever do you mean?'

'There was one outside Christina's window all night, and it kept her awake.'

'Really? Actually on the house? How strange, we don't usually have them honoring us with their presence. Anyway,' she went on more briskly, 'let's to breakfast. I intend to twit your dear father, it's a pastime I always used to enjoy, and one which has apparently not lost its appeal.'

As she went on down the staircase, Jane turned urgently to Christina. 'You won't say anything about seeing me in the garden last night, will you? I ... I don't want Lady Chevenley or Father thinking I've misbehaved in any way.'

'My lips are sealed.'

'Thank you.' Jane linked her arm again, and as they followed Lady Chevenley down to the hall, she changed the subject. 'I still don't believe that Robert's aunt was Father's great love. It came as quite a shock when I joined you all for tea yesterday and gradually began to put two and two together.'

'You were at a disadvantage. Robert and I had, rather reprehensibly, earwigged at the door first.'

They entered the sunny breakfast room, which had windows facing the moors behind the house. Robert and Mr Richmond had already risen from the table to greet Lady Chevenley.

Mr Richmond wore a plum silk dressing gown over his shirt and breeches, and in place of his usual wig he had on a tasseled black cap. Robert was fully dressed, in a sky-blue coat over a charcoal waistcoat, and light-gray cord breeches. His hair was a little tousled, and there was something about him that told Christina he'd slept very little after his secret assignation with Jane. Or was it because of what had happened before that, in the great parlor?

Mr Richmond hastened to draw out a chair for Lady Chevenley, and she smiled at him. 'Why, thank you, Hal. I trust this means you're in an agreeable mood this morning?'

'I'm always agreeable,' he replied.

Robert had come to meet Jane, taking her hand and raising the palm to his lips. 'Good morning, Jane, I vow you're looking lovelier than ever today.'

Jane hesitated, a strange look in her eyes, but as he smiled at her, she seemed to relax, smiling in return. 'Good morning, Robert,' she said softly.

The moment was almost upon Christina; in a few seconds Robert would speak to her. How would he address her? Would his embarrassment show?

He drew out a chair for Jane, saw her settled, and then turned to Christina. 'Good morning,' he said, holding her gaze.

'Good morning.'

He took her hand, cupping it briefly in both his and squeezing it in a secret gesture of reassurance that no one else could see. 'I must say that you're looking very lovely as well,' he said quietly, smiling at her.

Relief swept through her that he was endeavoring to behave as if nothing had happened, but his kindness brought her close to tears.

Mr Richmond surveyed her suddenly. 'Upon my soul, miss, you don't look at all well. Is the headache still with you?'

'No, I'm quite all right now,' she replied, taking the seat Robert drew out for her.

Lady Chevenley was settled now. 'I'm afraid poor Christina has had an owl to contend with. The horrid bird chose to perch by her window all night.' She glanced at her nephew. 'That must have been the noise you heard.'

'Yes.' He glanced fleetingly at Christina, who gazed steadily at her plate.

A discussion about the habits of owls ensued, giving Christina a little time to collect herself. She looked around the room. It was a cheerful chamber, its walls hung with blue-and-white painted silk above half-paneling. The immense sideboard, a weighty sixteenth-century item that looked as if it had been built where it stood, was laden with silver-domed dishes presided over by Campion. The table was laid with a crisp white cloth, and on it there was an array of fine porcelain. A bowl of yellow chrysanthemums graced the center, and around it were ranged bowls of fresh bread rolls, racks of toast, jars of preserves, a cold beefsteak pie especially for Mr Richmond, and a dish of crushed ice on which reposed a large pat of creamy butter.

Christina's appetite was nonexistent, although for the sake of appearances she endeavored to eat a buttered bread roll with her cup of thick, dark coffee. A glance at Robert's plate told her he felt much the same.

They'd almost finished their meal when a note was delivered from Grenfell Hall. It was handed to Lady Chevenley, who immediately beamed with delight. 'William has sent word that today is quite perfect for an ascent in the balloon! He says that if we drive over there at our earliest convenience, he'd be honored to take us all up.' Her eyes shone as she looked around the table. 'Isn't that *splendid*?'

Jane's eyes brightened; evidently memories of Major General Sir Penn-Blagington's roof were short-lived.

Mr Richmond looked sour. 'A plague on the fellow,' he grumbled.

'Hal, you gave your solemn word last night,' pointed out Lady Chevenley.

'Under duress.'

'You still gave it.'

'I know, devil take it.'

Satisfied that he couldn't wriggle out of the undertaking, she smiled at Christina. 'Won't you change your mind, my dear? I do think you'd enjoy it, you know.'

'I'd really rather not, Lady Chevenley. Truly, I'd be just as happy staying here and reading.'

Mr Richmond groaned. 'Oh, if I only had a golden guinea for every time I've heard *that*!'

Lady Chevenley tossed him a cross look. 'Christina is quite at liberty to read if she so chooses.' She turned her attention to her nephew then. 'And what about you, Robert? Are you still intent upon remaining on the ground?'

'I am.'

Jane gasped, suddenly remembering something. 'Oh, and I promised to ride with you later on, didn't I?'

He smiled. 'You did, but I release you from the promise.'

'Are you sure?'

'I am, but if your conscience troubles you, I'm sure Christina will oblige by riding with me in your place.' His gray eyes rested on Christina.

Jane looked at her as well. 'Oh, *would* you, Christina?'

'I ...'

'Oh, please say you will, otherwise I shall not be able to go, you know I won't.'

Christina looked reluctantly at Robert. 'Do you really wish me to ride with you?'

'If I didn't, I wouldn't have asked.' He smiled.

'Then of course I'll accompany you.' But she didn't want to; indeed it was the last thing she wanted.

The others left the table immediately to prepare to drive to Grenfell Hall, but as Christina rose to follow them, Robert called her back.

'If you think I've trapped you into the ride, Christina, then you're quite right. I make no apologies, because we have to talk in private, and I can think of no place more private than the high moor.'

'We don't have anything to say to each other,' she said quietly, looking unwillingly at him.

'On the contrary, we have a great deal to say.'

'I would rather not. I just want to leave it as it is.'

'I'm not prepared to allow you to do that, Christina.'

She looked pleadingly at him. 'Robert, I'm ashamed of—'

'Ashamed? Christina, you have nothing to be ashamed about.' He seemed about to come toward her, but at that moment there was a discreet tap at the door and Campion came in.

'Excuse me, my lord, but the rector of Darchford has called.'

'Oh, very well,' replied Robert, more shortly than he otherwise might. 'I'll be there directly.'

'Yes, my lord.'

Christina moved determinedly toward the door as the butler began to close it, but Robert spoke again. 'We *are* going to talk, Christina.'

She didn't say anything, but hurried on out.

24

A N HOUR AFTER the carriage had set off for Grenfell Hall, Christina was ready and waiting in her room for word from Robert that his interview with the rector was over. She paced nervously, her riding crop tapping in the palm of her hand. Her riding habit was made of beige corduroy, its beautifully tailored jacket trimmed with black braiding, and there was a flouncy ostrich feather curling down from her black beaver hat. It was an outfit stylish enough for Hyde Park, but she was too agitated to feel stylish.

The thought of the coming few hours filled her with great unease. What a fool she'd been to succumb to emotion, for that moment of weakness was costing her very dearly. Why had she departed so far from her firm purpose to conceal her feelings for him? It had been an act impetuous enough for Jane, not sober, commonsensical, usually wise Christina. Guilt struck through her again as she thought of her sister.

There were steps approaching, and then Campion knocked. 'His lordship awaits, madam.'

'Thank you, Campion,' she replied, pausing to compose herself as best she could. Please let her carry this off with at least a little panache, let *something* be salvaged of her pride. Taking a deep breath, she left the room.

Robert was waiting in the hall. He stood by the fire, his top hat, gloves, and riding crop lying on a table. Hearing her on the staircase, he turned quickly. 'Forgive me for keeping you waiting,' he said, speaking quite naturally because there was a footman by the main door.

'That's quite all right,' she replied as evenly as she could.

'We won't delay any longer,' he said, putting on his gloves and picking up his hat and crop.

Reluctantly she accepted the arm he offered, and they emerged from the house into the crisp sunshine, where two grooms waited with their horses. Robert's mount was a large, rather mettlesome bay, hers a strawberry-roan mare that quite obviously had some Arabian blood.

The thought of the ride was suddenly too much, and as Robert prepared to assist her to mount, she turned urgently to him. 'Couldn't we say it all here?' she asked quietly, keeping her voice low so that the grooms wouldn't hear.

'We need to be private, Christina.'

'Please, Robert.'

He shook his head, putting his hands firmly to her waist and lifting her on to the saddle. Their eyes met briefly as he handed her the reins; then he turned to mount his own horse, pausing only to tap his top hat on before riding away from the house. Christina hesitated a moment, then urged the mare after him.

They rode down through the park, and as they neared the lodge they heard the roar of the swollen river as it swept beneath the bridge and then over the rapids downstream of the little island. The noise echoed out of the trees, and as the horses crossed the bridge Christina saw how dirty with churned-up mud the water was. Broken branches swirled on the swift current, twisting like corkscrews beneath the arches of the bridge.

Robert's bay was uneasy about the river, tossing its head and fighting the bit until it reached the far side of the bridge, but then it moved easily upstream along the track that ran along the riverbank toward the high moors.

The Darch pounded through its valley, filling the air with its thunder, and the sharp smell of autumn was released from the fallen leaves as the horses passed over them. The ground was a carpet of russet, crimson, and gold, and almost directly ahead, the sun shone brightly down through those that had yet to fall from the branches arching overhead. Dappled shadows moved softly, stirred into life by the soft breeze breathing down from the moor.

There weren't any wheel ruts in the track, for Bellstones was the furthest into the moor that carts, wagons, or carriages could travel. The isolated farms and hamlets dotted over the wild landscape were served solely by strings of horses that were so used to certain routes they needed no drovers.

Christina's misery increased with each yard they rode, and she wondered how far they would have to go before he considered them to be sufficiently private for the delicate and embarrassing matter to be safely broached.

The hoarse cry of a raven jarred through the trees, startling both horses, and Christina saw the bird's black silhouette on the shiny green of a holly bush. Startled in its turn, the bird broke into noisy flight, swooping low over the track directly ahead, and then vanishing across the river among the crowding branches on the far bank. Christina's mare was a little frightened, shying and refusing to proceed. Robert reined in, coming back to take her bridle, and leading the unwilling mare past the place where the bird had been.

He looked at Christina. 'Are you all right?'

'Yes.'

'Horses can be difficult.'

'Yes. Robert, I'm sure we've ridden far enough—'

'No, Christina, for I'm taking you to a particular place.'

'Where?'

'The old bell tower.'

'But why?'

'I'll explain when we get there. Bear with me, Christina. This is too important to be rushed.'

'I wish ...'

'Yes?'

'I wish you'd have done with this torture,' she whispered, her voice barely audible above the thunder of the river.

He leaned over suddenly, resting his hand briefly on hers. 'I'm sorry if you feel it is torture, for I truly don't mean it to be, as I think you'll understand well enough in the end.' Releasing her, he turned his horse again, urging it on along the track.

For a moment she remained where she was, gazing after him. What did he mean? All she was going to understand in the end was what she understood right now: she'd made a humiliating *faux pas*, and would have to live with the shame of it for a very long time to come. With a heavy heart she rode on as well.

The Darch became narrower, and the valley began to climb toward the moors, which loomed high all around. Far above, the sky was still a matchless blue, arcing flawlessly from horizon to horizon, without even the smallest cloud to mar its perfection. High on an incline there was a farm, its stone buildings huddled against the slope. A flock of sheep moved up toward it, driven by a shepherd with two black-and-white dogs, but then the Darch curved away and the farm vanished from view.

The sun shone straight into their eyes now. The trees thinned out, and the ground changed to springy moorland grass, dotted with heather and the occasional tangle of gorse. Up here the air was crisper than ever, and the Darch's water was clear and sweet, babbling among rocks as it was joined by several small tributaries. Christina looked back. The wooded valley curved away behind, and in the distance, detectable only by the glint of sun on its windows, she could see Bellstones.

There was a shallow cleft in the moor directly ahead, and Robert rode toward it. The Darch gurgled between mossy banks, little more than a mountain stream now, and because the thunderous roar of the valley was far behind, the joyous warbling song of a skylark could be heard, although the bird itself was too high to be seen.

Riding through the cleft, Robert reined in, turning in the saddle to smile at her. Then he pointed ahead. 'The source of the Darch, and on the hill beyond, what's left of the old bell tower.'

Christina drew her mount to a standstill, gazing at the wild beauty of the scene. A small lake lay in a dip in the moor, its waters gleaming in the sunlight. Reeds swayed as the moorland breeze moved over the surface, and the song of the skylark gave way to the lonely call of a curlew. Some wild ponies had been drinking in the shallow water by the shore, but as the two riders appeared, they took flight, cantering away across the moor. Christina watched them for a moment, and then looked at the ruined bell tower. It stood foursquare on the top of its hill, and although only the lower walls remained, she could tell that at one time it would have been visible, and audible, for many miles.

Robert glanced at her. 'The view from up there is quite spectacular. Come on.'

Before she could say anything more, he kicked his horse into action again, riding down toward the lake, around its southern shore, and then up the incline to the ruins. He dismounted and tethered the bay, turning to assist Christina as she reined in. She was conscious of his strength as he lifted her down.

She moved quickly away, making much of gazing at the truly staggering view over Exmoor. The hills rolled away on all sides, and to the north, visible as a thin purple line on the far horizon, she could see the Bristol Channel. The breeze murmured around the ruined bell tower, and the air was very sweet, as only moorland air is.

He came to stand just behind her, resting a boot on a fallen stone. 'The devil's said to have had a hand in the making of Darch Pool.'

'The lake, you mean?'

'Yes. The story goes that Old Nick fell in love with an Exmoor maiden who lived with her father in a farm where the lake now is. The girl spurned the devil's advances, and her father took a stick to him, which so enraged the devil that he seized the farm, ripping it out of the ground, land and all, and tossed it over the moor into the sea. It became Lundy Island, and the hole that it left behind filled with water and became Darch Pool.' He laughed a little. 'A fanciful tale, is it not?'

'Yes.' She tried to smile at him, but couldn't.

'Perhaps this isn't the time for small talk, Christina,' he said quietly. 'Besides, I didn't bring you here in order to regale you with rustic Exmoor folklore, I brought you here to clarify certain very important, very personal matters.'

Ashamed color immediately flooded into her cheeks again, and she had to move away. She leaned a trembling hand on the side of the bell tower, and the breeze streamed through the ostrich plume in her hat. 'Robert, there's no need to clarify anything, for I already know in what way I've transgressed. You'll never know how much I regret what happened last night, but happen it did, and now you're fully aware of how I feel about you. I won't embarrass you again, for I intend to leave Bellstones as soon as I possibly can. I haven't thought of a suitable excuse yet, but I will.' She drew a long breath. 'I'm grateful to you for not mentioning anything of this to my father or sister, for I don't think I could bear it if they knew. I feel so … *disloyal*.' She lowered her eyes unhappily.

'Disloyal? Why? Because your heart is a free spirit that cannot be dictated to by arranged terms?'

'That's not what I mean, and I think you know it,' she answered, looking quickly at him.

'Don't think I'm making light of this, Christina, because I've never been more serious in my life. You seem to be blaming yourself for all of this, but the truth is that I am equally to blame.'

'You?' She turned quickly. 'I don't understand.'

'Do you think my hands rested *innocently* on your shoulders last night? Do you think I *accidentally* caressed you? I'm no novice in such things, Christina, and everything that happened happened because *I* initiated it.' His gray eyes were intense.

He gave a slight laugh then, removing his top hat and running his fingers through his dark hair. 'Do you remember the words of that song last night? The one about marriage being a lottery contest?'

'Yes, I remember,' she said slowly, her thoughts milling in confusion.

'I watched you while it was being sung, and I knew what you were thinking, because I was thinking the same thing. The lottery contest has played us a very shabby trick, Christina, and if I allow things to go on as they are, I'm going to find myself marrying the wrong Miss Richmond.'

25

THE AIR SEEMED to stand still around her. What was he saying? Did she dare to believe she was understanding him correctly? She looked helplessly at him, unspoken questions trembling on her lips.

'Christina ...' Whatever he'd been about to say froze as something in the sky behind her caught his full attention. 'Damn!' he breathed, not attempting to conceal his swift anger.

She turned, and saw William Grenfell's balloon drifting serenely through the air toward them, about fifty feet above the moor.

The crimson-and-blue globe floated silently on the breeze, its silk-covered wings wafting gently up and down, and its red pennants fluttering. But if the balloon itself made no sound, the same couldn't be said for its four occupants, who began to call and wave the moment they saw the two by the tower. They leaned over the side of the silk-swathed car, making it swing slowly to and fro.

Mr Richmond clung to a rope, looking less happy than his companions, but he still waved and smiled. Lady Chevenley was at his side, the tall plumes on her green velvet hat fluttering as gaily as the balloon's pennants.

Jane stood with William, her hair very red in the sunshine. She'd removed her bonnet, and was waving it in her hand so that its ribbons flapped. Her voice carried clearly as the balloon drifted nearer. 'Christina! Robert! Oh, you should have come with us! It's *wonderful* up here!'

Christina stared up at them. The spell of what had been happening a moment before still enveloped her, and she felt a sharp pang of conscience as she looked at her smiling, happy sister.

Robert recovered from his initial anger, waving in return.

William discarded the wings for a moment, cupping his hands to his mouth to call down, 'I trust you enjoy the rigors of the return ride, *mes enfants*. We'll be traveling in much greater style!'

'That depends upon your definition of style!' Robert shouted back.

This brought forth a gust of laughter, except from Mr Richmond, who looked as if he had very firm notions indeed concerning what was and wasn't style.

The breeze was playful, veering its direction a little so that the balloon shuddered. Jane gave an excited squeal, and William reached out instinctively to steady her. She held on to his arm for a moment, then the balloon settled again, and he bent to retrieve the wings, moving them quickly up and down in an attempt to gain a little more altitude.

Lady Chevenley, evidently already a seasoned aeronaut, hastened to check that the flap valve was fully closed. The breeze veered a little more, and the balloon revolved slowly, drifting perceptibly away from the bell tower toward the lake. Its reflection shimmered in the water, spangles of crimson and blue that broke and reformed with every ripple. The cleft in the moor lay ahead, and, unseen beyond it, the Darch valley; the balloon floated slowly on the gentle current of air, its path taking it toward distant Bellstones.

Neither Robert nor Christina spoke as they watched the taffeta globe move further and further away, and Christina found that she was holding her breath until it vanished from sight beyond the hill. Suddenly everything was quiet again, and the only sounds were the murmur of the breeze and the distant call of the curlew.

Robert turned to her, his voice soft. 'Don't listen to your conscience, Christina, listen to your heart. Jane is the wrong Miss Richmond for me. It's you that I want, you that I've wanted for a long time now.'

It was too much to take in, and she recoiled. 'No ...'

'Yes.'

'You can't mean it,' she whispered, confused and disbelieving.

'I've never been more earnest in my life, and if words alone don't convince you, maybe actions will.'

Without warning, he pulled her close. His lips were soft and warm, tender jailers that allowed her no chance to escape. He kissed her slowly and seductively, extinguishing all resistance, and assaulting her helpless senses in a way she'd never dreamed was possible. A wanton, voluptuous desire moved richly inside her, and with a sigh that was almost a moan, she surrendered, returning the kiss with all the heady passion she'd felt from the first moment she'd seen him.

As she responded, so he held her more tightly, and his lips became more urgent. She could feel the hardness of his body, and his warmth and strength seemed to invade her. She wanted to submit completely, to allow him full possession, for she needed him, needed his love.

His fingers curled in the warm hair at the nape of her neck, and he whispered her name as he bent his head to press his lips against the pulse throbbing at her throat.

She closed her eyes, sensuous shivers of joy trembling over her entire body. She felt as if she was alive for the first time, and she was intoxicated by the abandonment of restraint. Thoughts of Jane receded into oblivion; all that mattered was the ecstasy of this wild, incredible moment.

He drew back at last, his eyes dark as he cupped her face in his hands. 'This was meant to be, Christina, and we both know it. I can taste it on your lips, and see it in your eyes. You're the one who should be my wife, not Jane.'

Jane's name sent the spell reeling away, allowing the cold touch of truth to return. Remorse swept icily over her. 'No,' she breathed, 'no, this is all so very wrong....'

'My betrothal to your sister is far more wrong.'

'No.' She began to pull away from him.

He held her. 'Look at me, Christina.'

'Please ...'

'Look at me!'

Unwillingly she did as he commanded, and as her eyes met his she felt the current leap through her again, a compelling and magnetic force.

'Oh, Christina,' he said softly, 'you're mine, and I'm not going to let things go on as they have been. I've loved you since the night I saw you in the theater in London; *you*, Christina, not Jane. It was Henry Richmond's dark-haired daughter I wanted, his dark-haired

daughter I expected to meet at last at the Assembly Room ball. I
didn't know it was a second daughter I was engaging to marry, and if
I'd realized, I wouldn't have allowed things to progress at all. I loved
you at first sight, and now, having at last held you close and kissed
you, I know that it was the same for you. It was, wasn't it? That night
at the ball?'

She lowered her eyes, nodding reluctantly. 'Yes,' she whispered.

'And, like me, you tried with all your might to resist?'

'Yes.'

'I thought you'd succeeded, for you avoided me all the time, and
you hardly spoke to me when we were in company.' He paused,
momentarily touching her cheek with his fingertips. 'I tried to do the
honorable thing by Jane, for it wasn't her fault, and although I knew
that William loved her, I was convinced that she didn't welcome his
advances because she was happy to be marrying me. Even after that
business with the balloon, I was still determined to conduct myself
with all honor. I invited her for a drive the following morning,
intending to be sure of her feelings, and she convinced me that I was
the one she wanted. I was set on proceeding with the match, and my
resolution wasn't shaken until last night, when I stood by the window
in your room, and you came in. I knew then that I couldn't hold out
against my love for you.' He gave a wry laugh. 'I meant it when I said
that diplomacy was an art I'd had to perfect recently, for never before
have I had to so call upon my powers of tact, discretion, and
prudence. I came very close to telling you how I really felt, especially
when we went down to dine; in the end I confined myself to telling
you how much your answers to my questions mattered to me.'

She looked weakly into his eyes. 'I ... I had no idea ...'

'And if you had?'

'I don't know.'

'Your conscience?'

She looked quickly away. 'Yes.'

'Damn your conscience, I'm not going to let it blight both our
lives.'

'And what of Jane's life?'

'Do you think she'll be happy in a marriage that's so one-sided? I
can't marry her now, not when there's so much between you and me,

Christina. Last night, when my aunt suggested that song, I knew I couldn't ignore the words. "But if my fair one will be wise, I will ensure my girl a prize, Though not a prize to match thy worth, Perhaps thy equal's not on earth." Be wise, Christina, accept that what's happened between us today was meant to happen.'

'But …'

He put a finger to her lips, shaking his head. 'Jane and I would be disastrous together, for we're chalk and cheese. She longs for London, the Season, and socializing on an endless scale, whereas I love it here, far away from the capital and the sort of life she adores. She doesn't anticipate my thoughts, nor I hers, but you anticipate my thoughts all the time, and I can sense exactly how you feel about things. We're the perfect match, and I'm not about to let anything destroy the future that we're meant to share.'

She closed her eyes to shut out the urgency in his gaze.

'You have to look at me, Christina, for this is happening, it isn't a dream. Admit how much you love and need me, that's all I want to hear, then we can return to Bellstones and face them all with the truth.'

Unwillingly she looked at him again. 'I … I admit that I love you,' she said softly, 'but I love my sister as well, and *she* loves you.'

'Does she? Are you sure of that? Christina, you may think you know your sister, but you don't. If her heart is given anywhere, it's to William Grenfell, not to me.'

'No!'

'Yes. Oh, I admit that I thought she wanted me, but I was as deceived as you in that respect. I'm not inventing this, Christina, you must believe that. I watched them both at the dinner table last night, and it was clear to me that although William had promised to keep away from her, he was finding it as impossible as I was finding it impossible to deny my love for you. It was also clear to me that Jane was far from immune to him, and so after William had supposedly left Bellstones later on, I'm afraid I stooped to keeping a watch on her room. Sure enough, when she thought the house was asleep, she slipped out, went down through the gardens, and out into the combe, where William Grenfell was waiting. The kisses and embraces they shared were as telling as the one we shared a few minutes ago.'

She stared at him. 'No, it can't be so....'

'It *is* so.' He put his hand gently to her cheek, his thumb moving softly against her skin. 'They are as perfect a match as we, Christina, for William adores London, revels in the Season, and would sally forth to every occasion, given the chance. Believe me, my darling, for every word I've told you is the truth.' He drew her close again, kissing her on the lips.

But as she softened in his arms, giving in to the desire that had lingered, close to the surface, she suddenly heard an echo of a conversation that had taken place that very morning, when she'd met Jane on the staircase. She heard her own voice asking a question. *Am I to understand from this that you and Robert now have a love match?* Then came Jane's reply. *Yes, Christina, I love him so much I'm all at sixes and sevens.*

With a gasp, Christina pulled abruptly away from him. Jane *did* love him, and she *had* met him last night! He'd spoken of conducting himself honorably, but the truth was very different. Last night, after making advances toward her, Christina, he'd then kept an assignation with Jane as well!

'Christina?' Sensing the change in her, and not understanding, he made to draw her into his arms again, but she pushed him away.

'How could you do it?' she breathed. 'How *could* you?'

He looked uncomprehendingly at her. 'Do what? Christina, I don't know what you're talking about.'

'You've lied to me, and to Jane, you've made base advances to us both!' she accused distractedly.

'No!'

'Jane didn't meet William last night, she met you, she told me so, and what's more, I saw you returning from that tryst, just after she went into the house.'

'If she told you she'd been meeting me, she wasn't telling the truth.'

'She *told* me she'd met you, and she said she loved you so much she was all at sixes and sevens.' Tears were wet on Christina's cheeks. Her heart was pounding unbearably in her breast, and her composure was in utter chaos. She was shaking uncontrollably, engulfed in a bitter wretchedness that seemed to be tearing her apart.

'Christina ...'

'You're false, Robert Temple, and I know now that your reputation as a womanizer has been well-earned!'

Blinded by the tears, she gathered her skirts and ran to her horse. He ran after her, trying to stop her, but somehow she managed to mount, kicking her heel and urging the frightened mare away from the bell tower.

'Christina, you're going the wrong way!'

She didn't hear him. A tumult of pain filled her, and choking sobs caught in her throat. How easily he'd gulled her, and gulled Jane as well. The real Robert Temple was all that was shabby and cruel, all that was silken and seductive.

There were trees around her now, not the open moor, but she hardly saw them. A blur of autumn leaves fled past, and the mare's flying hooves scattered the crisp carpet cloaking the ground. She was vaguely aware of Robert calling her, and knew he was pursuing her; she spurred her mount to greater effort, unable to think of anything but getting well away from the source of her agony and guilt.

At last she reined in. She couldn't hear him anymore. Through the trees ahead she saw a broad, shallow river, but it wasn't the Darch. For the first time she looked around, and knew she was lost, for there was nothing familiar at all. A breeze stirred through the trees, rustling and whispering. It was a lonely sound that brought fresh tears to her eyes.

Slowly she dismounted, and the mare nudged her, making a soft noise. Christina slipped her arms around the animal's neck, burying her face in its long mane and giving in to the fresh, sharp pain of heartbreak.

26

MEANWHILE, IN THE balloon the mood was lighthearted and care-free, except for Mr Richmond, who still clung to the rope, wishing the voyage would end as soon as possible. The wonder of flight hadn't impressed him a great deal, and the possibility of calamity by far outweighed the awe of gazing down upon the ground from a great height. He found himself heartily in agreement with Christina and Robert, and wished he was with them by the bell tower, anticipating the long ride back to Bellstones, instead of up here in this flimsy car, supported by ropes and an invisible substance rejoicing in the peculiar name of hydrogen. The Almighty had never intended man to fly, as the likes of Icarus and William Grenfell had already found out to their cost; he, Henry Richmond, had no wish to provide further proof that it was ill-advised for man to defy the laws of nature.

Lady Chevenley moved closer next to him, smiling as he gazed uneasily down at the Darch in the valley below. 'Is it not a splendid sight, Hal?'

'It will do.'

'Is that all you have to say?' she chided, tapping his arm reprov-ingly. 'It's a *wonderful* sight, and you should he grateful to William for permitting you to participate in this aerial adventure.' She leaned over the side of the car, looking down at the valley again. 'My, how *strong* the river still is after all the rain. I don't think I've ever seen it in such spate. Look at that tree trunk in the water – it's like a frigate before the wind.'

Mr Richmond looked cautiously down, and then straightened again. 'If it strikes the bridge at Bellstones, there will probably be damage. A bridge was brought down in Stroud a year last spring.'

'Oh, *really*, Hal, must you always look on the black side?' she replied a little crossly. 'The Darch runs fast every year, trees fall into it every year, and they strike the bridge every year, but it's been standing there unharmed for centuries now.'

'Nevertheless ...'

'I vow you'd find fault with the Angel Gabriel today, Hal Richmond,' she interrupted, determined not to let him spoil things with his grumbles.

'Alicia, I merely made an observation. That bridge in Stroud *did* come down.'

'No doubt Gloucestershire bridges are inferior,' she responded, the light in her eyes terminating the argument.

Bellstones appeared ahead now, the house looking very beautiful in its sloping park. William grinned triumphantly at the others, for the breeze couldn't have served him better had it tried. 'How's that for tidy planning, sir?' he said to Mr Richmond. 'I do believe I'll be delivering you directly to your door.'

'We aren't safely on the ground yet, sir,' replied Mr Richmond.

'We will be, sir, we will be.' William turned back to Jane, speaking in an undertone. 'I vow the old boy almost hopes we come a cropper.'

'Don't be horrid about him,' she replied, but with a stifled laugh.

'Jane, we have to talk.'

She met his eyes. 'I know.'

'Things can't go on like this. Something has to be done, and quickly, or events will overtake us all.'

'I know.'

'I intend to bring the balloon down at Bellstones. Somehow we'll manage to speak privately then.'

She nodded, and unseen by the others, his hand closed briefly over hers.

The bridge and lodge lay directly below now, and the roar of the Darch rose clearly in the air. The river sped beneath the bridge, parting around the islet downstream, and then thundered over the rapids toward Darchford village further down the valley.

Lady Chevenley had been observing the progress of the tree trunk in the water, and she held her breath as it swooped toward the bridge, somehow finding a path directly beneath one of the arches, spinning out the other side, and swirling away past the islet to the rapids. 'There,' she remarked to Mr Richmond, 'the bridge remains intact, not so much as a chip of stone out of it.'

He sniffed, and said nothing.

They floated silently on, and then the park was below them. William reached up to the line of rope vanishing through the neck of the balloon, pulling it slightly in order to open the flap valve at the top of the taffeta sphere billowing overhead. As the valve opened and hydrogen was released, the balloon was put into a long, slanting descent toward the ground. A tall, spreading cypress tree loomed ahead, and quickly he bent to throw out two sandbags. The balloon's descent checked, it lifted slightly, drifted neatly over the tree, and then sank again as the valve was operated once more.

The servants in the house had already seen the balloon, and came out to watch as it came down. William worked hard now, picking up the silk-covered oars to attempt to maneuver the balloon to a particularly inviting and level portion of the park, directly in front of the house. The breeze was blessedly light, allowing the balloon to come to earth with more grace than was frequently the case.

Mr Richmond held on to the rope and his hat as the balloon bumped gently along the grass, and he exhaled with utter relief as it came to a standstill at last. Jane's eyes shone with excitement, and Lady Chevenley laughed delightedly, gazing up at the crimson-and-blue taffeta looming above.

William tossed out an anchor, and then vaulted out after it, making certain it was firmly embedded in the ground. Seeing the servants in front of the house, he called the men over, instructing them to take the various ropes and make them fast with wooden pegs, so that a sudden gust of wind wouldn't lift the balloon off the ground again. Climbing back into the car again, he made certain the flap valve was closed, so that no more hydrogen would escape; then he grinned at his three passengers.

'We're safely on Mother Earth again, never more safely, and I trust the voyage was as illuminating an experience as you could have wished.'

Jane clasped her hands, her eyes shining. 'Yes, oh, *yes!*'

Lady Chevenley nodded as well. 'William, my boy, it was a marvelous diversion, and I wish now that I'd imposed on you before. Why, I think I should have a William Grenfell medallion struck.'

'Medallion?' asked Jane curiously.

Lady Chevenley's glance stole wickedly toward Mr Richmond. 'Yes, for there was a time when no English lady felt properly dressed if she didn't sport a Lunardi medallion on a velvet ribbon around her neck.'

Mr Richmond wasn't prepared to let *that* pass without comment. 'All of which goes to prove that women can be exceedingly foolish creatures,' he observed caustically.

William alighted again, reaching up to assist Jane down first, and then Lady Chevenley. Mr Richmond ignored the proffered assistance, choosing to clamber down by himself, and then standing on the ground as if he'd come ashore after a long voyage at sea, instead of an hour or so aloft in a balloon.

Lady Chevenley went to him, laughing a little as she linked his arm. 'What a fuss, Hal Richmond. I vow I'm infinitely more brave than you.'

'Rubbish.'

She smiled fondly, knowing him so well. 'Have it your way. Now, then, I'm sure the vigilant Campion will be hastily organizing tea for us all, he being the jewel he is, so I suggest we give him a little time by taking a stroll in the gardens.'

'You and your strolls in the garden,' grumbled Mr Richmond. 'I vow you were forever suggesting such exercise when we were young.'

'Because I wished to get you alone, Hal,' she replied tartly, 'although for the life of me, I sometimes wonder why. Shall we take that walk, then?' Her glance encompassed the other two as well.

Jane smilingly declined. 'I think I'd rather go inside, Lady Chevenley.'

William quickly agreed with her. 'We'll leave you two to enjoy your stroll together,' he said, offering Jane his arm, and without waiting for anything more to be said, they walked away toward the house.

Mr Richmond looked darkly after them, but Lady Chevenley

pulled his arm. 'Leave it in the lap of the gods, Hal, and put your mind to enjoying my society instead.'

'But ...'

'My advice is that you leave it, Hal,' she repeated, glancing at the other two. 'I believe all will soon be satisfactorily resolved.'

'I don't think you have any idea—'

'On the contrary, Hal, I think I have a very shrewd idea. Now, then, forget about them and be agreeable to me.'

He hesitated, and then allowed her to steer him in the general direction of the gardens. Alicia Partington had always been able to wrap him around her little finger; he'd adored her in the past, and, so help him, he adored her still. She was quite the most captivating woman he'd ever met, and that included both his beloved wives, and his male vanity had taken a terrible bruising when the infernal Lunardi hove into view over London.

She smiled at him. 'What are you thinking, Hal?'

'I was wondering what you ever saw in me.'

She paused, turning to face him. 'I saw an honest man, a man who was gentle, shy, and sympathetic, but who was also – forgive me – inclined at times to be a little stuffy. Like all women, I suppose, I thought I could iron that wrinkle out of you, which was why I played up to Vincenzo. I shouldn't have laughed when you were tossed into that pile of, er, something unmentionable, but I couldn't help myself. It was a moment's amusement that cost us both dearly, but we have another chance now, Hal, and I don't intend to let you escape so easily again.'

He stared at her, totally taken aback.

'Don't say anything, Hal, just think about it.' She made him walk on toward the gardens.

In the house, Jane and William proceeded across the hall to the great parlor. A footman opened the door for them, and they stepped inside. As the door closed again, William immediately turned to her, pulling her close and kissing her full on the lips.

She offered no resistance, indeed she came to meet him, slipping her arms around his neck and returning the kiss.

He gazed into her lovely eyes. 'I've wanted you from the moment I saw you looking from the window in Johnstone Street.'

She pulled guiltily away. 'But I'm here to be betrothed to Robert, and I shouldn't even be thinking of you, let alone kissing you.' She pressed her hands to her cheeks. 'I've been behaving very badly, William.'

'We both have, if it comes to that, but our conduct has been brought about by circumstances beyond our control. If you marry Robert, you'll be making a terrible mistake.'

She bit her lip. 'I know, but how can I possibly withdraw from the match now? And how can I face my father?'

'Listen, Jane, I know that your father and I haven't exactly seen eye to eye, but I'd be doing him a grave injustice if I said I thought he'd put the St Clement match before his daughter's happiness. I may not have a title, and I may not be as wealthy as Robert, but I'm not exactly a poor match, am I? There have been Grenfells at Grenfell Hall since just after the Norman conquest, which lineage is actually more impressive than Robert's.' He hesitated. 'We have to come out into the open about our feelings for each other, Jane, and not for just our own sakes.'

'What do you mean?'

'I'm thinking about Christina.'

'Christina?' She looked at him in surprise. 'But what has she to do with it?'

'She's in love with Robert.'

Jane stared incredulously at him. 'Oh, what nonsense—' she began.

'It's true, Jane, believe me.'

The serious note in his voice arrested her. 'How do you know?' she asked.

'Observation, originally. Then I faced her with it, and she admitted I was right.' He smiled a little, remembering. 'She was taking me to task for attempting to come between you and Robert, even though she loves him herself and it would be to her benefit if you and I ...' He didn't finish, but looked at her again. 'She really does love him, Jane, and she's doing all in her power to hide the fact.'

She turned away. 'Oh, poor Christina, and to think I've been so selfishly wrapped in my own problems that I didn't even notice. Why, I even lied to her this morning about it. She asked me if he and I had a love match now, and I said we did. I only said it because I was afraid.'

'Afraid?'

'She caught me off guard by telling me she'd seen Robert returning to the house last night after me. She put two and two together and deduced that Robert and I had had an assignation. I was alarmed, for if Robert had been in the gardens last night at that time, then he might have seen us ... I hardly dared go down to the breakfast room after that, but he was all charm and attention, and I knew he hadn't realized what I'd done.' She looked guiltily at him. 'You're right, we can't go on like this, for one lie is inevitably leading to another, and the longer we leave it, the worse it will get.'

He smiled, pulling her close and hugging her. 'You won't regret it, I promise you.'

She hid her face against his shoulder. 'I wish I hadn't fibbed to Christina.'

'You weren't to know.'

'No, but I should have done. I've told monstrous untruths ever since I met you, and although I've admitted some of them to her, I wasn't honest enough to say how I really felt about you.' She drew back a little. 'I came here fully intending to be all I should be to Robert, but when you came to dinner last night ...'

'It was the same for me. I meant to stand by my promise where you were concerned, but once faced with you again, I knew I couldn't.' He put his hand to her chin, tilting her head and smiling into her eyes. 'When shall we tell them?'

'As soon as we're all together.'

'When Robert and Christina return from their ride?'

She nodded. 'I wish ...'

'Yes?'

'I wish that Robert and Christina ...'

'A fairy-tale ending?'

'Yes,' she whispered, blinking back tears for Christina. 'Kiss me again, William.'

He wasn't one to decline such an invitation, but as he embraced her again, his lips warm over hers, the door opened and Mr Richmond came in with Lady Chevenley.

The lovers leapt guiltily apart, and Jane was dismayed. With a mortified gasp she ran from the room.

William hurried after her. 'Jane!'

She ignored him, fleeing up the staircase without looking back. A moment after she'd vanished from sight along the gallery, he heard her door close. Taking a deep, reluctant breath, he turned back to face the others, clearing his throat awkwardly. 'I, er, think I have a confession to make.'

'You do indeed, sirrah!' snapped Mr Richmond.

Lady Chevenley went to sit down on one of the settles. 'Hal, I think that what William is about to say is that he and Jane are in love with each other, a fact that may have escaped your attention, but certainly hasn't escaped mine. Come and sit down, and we'll hear him out together.' She patted the settle next to her.

27

ALONE IN THE woods, Christina tried to pull herself together as her sobs subsided at last. Somehow she had to find her way back to Bellstones, she had no option. The trees whispered in the light breeze, and through the branches the sky was clear and blue, but down here, in this unknown valley, she was trapped and lost.

She looked up at the sunlight, trying to think. The sun. When she and Robert had left Bellstones, the sun hadn't been quite in front of them, then, when they'd passed the farm on the hill, turning their direction, the sun had shone straight into their eyes. It had moved on now, but by the shadows she knew where it would have been an hour or so before.

With sudden hope, she remounted, turning the mare away from the sun and riding back through the trees. She had no hoofprints to follow because of the fallen leaves, but had to keep glancing behind at the sun, and she rode slowly, unable to stop her thoughts turning upon Robert. She now knew how false he was, but her treacherous pulse still quickened at the memory of his kiss. Would that her heart had remained asleep, safe from the pain she knew now. But she wasn't alone, for Jane loved him as well, and would have to be told the truth, not only about him, but about her, Christina's, disloyalty.

The trees were beginning to thin, and the land was rising. Suddenly she could see the moor ahead. With a glad cry, she urged the mare a little faster, and at last she saw a very welcome sight, the ruined bell tower on its vantage point above the lake.

She reined in at the top. The sun still glinted on the lake, and in the distance she could see the cleft in the moor that marked the commencement of the Darch's deep, winding valley.

Kicking her heel, she moved the mare on again, riding down around the shore of the lake and then up to the cleft, where she paused to look back at the tower. She could still feel his lips on hers, and see the warmth in his eyes as he'd smiled at her; and she could still feel the utter devastation of the moment she'd seen through him. With a bitter heart she urged the mare on again, through the cleft and down toward the cloak of the trees in the valley.

Unknown to Christina, Robert was about a mile ahead, having temporarily abandoned his fruitless search. He knew the moor and valleys well, and knew that it was possible for her to have found her way back to Bellstones by another route. He had to find out if she was safe; if she hadn't returned, then a search party would have to be organized immediately. The Exmoor nights could be bitterly cold at this time of the year; freezing mists could materialize without warning, and the first snow of winter often fell after a clear autumn day.

He rode the bay swiftly along the riverbank, gathering the startled animal together when a small herd of red deer suddenly burst from the trees on the far bank, leaping and springing along the under-growth for a moment before vanishing among the trees again. He could hear the roar of the river beneath the bridge, and then saw the curl of smoke from the lodge. As he rode into the park, he saw the balloon in front of the house, and the small gathering of servants around it. The pounding of the hooves caught their attention, and a senior footman detached himself from the group as his master reined sharply in.

Robert controlled the capering horse. 'Has Miss Richmond returned?'

'Yes, my lord, she, Lady Chevenley, Mr Richmond, and Mr Grenfell returned about an hour ago.'

'I mean Miss *Christina* Richmond.'

'Oh, no, my lord, not that I know of.' The man turned question-ingly to his companions, but they all shook their heads. No one had seen the elder Miss Richmond.

With a curse, Robert urged the tired horse on toward the house. A groom hurried from the stables, and Robert tossed the reins to him before hurrying into the house. He heard voices in the great parlor and strode in, hoping against hope to see Christina's face. But he didn't; he saw only his aunt, Mr Richmond, and William.

Lady Chevenley was seated by the fire, and rose to her feet. 'Ah, there you are, Robert.'

'I take it Christina hasn't returned?' he said without preamble.

'Christina? Why, no, I thought she was with you.'

'She was. I was hoping she'd found her way back here.'

Mr Richmond stepped forward anxiously, his quick anxiety for Christina overshadowing his anger about Jane and William. 'Robert, where is she?'

'Lost somewhere on the moor, I fear,' replied Robert grimly, removing his top hat and running his fingers through his dark hair.

'Lost? But how...?'

'A misunderstanding,' answered Robert, glancing at William, who had yet to meet his eyes.

Lady Chevenley was very concerned. 'How long ago was it when you last saw her, Robert?'

'At least two hours. I searched for an hour or more without success, and then I rode here as quickly as I could. Since she doesn't appear to have found her way back, we'll have to organize a search party immediately.' Robert turned on his heel, striding back into the hall and calling for Campion, who came immediately.

'My lord?'

'Get as many men as possible, have horses saddled, and make ready for a search of the moor. Miss Christina Richmond is missing.'

'Yes, my lord.'

'And have a fresh horse saddled for me.'

'My lord.' Campion hurried away.

From the door of the great parlor, William spoke to Robert. 'Robert, I know this may not be the time ...'

'But you think I should know about you and Jane?' Robert turned to look at him.

William stared. 'I ... Yes.'

'I already know, as you will have gathered. I know you met her last night, and I know the nature of your meeting because I followed you.'

William colored a little. 'I … I had no idea.'

Robert looked past him at Mr Richmond and Lady Chevenley. 'I'm not concerned that Jane and William find themselves in love – indeed I gladly absolve Jane of any obligation toward me, for my conduct in recent days hasn't exactly been loyal to her.'

Mr Richmond was at a loss. 'Eh? Robert, my boy, what on earth is all this about?'

Lady Chevenley tapped his arm. 'It's obvious to me, Hal. Robert is in love with Christina, not with Jane. He told me he'd fallen for the dark-haired Miss Richmond he'd seen at the theater in London, and by no stretch of the imagination is Jane dark-haired.'

William exhaled with relief. 'Robert, if only you knew how glad I am to hear this.'

'Spare me your joy until I know what's become of Christina.'

William nodded. 'I'll help with the search.'

'I'd be grateful.' Robert smiled, but the smile was touched with his anxiety for Christina.

William went to him. 'We'll find her, I know we will.'

'I trust so, my friend, for I love her with all my heart, and I only hope I can convince her of that fact, but at the moment she sees me as the devil with two tails.'

William was puzzled. 'I don't understand.'

'She was in the gardens last night when Jane returned from her rendezvous with you. She saw me creeping in behind Jane, and thought *I* was the one Jane had been meeting. Jane, for reasons which are crystal-clear, chose to pretend that I had indeed been with her last night, and when I had at last faced Christina with my love, and extracted a similar confession from her, she suddenly remembered what Jane had said.'

'That's when she rode off and you lost her?'

Robert nodded. 'That's when she rode off and I lost her,' he murmured.

Mr Richmond was stunned by the turn romantic events had taken, but above all else he was worried about Christina. 'I wish to accompany you on the search,' he declared firmly.

Lady Chevenley shook her head. 'Hal, I don't think that's a very good idea.'

'She's my daughter.'

'And your gout will make you a hindrance rather than a help. You and I must stay here, with Jane.'

'Dammit ...'

'Believe me, Hal, in this particular instance I'm offering you good advice.'

Robert was in agreement. 'My aunt is right, sir – it would be better if you remained here.'

Mr Richmond didn't want to concede, but knew he had to. 'Oh, very well. Robert, my boy, bring her back safely.'

'I'll do my utmost, I promise.'

While the search party was preparing at Bellstones, Christina was nearing the bridge. She didn't see the large tree trunk sweeping downstream. Lying low in the churning water, it traveled swiftly, striking the bridge squarely just as she'd ridden halfway across. The blow was resonant, like that of a huge hammer in a cave, and the sound echoed loudly around the trees, startling the birds. It terrified the mare, which reared immediately with a squeal of fear, lurching sideways as it did so.

Christina screamed, struggling to cling on as the mare fell heavily against the parapet. She felt her grip slipping, and wasn't strong enough to hold on. With a sickening jolt she was flung over the bridge and into the foaming, bitterly cold torrent below.

The current was strong, seeking to drag her beneath the surface, and the water washed chokingly into her mouth and nostrils. She was blinded by the cold of it, and her corduroy riding habit was swiftly saturated, making it so heavy that it began to pull her under.

She was filled with panic, struggling violently in the water. Help me, please help me! The scream was silent, shrieking through her as she felt herself drowning. The water had her in its power now, spinning her helplessly in a vortex of current. She tried to reach out, but there was nothing to save her. She caught a blurred glimpse of the bridge and of her frightened horse cantering on through the gates into the park; then the Darch swept her on downstream toward the islet.

The tree trunk that had been the cause of it all was being swept downstream as well, lurching so harshly against her in the water that it almost jarred the last of her breath from her lungs. It was the moment of salvation, the only tiny moment when she could claw herself back from the brink of death. Finding a vestige of strength from somewhere deep inside, she tried to grab at the trunk. Her fingers slithered uselessly on the wet bark, and another wash of water flooded her mouth as she tried to gasp for air. Coughing and choking, she tried again, managing to grab a small broken branch projecting from the trunk. She was swept on downstream, but could hold her head above water now, and thus take huge gulps of life-giving air.

A new roar filled the valley, the thunder of the Darch as it foamed over the rapids. She'd be dashed on the rocks! Renewed panic surged through her, but even as it did, she briefly felt the riverbed beneath her feet. Twisting, she saw that she was closer to the islet than she'd realized. If she could only reach its shore! The pounding of the rapids was still louder; she had a second or two to make up her mind before it would be too late and she'd be swept past the islet.

Taking a huge breath, she released the log, trying desperately to find purchase with her feet. Stones slipped away beneath her, and it seemed hopeless. The river was too deep and strong ... she'd never reach the shore ... Suddenly her foot was on a much larger rock, a rock that didn't break loose from the riverbed as she tried to push against it. Then there was an overhanging branch from one of the islet's low trees. With a sob she clung tightly, praying the branch wouldn't break. Slowly, inch by painful inch, she hauled herself toward the shore. Her strength was failing, she was so cold, and her riding habit was weighing her down. Her fingers began to slip on the branch, and a cry of dismay escaped her.

With a superhuman effort she held on, struggling again to cross those final inches to the islet. Miraculously, there was another rock, just where she needed it. With a desperate sob she forced her feet against it, dragging herself out of the water and on to the shore, where she lay on the damp grass, the water swirling eagerly past, as if it would snatch her again.

Her heart was pounding, and a deathly cold spread through her.

She could hear the river, but as she tried to see, the colors became strange. The grass was blue, and the sky a deep, bloody crimson. Sound began to fade, as if she was slipping into a bottomless pit. Darkness folded over her, and she lost consciousness.

28

A LARGE GATHERING of men and horses waited in front of the house, ready to leave the moment Robert and William joined them. Two fresh horses were being held by a groom by the porch, and Campion stood nearby, his hands clasped behind his back, his glance moving sternly over the men to silence their whispers. Rumor was rife among the servants, for nothing happened in a big house without the staff finding out about it, and there were already murmurs about his lordship and the elder Miss Richmond, and Mr Grenfell and the younger Miss Richmond.

Robert and William emerged at last, followed by Mr Richmond and Lady Chevenley, but as the two men were about to take the reins of their waiting mounts, the sound of galloping hooves carried up the park toward them. They turned sharply, looking past the balloon toward the riderless mare that was bolting in the direction of the stableblock.

Robert's lips parted on a sharp intake of breath. 'It's Christina's horse,' he said quickly.

William and Lady Chevenley watched the animal in dismay, and Mr Richmond closed his eyes, turning heavily back into the house, unable to bear the thought of what might have befallen his beloved elder daughter.

Lady Chevenley followed him, linking her arm tenderly through his, and saying nothing, but as they entered the hall, Jane's distraught voice startled them. She was flying down the staircase, her tearstained face pale with anxiety. 'It's Christina! We must go to her quickly!'

Lady Chevenley went to her, seizing her arms. 'The men are leaving now, my dear – they're going to search the moor.'

'But she isn't on the moor. I s-saw it all from my window …' Jane could hardly speak, and fresh tears stung her eyes. 'She was thrown from the bridge, Lady Chevenley – she … she's in the river.'

Lady Chevenley stared at her in horror, then gathered her skirts and hurried outside again, calling out to Robert just as he and the men were urging their mounts away.

He reined his horse in, looking back.

'She was thrown into the river from the bridge. Jane saw from her window.' Lady Chevenley was close to tears herself, for she knew how dangerous the Darch was when in spate. Christina had little chance of survival.

Robert didn't hesitate. He kicked his horse forward again, flinging it down through the park toward the lodge and the bridge. The pounding of many hooves echoed across the grass as the search party followed him past the balloon, their horses kicking up pieces of turf.

The roar of the Darch seemed to leap up toward Robert as he drove his horse down the slope to where the autumn trees choked the valley. Dear God, let her be safe. Let her be safe.

He reined in on the bridge, staring downstream into the thundering, foaming water. No one could live in that. Even if Christina had survived the fall itself, she was certain to be dragged under, or dashed to death upon the rapids. A deep pain spread through him, a sense of certain loss that seemed to squeeze his heart in his breast.

William maneuvered his horse next to him. 'We can search downstream, Robert. The rapids may not have claimed her.'

Robert didn't reply. He knew his friend was trying to comfort him, but such comfort was in vain when the fury of the Darch resounded so ferociously all around them.

The rest of the search party had reined in as well, their horses capering and tossing their heads. The lodgekeeper, who'd been unaware of what had befallen Christina, now came to an upstairs window, drawn by the unmistakable sound of a great many horses. Learning from the men closest to him what had happened, he stared downstream as well, and from his vantage point he saw something lying just on the shore of the islet. He strained his eyes, trying to make it out. It looked like a bundle of wet beige cloth, but the more he stared at it, the more it seemed to take shape. It was a woman.

Excitedly he shouted to Robert. 'My lord, I think Miss Richmond may be on the island – I'm sure I can see her from here! On the Darchford track bank!'

Robert's head jerked around toward him, and then he urged his mount on across the bridge, reining in again on the far side. He could see her then, lying motionless on the grass, the hem of her riding habit dragging in the furious current. There was no sign of her hat, and her dark hair had fallen loose from its pins, tumbling wetly over her shoulders and clinging to the corduroy of her jacket. Was she still alive?

He rode slowly along the riverbank, reining in again directly opposite her. He could see her face now. It was ashen, and her eyes were closed. The breeze fluttered a stray curl of her hair across her cheek, catching some strands on her lips, but that was the only movement he could see.

His heart twisted within him, and he leaned forward on the pommel. 'Christina?' he called above the thunder of the river.

She didn't move.

'Christina! Can you hear me?' His voice shook with emotion, but he still called clearly.

At first he thought she wasn't going to respond, but then he was sure he saw her eyelids flutter. Hope surged into his heart, and he called again.

'Christina! Answer me!'

The men by the lodge watched silently, and William rode slowly along the track to join Robert.

'Christina!' shouted Robert again, refusing to accept that he'd imagined that movement of her eyes.

William leaned across sadly to touch his arm. 'Robert ...'

'I saw her eyelids move, William.'

'A trick of the light.'

Robert's eyes flashed. 'She's alive, I know she is!' He looked across at the island again. 'Christina! Can you hear me!'

He could hear his heart beating as he waited, watching for the tiniest movement. The seconds ticked past, and still she lay there, but then, barely perceptibly, her hand moved on the grass.

Exultation throbbed wildly through Robert, and he looked triumphantly at William. 'Did you see? Did you see?'

'Yes.' William nodded, a half-laugh catching in his throat.

'We have to get to her, and quickly.'

'But how? Look at that water ...'

Robert stared helplessly across at the island. Somehow they had to reach her, but the Darch might as well have been a mile wide.

A thought suddenly struck him, a wild thought maybe, but it at least offered a little hope. 'The balloon, William,' he said quietly, his voice barely audible above the thunder of the water. 'Four teams of men, holding the balloon by ropes, two sets moving down each side of the river until the balloon is directly over the island. There's a rope ladder in the stables, a relic of my grandfather's Royal Navy days....'

William's thoughts raced ahead of him. 'The ladder could be fixed inside the car, and someone could climb down to the island!'

'It can be done?'

'I believe so. The balloon has hydrogen enough, and there isn't much of a breeze.'

'Then let's get to it. Every moment we delay puts her more at risk.' Robert turned his horse, spurring it back along the bank toward the bridge. He ordered the lodgekeeper to keep watch on the islet, then shouted instructions to the waiting men as he rode, and within moments they were all riding swiftly back to the house.

Lady Chevenley, Mr Richmond, and Jane were waiting by the porch, their faces pale with anxiety, but by the manner of the returning search party they soon knew all was not yet lost. They hurried forward as everyone reined in by the balloon, and Lady Chevenley drew Robert aside for a moment.

'What's happening? Have you found her?'

'She's on the island, Aunt, and she's alive, but barely conscious.'

Lady Chevenley looked inquiringly at the balloon. 'But why...?'

He quickly explained the plan. 'William says it can be done, and so that's what we intend to do. I'll climb down the ladder to her.'

'Oh, you *will* be careful?'

He kissed her cheek. 'If I have to take risks, then I will, for she means everything to me.'

She managed a fond smile. 'I know, my dear, I could see the way the wind was blowing as soon as you arrived. Christina is the one for you, just as Jane is the one for William.'

William was hastily preparing the balloon, but he straightened the moment Mr Richmond addressed him.

'Mr Grenfell?'

'Sir?'

'I, er, realize that our acquaintance may not have started out on the best foot, and I accept that a great deal of the blame lies with me for allowing my prejudices to cloud my judgment where you and Jane are concerned, but if you can save Christina now ...' Mr Richmond paused, almost overcome. 'If you can save her now, I'll be eternally grateful.'

'If she can be saved, we'll save her, sir. I like and admire her very much, and I intend her to be present when I marry her sister.' William looked directly at him, to emphasize how much he meant every word.

Mr Richmond nodded. 'I accept the situation, sir, and I gladly put the past behind us. If you are the one who will make Jane happy, then so be it, for her happiness is all that matters to me.'

William reached out to rest a warm hand on the older man's arm. 'Thank you, sir. I promise that you won't regret it. But now ...' He looked at the balloon, for there were still many things to be done before the rescue attempt could commence.

Mr Richmond understood, and nodded. 'Take care, my boy.'

'We'll do all we can, sir.'

Mr Richmond turned away, moving slowly to join Lady Chevenley and Jane. Jane was crying, for she now knew the cause of the misunderstanding by the bell tower, and she blamed herself for what had befallen Christina.

Lady Chevenley did her best to offer comfort. 'My dear, when you told your fiblings, you didn't know Christina loved Robert, so ...'

'B-but if I ... I hadn't lied, she'd n-never have ridden away on her own, she'd have come b-back safely with R-Robert, and we'd all be inside now, t-toasting our future h-happiness.'

Mr Richmond put his arm around her, patting her shoulder. 'We'll do that yet, sweetheart, and with the best champagne Bellstones can muster. I'll raise my glass to you and William, and to Christina and Robert.'

Realizing that this meant he accepted her love for William, she burst into tears again, flinging her arms around his neck. He held her close, watching as Robert and William marshaled the teams of men they'd selected for the task in hand.

The rope ladder had been found in the stables, and while it was being firmly fixed to the car, four anchor ropes were put in place at the corners of the car, so that the balloon could be held as steadily as possible while it was being maneuvered.

When the teams were ready, and Robert and William were in the car, the anchor itself was pulled out of the ground. The men on the ropes took the strain as the balloon began to rise, the crimson-and-blue taffeta shivering slightly as the ropes became taut, arresting the ascent about twenty-five feet up. Then, very slowly and carefully at first, the teams of men began to move down the park toward the lodge and the bridge.

Mr Richmond, Lady Chevenley, and Jane followed the strange procession, and so did the Bellstones servants not employed on the ropes. It seemed to take an age to reach the gates, where the lodge-keeper told them that Christina was still safe on the island.

Trees overhung the gates, and leaves and broken twigs showered down as the teams eased the balloon through. They moved to the center of the bridge, holding the balloon steady, still about twenty-five feet above the river; then the teams parted, two moving to the far bank, and two returning to the near bank. With great care, they began to maneuver the balloon downstream toward the islet.

The golden car swung a little as Robert and William leaned over, watching every slow inch of progress. Robert's anxiety grew with each minute. He could see Christina, lying so very still by the eager water; then the island's low trees obscured his view, and the balloon shuddered as the teams on the banks came to a standstill, halting the car directly over the island.

William tossed the rope ladder over the side, watching as it disappeared into the foliage below; then he looked at Robert. 'Take care, my friend.'

Robert didn't reply, but climbed over the edge and began to go slowly down. The ladder swung alarmingly, and everyone on the shores gasped, fearing he would fall. He paused, waiting until the ladder was still again; then he continued his descent.

The topmost branches splintered as he pushed down through them, and leaves fluttered loose, some falling to the grass below, others on to the swift-flowing water, which snatched them away toward the thundering rapids.

Looking down as he emerged beneath the trees, he could see Christina lying directly below. He climbed down to within four feet of the grass, then jumped lightly down, kneeling beside her.

The profile of her face was ashen, and her eyes were closed, her dark lashes resting against her cheeks. The stray curl of hair still fluttered softly in the light breeze, partly caught on her lips, and the hand that had moved before now lay perfectly still. He was very conscious of the river as it slid hungrily by only inches away, the current still dragging at the hem of her riding habit, as if awaiting the opportunity to pull her into its depths again.

He took his coat off, laying it carefully on the grass; then he took gentle hold of her, moving her so that she was resting on the coat, and he could wrap it around her to keep her as warm as possible. He pulled her up into his arms, and her head lolled lifelessly back, her wet, tangled hair clinging to his shirt sleeve.

Her cheek felt cold to the touch. 'Christina, can you hear me?'

She made no movement.

'Christina!' He spoke more imperatively, shaking her slightly. 'Look at me!'

There was still no response. He felt helpless. She had to come around, she *had* to! He hesitated, then gently slapped her face. As she continued to lie motionless in his arms, he slapped her again, harder this time. 'Look at me, Christina, for pity's sake,' he whispered.

Her lips parted, and her eyelids fluttered. Suddenly she was looking at him, her eyes dull but alive. Gladness surged through him, and he held her close again for a moment, gesturing to those on the bank that she'd responded at last.

On the shore, Jane leaned weakly against her father, blinking back tears of relief, and Lady Chevenley drew a long, steadying breath, praying that the rescue itself would proceed without hindrance. There was many a slip betwixt cup and lip, and as she looked up at the balloon, it seemed to be a very long way from the ground.

On the island, Robert was looking into Christina's eyes again. 'Can you understand me, Christina?'

'Yes,' she whispered.

'Are you in any pain?'

'No.' She was puzzled. What had happened? Where was she? All remembrance of the accident and what had gone before had fled, and she couldn't understand why he was looking so anxiously at her.

He put his hand gently to her cheek. 'I have to get you up to the balloon.'

She stared at him; then her gaze moved beyond him, to where the balloon was just visible above the low trees. Alarm crept through her, and her eyes widened.

He tightened his hold reassuringly. 'I'll take care of you, Christina, you mustn't be afraid. Do you think you can put your arms around my neck?'

'I ... I think so.' She looked at him again, recollection stirring. They'd quarreled, she'd ridden away from him....

He glanced up at the rope ladder. 'If you can hold on to me, I can grip you with an arm around your waist, and I can climb back up to the balloon with you. Are you strong enough for that?'

She hesitated, memories still returning.

'Christina? Are you strong enough for that?' he repeated.

'Yes. I think so.'

He could see the thoughts in her eyes, and knew she was begin-ning to remember what had happened. 'Trust me now, Christina, for I have to get you to safety. Put your arms around my neck.'

She did as she was told, linking her arms as tightly as she could. Holding her firmly around the waist, he stood up, looking up through the foliage toward the balloon. 'Can you hear me, William?' he shouted.

'Yes, Robert, I hear you.' William's voice drifted down, just audible above the noise of the river.

'I'm climbing up with her now.'

'Right.'

Robert put a foot on the ladder, holding it with his free hand, and looking at Christina. 'Are you ready?'

'Yes.'

'Hold tight, whatever you do.'

She nodded.

'Close your eyes – it won't be as frightening.'

She again did as she was instructed. He began to climb, easing up the ladder step by slow step, and pausing when it again began to sway. As it steadied, he continued to climb, pushing up through the trees, but as he cleared the topmost branches, the ladder began to sway again, more alarmingly this time.

Christina could feel the motion, although her eyes remained closed. She was holding on to him as best she could, but her strength was already fading. She didn't feel as if she was really awake, and she opened her eyes to prove that she was. She saw the sky, and the balloon billowing above. The sky wasn't blue anymore, it was a strange shade of mauve, and the balloon was turning to green and gold. She was afraid, and tried to say Robert's name, but no sound came from her lips. Her arms began to relax, falling away suddenly as unconsciousness overtook her again.

Without warning, Robert found himself holding her limp body. He heard Jane's distant scream, and the horrified cries of the onlookers as it seemed he couldn't possibly keep his grip on her. He gritted his teeth, holding on for all he was worth, then, more slowly, continued to climb.

At last he could see William reaching down only a few feet above.

'Robert? Just another two steps, and I'll be able to take her.'

Robert nodded, easing himself up. He clung to the ladder as William caught Christina under the arms, dragging her strongly up into the safety of the car. There were cheers from the onlookers as Robert climbed wearily in as well, and then William gestured to the teams on the ground to begin pulling the balloon back toward the bridge.

Christina lay on the floor of the car, as limp and unconscious as she had been on the island, and although Robert knelt beside her, trying to arouse her again, she remained still.

The balloon was drawn upstream to the bridge, and the teams maneuvered it to the Bellstones side. For a moment it seemed one of the ropes would be trapped on a sturdy branch, but the men heaved, and with a crack the branch broke, leaving the balloon free again.

William called to the men to drag the balloon right to the house, and after what seemed like a lifetime, it was at last being lowered to the ground right in front of the porch.

As the anchor was made fast, Robert gathered Christina's limp body into his arms and climbed carefully out of the car. He ignored helping hands as he carried her into the house.

29

FIRELIGHT FLICKERED IN the garden room, setting shadows
dancing on the walls. The colors on the tapestries glowed, and
the faces of the Tudor miniatures on the wall opposite the window
seemed almost alive. There was a sudden brightness as the fire
shifted, sending a cloud of sparks fleeing up the chimney to the cold
autumn night.

Robert sat on the window seat, gazing down at the moonlit
gardens below. He wore a blue paisley dressing gown over his shirt
and breeches, and the shirt was unbuttoned at the throat. There was
an untouched glass of cognac in his hand, and his hair was ruffled by
the number of times he'd run his anxious fingers through it.

Jenny sat unhappily in the chair by the fire, her hands clasped
neatly in her lap. It was three o'clock in the morning, but she
hadn't changed out of the clothes she'd worn when her mistress
had been brought back. Her eyes were tired and strained as she
glanced at the figure by the window, but her attention was mostly
on the green four-poster, where Christina lay without moving, her
dark hair spilling over the lace-edged pillow. The maid blinked
back tears, for she loved Christina, and feared she would die. The
doctor from Darchford had examined her, and said that although
she was very ill, she would recover. Jenny looked at the pale face
against the pillow. So many hours had passed now, and there
hadn't been any sign of consciousness; how long would it go on
like this?

There was a tap at the door, and Jane came in in her frilled pink
muslin wrap. Her red hair was brushed loose, and her face was rather
pale, still bearing the traces of all the tears she'd wept. She looked

inquiringly toward Jenny, hoping to hear at least some optimistic news, but the maid shook her head. The hope died in Jane's eyes, and a little dejectedly she turned to go out again, but then hesitated, looking uncertainly toward Robert. 'May ... may I speak to you?' she asked.

He nodded, swirling the cognac in the glass. 'We do have things to say, do we not?'

She came closer, her lovely eyes filled with unhappiness. 'Can you ever forgive me for this?' she asked in a low, shaking tone.

He held his hand out to her, his fingers closing reassuringly over hers. 'You were as much a victim of circumstances as I was.'

'I'm so very sorry,' she whispered, her voice breaking. 'If I hadn't lied to her so that she thought it was you I'd met last night ...'

'And if I hadn't held my tongue when I first realized I was going to marry the wrong Miss Richmond ... if your father hadn't wanted his younger daughter to secure an aristocratic husband ... if William hadn't held back from confronting your father with the truth before you left Bath ... It's an endless list, Jane, and the blame has to be shared.' He put his hand briefly to her cheek.

She drew away, searching for a handkerchief in her sleeve, and dabbing her eyes. 'I didn't want to deceive you, truly I didn't.'

'Nor I you. Please, Jane, we're both guilty, so shall we leave it at that?' He managed a smile. 'Besides, I'm sure you and I would have made an appalling match of it, whereas you and William ... well, you're ideally suited, are you not?'

She shyly returned the smile. 'If William and I are an ideal pair, Robert, then I have to admit that so are you and Christina. I was blind to it, but now that I know, I can see that you're perfect for each other.'

His lips twisted a little wryly, and he looked out of the window again. 'We *would* have been perfect together,' he corrected quietly.

'You will be still.'

'What happened between us on the moor may prove irreparable.'

'But when she knows that I lied, and that I love William ...'

'She doubted my character then, and I fear she may doubt it still. She also has her own conscience to bear.' He smiled a little sadly. 'Christina is a very honorable creature, Jane, and no matter what has since come to light, one thing remains: she briefly – oh, so briefly – accepted my advances even when she thought you were in love with me. She won't forgive herself for that.'

'Then we'll have to see that she does, Robert, for otherwise no one will be really happy.'

There was a soft sound, like a sigh, and Jenny sat forward suddenly, looking at Christina. 'My lord, Miss Jane, I think she's waking up!'

They hurried to the bedside as Christina's head turned slightly. Her eyes opened, and at first she saw only the maid. She smiled. 'Jenny,' she murmured weakly. Then her glance moved on to Jane and Robert. The smile faltered when she looked at him. Vague memories returned again, unpleasant memories of mistrust and deception, disloyalty and shame.

He knew his fears were being realized, and without a word he turned and left the room.

Jane looked quickly after him, about to call him back, but then changed her mind; it would be better to speak to Christina first. She turned to Jenny. 'Go and tell the others that Miss Christina is awake again, but tell them not to come up because she's weak and needs to rest all she can.' She didn't want the others to come, not until she'd tried all she could to put things right between Christina and Robert.

'Yes, miss.' The maid hurried out.

Jane sat on the edge of the bed, taking her sister's hand. 'How are you feeling?'

The kindness in her voice made Christina feel more guilty than ever. 'Well enough, I suppose,' she said quietly, avoiding Jane's eyes.

Jane knew what she was thinking. 'Look at me, Christina, for I understand everything. I know how you feel about Robert.'

Christina's glance fled incredulously toward her. 'You ... you know?'

'Yes.'

'Will you ever be able to forgive me?'

'If you can forgive me.'

'I ... I don't understand. What is there for me to forgive?'

'My untruths. It wasn't Robert that I met in the gardens last night, it was William. Robert was telling you the truth – he followed me and saw me with William. He loves you very much, Christina.'

Christina stared at her.

Jane squeezed her hand. 'I fibbed to you because you startled me so when you said you'd seen me, and then I was alarmed when you said you'd seen Robert as well. I wouldn't have done it if I'd known how you felt about him, and I feel very guilty indeed that it was my fault you misunderstood him on the moor. You might have died in the river, Christina, and I would have been to blame.'

'Oh, no, please don't think that.' Christina's fingers curled around hers.

'I don't think badly of you, Christina, for I know that if things had been different, and William had been about to be betrothed to you, I would have done what you did, I wouldn't have been able to help myself.'

Tears sprang to Christina's eyes. 'Oh, Jane ...'

'Guilty consciences have no place in our lives anymore – you do know that now, don't you?'

'But Father—'

'Knows everything. He was a little, er, startled at first, but he accepts everything now. Why, he's even friendly with William.'

'He is?' Christina searched her face. 'You wouldn't fib to me, would you, Jane? You wouldn't say all these things because of my accident?'

'Of course I wouldn't! Whatever do you take me for?' Jane smiled then. 'Don't answer that last question, for to be sure I've been a horrid wretch to you of late. When I think of how badly I behaved, and what a trial I was to you, I'm very ashamed of myself.' Jane glanced toward the fire. 'My only excuse is that when I met William for the first time, it was like being struck by lightning.'

'I know exactly what you mean.'

'You and Robert?'

Christina nodded. 'Until he walked into the Assembly Room, I was myself, but the moment I looked at him, I was a completely different person. It was like being shaken into life.'

'What a strange pair we are. I don't think poor Father knows quite what's hit him, but he has wit enough left to be determined to soon toast all our healths, mine and William's, yours and Robert's, and, I do believe, his own and Lady Chevenley's.'

Christina smiled, but then her eyes clouded over. 'Oh, Jane, I said some dreadful things to Robert on the moor. I accused him—'

'It doesn't matter anymore, Christina. All that matters is that you and he make up your differences. He wants you, and now it's time for you to tell him that you want him as well.'

Jane got up from the bed, hurrying out of the room, and Christina stared uneasily after her. 'Jane? I'm not ready yet....'

But Jane had gone, and the room was suddenly quiet. The firelight continued to flicker warmly over the tapestries and the hangings of the bed, and she turned her head away, closing her eyes tightly. So much had happened in one day, so many confessions had been made, accusations leveled, hurtful things said.

The door opened quietly, and Robert was silhouetted against the light from the passage and gallery.

She looked quickly toward him, unable to speak.

Slowly he came into the room. 'Jane tells me you wish to speak to me.'

'Yes. I ...' The words wouldn't come; it was as if her tongue were frozen.

He drew a long breath, going to the window and looking out into the night. 'You've remembered everything that happened by the bell tower?'

'Yes.'

'I shouldn't have taken you all the way out there, but it's a place that means a great deal to me. I meant to explain that to you at the time, but somehow it never got said. When I was a small boy, I used to ride there when I had problems, whether it was simply because my tutor had made me write a thousand lines or my father had tanned my hide for taking a pineapple from the pinery. It was a place I always went to when I had things to think about. Because I was there, my troubles didn't seem to matter anymore. I'd stand by the tower, gazing around the moor, and I was king of all I surveyed.' He glanced back at her. 'I know it's foolish, but I wanted it to be like that again today. I wanted all the misunderstandings and faults to go away, leaving only happiness behind, for everyone, not just you and me.'

'But it all went wrong instead.'

'Yes.'

'It went wrong because I was foolish,' she said quietly.

'The facts, as you knew them, gave you no reason to believe me.'

'My heart gave me every reason, though.'

He turned quickly. 'Your heart?'

'I loved you then, and I love you now.'

For the space of a heartbeat he didn't move; then he came quickly to the bed, sitting down and taking her hands urgently in his. 'And I love you, Christina, I love you with all my heart.'

She closed her eyes, tears stinging her lids as he bent to kiss her softly on the lips. 'Oh, Robert,' she whispered, 'I'm so sorry I said all those things....'

'It doesn't matter anymore.'

'Do you forgive me?'

'You don't need to ask,' he murmured, kissing her again.

'If I could turn the clock back ...'

'Time starts again from this moment, and the past is of no consequence.'

The tears were wet on her cheeks. 'I'm suddenly so happy,' she whispered.

'And so am I, for at last I have my quarry where she can't escape.'

'Your quarry?'

'The right Miss Richmond, the *only* Miss Richmond for me.'

There was a lump in her throat. 'I still don't believe this is happening. I can't believe you love *me*, dull, bookish Christina.'

'Then I must make you believe it,' he said softly, taking a small leatherbound box from his pocket. 'I intended to give this to you by the tower, but now is perhaps a better time.'

She watched as he opened the little box and took out a ring. It was a beautiful ring, set with a solitary diamond that sparkled and flashed in the firelight. He took her left hand, and slipped the ring on to the fourth finger; then he drew her hand, palm uppermost, to his lips.

'You're almost mine now, Christina Richmond, you're the future Lady St Clement, but when we say our marriage vows, and you become Lady St Clement in fact, then you'll be mine forever.' He pulled her into his arms and kissed her again.

She closed her eyes, surrendering to the kiss. There was no guilty conscience now, no pang of unease that she was being disloyal, just a deep, sweet sense of joy that at last all was as it should be.